MW01117975

Please Leave a Review

THE SEVENTH

SOUL

By Anne
Langworthy

Andrea
Happy reading

This book is a work of fiction. Names, places, characters, and incidents are the product of the author's imagination or used fictitiously. Any resemblance to actual people, places, or events is purely coincidental.

All rights reserved. Printed in the United States of America. No part of this book may be used or reproduced without express written consent of the author/publisher.

Langworthy, Anne Marie 1978 –
    The Seventh Soul/Anne Langworthy

For information/questions contact
a.langworthy.author@gmail.com

The Seventh Soul Copyright 2020 © by Anne Langworthy
Cover design by Richard B. Titus and Michael Langworthy

ISBN: 9798607705831
First edition—January 2020

For Michael

my love, my muse

Prologue

Her eyes lock on his from across the dance floor, the dust from the smoke machines obscuring his face, and from there she is lost. She knows this, but it does not stop her from moving slowly toward him, her body responding only to his presence.

Before she knows it, his arms are around her, their bodies tight against each other, grinding to the bass in the music. Never has she felt like this. Her body pulses with uncontrollable need. This is stupid and reckless and though she knows this, knows that nothing good could ever come from it, she takes the hand he offers her and follows him down a dark hallway.

The door is dark green to match the walls, scarred with scratches. The metal plate riveted to the bottom is dented where some of the patrons decided to kick it open, instead of just pushing on the brushed stainless steel square where a doorknob would have been. They are embraced in erotic passion as they push through this door marked 'MEN' and enter a world that she never would have thought to visit.

But she doesn't care. She can barely smell the urine that permeates the air. Doesn't care about the filth that streaks the counter-tops and the walls; the graffiti that boasts of true love and the exploits of men that consider themselves God's gift to women. All she cares about is him. *That he is kissing her, touching her in all of the ways she has dreamed of being touched.*

Her tongue eagerly explores his mouth, tracing the texture of his taste buds, the flavor of mint gum on

1

his breath. It is heady, and she is drunk with the taste of him. Not that she isn't drunk already. Later, she would use this as an excuse, a way to place the blame on something other than herself. But for now, she only knows what she wants, and thirsts to have it.

Without warning, he breaks off the kiss to nip at her ear. A moan escapes her lips, a deep husky sound of the type she had never had occasion to utter. He leans back and she is lost once more in the pools of molten gold that are his eyes. This is what dreams are made of, she thinks.

Nothing matters but what he is making her feel. The touching and the freedom that accompanies it. The beauty of his eyes, and his tanned face, and the planes of his chest that she imagines lurk beneath the silk shirt.

His tongue darts out and wets the length of her neck. She moans again. He seems to be less affected by her than she is by him; well, that is about to change.

Raking her nails sensuously over his chest, teasing him with her touch, she rips open his shirt. Buttons pop off, ricocheting off the porcelain sink and the mirror with a faint ting. Finally, he moans and the sound sends her teetering on the edge of ecstasy.

With an almost imperceptible movement, he cups his hands around her bottom, lifting her off her feet. He makes sure to grind his sizable erection against her before sitting her on the counter. For a moment she is afraid. How can she take that into herself and survive it? Surely he is too big for her body. But he kisses her again and the thought is vanquished.

She doesn't know him, not even his name, but

2

she is sure he is the one. The one she wants to give it to. She cannot explain it, even to herself, so she doesn't try; she just embraces the moment.

Her gaze moves once more to his face, but something has changed in the features. They seem to be moving around, morphing from shape to shape until nothing is familiar. His skin has become a dull shade of grey. His eyes are no longer the beautiful gold they had been, but a sickly shade of yellow; the pupils narrowed to vertical slits, like the eyes of a snake. Something moves underneath the skin of his cheeks.

The screams come unbidden from her throat, the sides of it constricting until it is just a thin tube, too small for even air to fit through. She screams again and again, until her throat is raw and the only sound that escapes is a tortured wheeze.

She is wrong about the dreams. She knows that now. Dreams are nothing more than sweet preludes to nightmares—and the nightmare is just beginning.

The room spins, turning her surroundings into a dirty blur and before her brain even has time to process what is happening, she is on her stomach with her bottom half hanging off the counter. The bridge of her nose cracks against the faucet and blood streaks down the sink basin. Blood surges down the back of her throat, so instead of the scream she is planning, she chokes on the coppery fluid.

She cannot breathe.

Nothing works. Not her lungs or her brain or her limbs. Those traitorous limbs that refuse to move, that will not perform even the simple actions that could save her life.

There are tearing sounds as he rips at her skirt with nails that are much longer than they were before. The underwear are gone in a matter of seconds, discarded onto the floor along with the other refuse.

Her hymen bursts with the first violent thrust.

"NO! NO!" she screams, with more force than she thought she had. "I don't want this! I change my MIND!"

The man stops for a moment to yank her head back once more and force her to look in the mirror. To behold him. His skin has taken on the faint bluish tint of asphyxiation; his eyes glowing menacingly.

"You cannot stop now," he croons. "We are just getting started. If you do not make me angry, perhaps you will survive this."

And she knows that he means it. She can see it in those hateful eyes. Feel it in his pulsing body. He will not hesitate to kill her.

She cries and whimpers, but bites back the screams that want to pour from her mouth. All she can do now is pray that it will be over soon.

But it is not. He takes his time, pounding against her with vigor and chuckling a deep, throaty laugh.

She is being ripped apart, torn from inside out and soon there will be nothing left of the woman she was becoming.

Just a shell.

After what seems like hours, an explosion of sorts erupts within her. A feeling of pure dread saturates each cell in her body. It is painful and horrifying and she is going to be sick. Her skin is

4

crawling, her every fiber wanting to run away. But she cannot move.

When he is spent, he lets her fall to the floor to weep in the dirt and trash that litters it. She lays there for a long time, with her eyes closed, hoping that he thinks she died. Hell, she wishes she had. She does not think about the pool of blood and semen that stains her thighs or the deep scratches that burn her skin.

She stumbles home in a daze, her vision cloudy and uneven. The memories fade from her mind with each step.

Chapter 1

They were lined up two by two like members of a jury, silently screaming their verdict: GUILTY!! Ivanya Devereaux begged and pleaded from her porcelain witness stand, trying to convince them to change their minds and grant her a reprieve, but they only stared, the twin blue lines on their faces unblinking. Uncaring. It was no use, the sentence had been handed down—life without parole.

Her breaths came in quick gasps. She white-knuckled the toilet seat so she wouldn't tumble to the floor. Pants still around her ankles, she contemplated the pile of small, unopened pink boxes with EPT emblazoned on the front. Below this was the promise: 99.9% ACCURATE. Ivanya supposed she could rip open the rest of the boxes, pee on twelve more sticks and perpetuate this ridiculous charade, but really, what was the point? The odds were not in her favor that she would get a different result.

"I'm pregnant," she whispered to the empty room. The words sounded much louder than they should have. She took a deep breath and forced the next sentence past her lips. "I'm going to be a mother."

It sounded even weirder the second time.

She had suspected the condition for about two weeks now. Pushing it to the back of her mind had worked for a while, but the symptoms soon refused to be ignored. Finally, after the churning nausea and the extra five pounds that took up residence around her middle, she had to own up to the facts. These were plain and simple: sometime in the recent past she had

had sex. So why couldn't she call up the memory in her mind? Or even the partner? She would settle for knowing who it was that took her virginity. Granted, many of her nights were ninety proof, accentuated by the occasional joint, but if she had taken the step into sexual adulthood, shouldn't it at least be memorable?

This is what you get for being shit-faced all the time! the annoying voice in her head shouted. Ivanya hated that voice. It sounded suspiciously like her grandmother—younger—but just as snarky as the old woman herself.

Holy hell! Grams! What would she say? Perhaps she would cluck her tongue as if she had known all along that Ivanya would do something immensely stupid—like get pregnant. Grams would look at her over the rims of her reading glasses with clear, blue eyes and lament about how disappointed she was. Ivanya would rather suffer grave bodily injury than the disappointment. Then Grams would demand a plan of action, which Ivanya did not have. She'd been in so much trouble lately that this could be the thing that got her kicked out of the house.

Forcing the rising gorge back down her throat, she stood and yanked her jeans up over her hips. She searched the mirror for evidence of her condition, perhaps the word pregnant stamped on her forehead, but other than a slight rounding of the cheeks, there was nothing. Evidence of her state of mind, however, was abundant. Her green eyes were large and ultra-bright, the whites stark and lined with red. Puffy purple crescents marked the fact that she hadn't slept much in the last few days. She looked tired, but not pregnant.

Good. She needed to hide it until she came up with a solution. Pretend everything was normal.

But she didn't feel normal.

She felt like her life was ending.

There was so much that she wanted to do before settling down. She wanted to travel and go to college; things that would be impossible with a child. Being barely eighteen, she could hardly care for herself, let alone a baby. Grams would probably end up raising the thing.

Ivanya scooped all of the tests into her arms and hurled them at the little trashcan in the corner. None of them landed inside, but she didn't care. She had bigger problems. Tears painted her cheeks as she mourned the life she had barely begun to live. She ran from the room, not bothering to shut the door behind her, and flopped her stomach onto the bed. Burying her face in the pillows, she sobbed as if she had lost her best friend. In a way she had; she had lost herself.

All she wanted was for it all to go away. Just fall asleep and never wake up again.

Ivanya sat up, hope glimmering in the back of her mind. She could do that. There was a way for this to be over. Reaching under the mattress, she fumbled around until she found what she was looking for.

Once upon a time, the velvet box had contained a sapphire bracelet that Grams had given her for her fifteenth birthday. The bracelet sat in her jewelry box gathering dust; she had never even put it on. Sitting on the satin lining of the box were a pair of razor blades. The shiny steel gleamed when the light hit it. She had considered this once before, but nothing ever came of it. Just collecting the blades had given her peace of mind, and whenever she felt the need, she would open the box and look at them. She had never needed to take them out.

Until today.

Carefully, Ivanya pinched one between two fingers and sat the box down on the bed. She was not afraid; in fact, she felt calmer than ever before. She winced a little as the blade bit into the skin of her wrist. A crimson ribbon of blood flowed over her porcelain skin. More bubbled to the surface with each heartbeat. She slid the razor over the other wrist, pushing harder this time. Blood spurted out of the veins, some of it spattering the wall. She watched in grim fascination as the drops lid slowly over the violet wallpaper.

Her head began to spin. Good; it wouldn't be long now.

Dying was a curious sensation and not entirely unpleasant. It was as if she were floating. Up and up as she became weaker. Blood pooled onto the sheets and the darkness closed in.

For the first time in months, Ivanya Devereaux knew peace.

Chapter 2

She often wondered of the soul. Why did some creatures seem to come equipped with one while others did not? Did a soul require maintenance to keep it functioning properly? And most importantly, how does one with no soul acquire one? Or six? Or however many one may require?

Lykah sat primly on her throne as she listened to Kabe rattle on about the prophecy. Normally, the subject interested her to no end, as the object of one's desire frequently does. Kabe's report, however, was dry and passionless, laced with the distinct ring of déjà vu.

"I know all of this, Kabe," she murmured, her voice soft but commanding, with a sharp edge of annoyance. "Tell me something new or leave my chambers."

She relished the quiver in his voice as he tried to recover. His pale face grew red and his throat worked up and down, choking on his words.

"Well, uh, the time spoken of in the prophecy? It is...it is..." he gulped, anticipating what was to come. "It is now."

"What?!" Lykah howled, springing from her perch. She stood over Kabe, glaring down with contempt. "You said the prophecy would come to pass in five years. You SAID your calculations were flawless. Am I to understand that you have misled me all this time?" This last was punctuated with a sharp rake of claws across his chest, neatly rending the fabric of his cloak.

"My calculations *were* flawless, Priestess. Some event that I could not foresee altered the time-line."

"So you are telling me that all the preparations for the ritual need to be moved up? That I must begin collecting the items now?" Her voice did not rise; it was calm and even—deadly.

"I am afraid so."

"You should be, Kabe. You really should be." After a pause, her voice deepened to a husky tone. She ran one talon softly up his throat and he shivered in response. "Now, Kabe. I know that this is not your fault. However, I need you to do what you can to help me accomplish our goals."

Kabe's breath was ragged with desire as Lykah kissed him full on the mouth. After a moment, she leaned back, just enough to fit a slip of parchment between them.

"When this is over, we will rule side by side. You will be a strong and mighty king, and I your faithful queen," Lykah crooned, placing a kiss on Kabe's brow. She smiled as his breath hitched and then pulled away from him. His longing eyes followed her as she strode across the room and opened the door.

"Until next time," she whispered. "I trust you will have better news for me then."

Kabe lowered his head, muttered a farewell, and scurried out into the corridor.

The fool. Kabe had been infatuated with Lykah since they were merely children. He followed her everywhere, even though he was painfully aware that he was beneath her. Kabe still harbored the hope that one day things would change. It was an advantage Lykah simply could not pass up. Now that he believed his dreams were coming true, he would work that much harder for her. People tended to be particularly malleable when they believe they were loved. Though Lykah's kind could not love per se, there something to be said for need and lust, the very machinations that make one vulnerable. Sometimes the appearance of love was more useful as a governing tool than fear.

But she liked fear better.

*****

The stool was hard and small, almost incapable of holding the bulk of the creature that sat on it. It creaked under his weight with a sound like one of those giant gas explosions that issued from the backsides of humans. He tried not to move. It would be unprofessional to make such noises during a job interview.

He waited, growing more irritated by the second. Not many dared to keep him waiting. That this prospective employer saw fit to try it did not endear her to him in the slightest.

After about five minutes (all of which he spent steeping in anger), she strode into the room, a thick red cloak billowing behind her. She exuded power and confidence, swathed in the aroma of magic. Strong magic, with bitter scents of sulfur and earth, truly intoxicating. He wanted to inhale it deeply into his lungs, but one look at her face told him that it would be a mistake.

Lykah, High Priestess of the Trynok, and perhaps his future employer, sat down across from him. Her face was a plain one, with skin that looked alien in the lamplight, much like the human invention plastic. The cheekbones were high, and the nose but a slight bump and two slivered openings. But her eyes burned with a hunger he could not name. They lit the rest of her face, taking it from plain to striking.

"Tarik, you are here because I was informed that you possess skills that could be of use to me. Are the rumors true?"

He smirked as sparks of electricity bounced over his fingertips. Lykah squealed with delight, her skin tone turning from paste to a soft mint.

Tarik's forked tongue flicked out to taste the sweetness of her envy. The intricate markings on his neck began to glow a neon crimson. He could feel it working, the strange disconnected feeling that came with this particular gift. The leathery black skin faded into near nothingness.

There was no delighted giggle this time. No, the reaction was a truly rewarding sharp intake of breath. She reached out a pale hand and passed it through his, which was now the color and consistency of smoke.

"So?" he asked, allowing his body to solidify again. "Did I pass the test?"

Lykah cocked her head to the side like one of those yapping Chihuahua creatures. "There is one more thing that I require. A thing that I have heard only you can accomplish."

Tarik inhaled deeply, allowing the deluge of

scents to take over his senses. Astringent eucalyptus, cinnamon, lemon, and poppies. Once he had the flavor profile he could interpret it.

"You are envious of my talents. Impatient, as well. You have been surprised this day, and it was not a good one." He favored her with a wry smile, revealing a row of sharply pointed teeth. "You also bear the scent of recent sex. With the guard outside."

"That will do," she snapped, her cheeks flushing. She rose, and waved a dismissive hand at him. "I will contact you soon with the details."

"Sit. Down." His voice had lowered to a deadly monotone. "We have more to discuss."

"No one gives orders to me. You will speak to me in a manner befitting of my station."

Lykah was obviously not used to being challenged. Tough. Just because he was offered the job did not mean he was going to take it. Only a fool would agree to something without knowing the particulars, and though he was many things, a fool was not one of them. He reached into the side pocket of his cargo pants and produced a squashed scroll of parchment.

"What is this?"

"This," Tarik answered, "is the contract stating the amount of money you will pay me. One hundred thousand dollars, in human currency. There also a subsection at the bottom where you will document the details of the task. Without a signature, in blood, I do not take this job. You can find yourself another demon."

She raised the ridge where an eyebrow would have been had she not been completely hairless.

14

"Human money. Are you serious?"

"Do I look as though I am not?" he asked. The red marks on his skin began to glow again, as they did whenever he was angry or called upon his powers. The distinct scent of fear radiated from Lykah's skin.

"Fine. When your task is complete, you will be rewarded handsomely. Come back tomorrow for the signed contract."

There was no shaking of hands, just a respectful bow between them. Then Tarik faded out and was gone.

Lykah fumed as she paced her chambers. Who did Tarik think he was? No one spoke to her that way; she demanded respect and had been known to kill for it. However, the aloof attitude and borderline disrespect he had displayed intrigued her as much as it angered her. Part of it was the fact that he was a truly beautiful specimen. He towered over her, easily seven feet tall, his bones covered in thick ropes of muscle. Deep crimson runes covered his ebony skin; they wound over his arms, up his neck, and even graced his bald head. She wondered if the markings continued down the rest of his body. A wave of heat moved over her skin, which turned a soft pink.

Also, he was ruthless. Though it was uncertain exactly how high his body count was (Tarik did not brag of his accomplishments), he truly enjoyed the kill. He employed many different mediums, spilling blood with an imaginative and dramatic flair. The carnage was always a sight to behold.

Tarik would be just fine for her purposes, provided she could keep him in line. That could prove to be difficult, though.   The only one that Tarik respected or cared for was himself. Lykah would have to watch him closely. She smiled as the planes of her face shifted, revealing a perfectly aligned row of white teeth.   With one tanned hand she brushed a newly sprouted mane of chestnut hair out of her face.

She looked forward to the challenge.

Chapter 3

Ivanya bolted upright in bed, screams dying on her lips. Her lungs greedily sucked in oxygen and she choked on the puddle of saliva that had collected in the back of her throat. Darkness clouded her vision, just a pinpoint of light was visible, swimming among the shadows. She remembered it all with such perfect clarity: his lips crashing against hers so feverishly that she tasted blood; fingernails sinking into her tender flesh while she cried out, each protest falling on deaf ears.

And his face. Never would she forget his face.

It's not that she knew what he looked like, at least, not exactly. Rather, she remembered his features changing from one face to another, the stages between each one resembling grey colored clay.

The blades of the ceiling fan whooshed these terrifying visions away. They whirred around, the steady hum bringing her back to consciousness. It was then that her brain made the connection—she was awake. Her eyes grew wide as the implications of that sank in.

"No way," she whispered to no one. She sat up and looked around the room, just to make sure this was all really happening and not just some purgatory designed to torture her. Sure enough, there were streaks of blood on her arms, some of it dry and flaky. The scarlet pool saturated the sheets, no doubt staining the mattress beneath.

You can't even kill yourself properly, the voice snickered. Ivanya didn't bother arguing this time—it wasn't like she was wrong.

The cuts on her wrists were no longer the open wounds she had inflicted, but bright ribbons of puckered skin. She fumbled for the razor and raked it up her arm again. This time she watched more closely and was rewarded with the impossible. Though blood shot from her veins, drenching her once more, the damage was slight. Before her eyes the gash began to close. The flow of blood slowed to a sluggish ooze as the skin knitted itself back together, and when she wiped it away there was scarring, but no wound.

Ivanya turned her eyes toward the ceiling, but seemed to look through it instead of at it. "Why won't you just let me die!" she screamed at whatever was up there. She wasn't sure whether she believed in God or not, but something had intervened and she was angry. The only way out—the only avenue for escape—was now blocked.

Since ending her life had proved futile, she supposed an abortion was out of the question. The only thing that had changed in the last few weeks was the pregnancy, so she assumed the fetus (she couldn't bring herself to think of it as a baby) was the reason for all this craziness. This led to one more disturbing thought: if she was being kept alive for the purpose of brining this thing into the world, what exactly was she carrying?

Eeewweeeeeooooohhh. X-files much?

18

Maybe it was a stupid idea.

Besides Grams, there was only one person who could help her now. She scrolled through the contacts on her cell, found the one labeled BIZATCH-and paused, her finger poised just above the little green phone icon.

What would she say? "Hey, so I'm pregnant with I don't know what, and I tried to kill myself, but the spawn wouldn't let me die?" It did not exactly roll off the tongue. Plus, odds were that her best friend in the whole world would think she was a lunatic. Not that Ivanya would blame her. If the roles were reversed, she would have a hard time swallowing that whopper herself. Steeling herself for the conversation ahead, Ivanya pressed the talk button.

It was answered on the third ring.

"Hola, chica! How are you?" her best friend chirped.

"Hey, Abs, you got a minute?"

"Sure thing. What's up?"

Ivana sighed, unsure of how to begin. *Just rip the Band-Aid off for God's sake!*

"I'm in a little bit of trouble," she croaked.

Abby snorted. "You're grounded again? Doesn't your grandma get tired of that? It's not like it works."

"No, I'm not grounded. Grams thought probation was good enough this time. She's probably given up on me." She cradled the phone against her shoulder and plucked a pad of paper off the nightstand. Slowly, deliberately, she began to tear a sheet of paper into long strips.

The confusion was evident in Abigail's voice. "Well, then, what trouble?"

Ivanya sucked in a deep breath, summoning all the courage in her body. "The kind that comes with a stroller."

Silence on the other end of the line.

"Abs?"

Still nothing.

"Abigail?"

Ivanya could hear short, gasping breaths in her ear.

"ABIGAIL!" she shouted.

"You're pregnant? How is that even possible?" Her voice raised an octave with each question, getting so high that Ivanya had to move the phone away from her ear or suffer a brain hemorrhage.

"Pipe down, Mariah! How is it that you sound more upset about this than I do?" Ivanya asked, testily.

"Because your grandma's gonna blame this on me!"

20

That did it, Ivanya had to laugh. Grams tolerated Abigail Kayne, but she did not like her. She thought the girl was a trust fund brat who depended on her money and status to get what she wanted. A bad influence who enabled every bad decision Ivanya had ever made. And to an extent, Grams was right. Ivanya felt free around Abby, independent. She could be who she wanted to be, not who Grams prescribed her to be.

"Relax; she's not going to think you got me pregnant."

"Yes, she will," Abigail whined. "She'll say that if you hadn't been friends with me you would have been working on your Nobel Prize winning plan for world peace. And you probably would have been, too. Who's the father?"

It was Ivanya's turn to be silent now; she concentrated, instead, on the strips of paper in her lap, which she now began to rip into squares. She mumbled something unintelligible under her breath.

"What?"

"I, uh, don't really know."

There was a heavy pause of surprise. "Seriously? I had no idea you were such a skank, Vani."

"Yes, thank you so much. This coming from the girl who is trying to develop her own brand of condoms and sex toys. What are you calling it? Kandy Kanyes?"

Abigail screeched with laughter. "You laugh, but when Kandy Kaynes' impressive line of dildos is paying for your kid's college tuition, you'll thank me."

And with that one sentence, the laughter abruptly stopped for Ivanya. It had been so easy to slip back into old patterns and laugh for a change, but there were bigger things at stake here, and she needed to deal with it. Somehow.

"Not to belittle your creativity, but I'm in crisis here. Can we talk about me?"

Ivanya could practically hear the sheepish expression crossing her friend's face.

"What are you going to do?"

She sighed. "I haven't figured that out yet, hence the phone call. I was hoping for a brainstorming session. Can you come over?"

"I'll be there in a few. Leave the window open; I don't want to be subjected to Mrs. D's scrutiny today."

Ivanya ended the call and opened the window, peeking out to make sure the ladder was still in place. Sometimes, Grams took it upon herself to move it. Once, taking for granted that it would be there, Ivanya almost fell to her death because Grams had placed it in the backyard.

Soon, everything would be okay, she assured herself. Abigail would be here and they could figure this out. Even the weird stuff.

*****

Ivanya bolted down the stairs with a plastic trash bag containing her bedding clutched in her left hand. She was hoping to make it out the back door and to the burn barrel before Grams caught her. If that happened, she would be ensconced on the fifth floor of Herbert Kayne Memorial before the day was out.

The creaking of the rocking chair assured her that Grams was in the living room, probably working on a crossword puzzle. Good. Ivanya leaped off the bottom step, the momentum almost sending her on her butt. She quickly zipped down the short hallway, pushed the back door open, and sprinted across the yard to the barrel. She tossed the bag inside, doused it with a healthy helping of lighter fluid, and tossed in a lit match. Soon, the evidence of her situation would be reduced to ash.

She trudged back to the house, her stomach heaving in an effort to catch her breath.

"Ivanya," Grams called. "Can you come in here, please?"

Damn it. There was a tense quality to Grams' voice, which could only mean trouble for Ivanya. As soon as she entered the living room she froze. On the end table lay a neat row of positive pregnancy tests, like pawns on a chessboard. Only they were not the sacrificial pieces; that honor went to Ivanya herself. And Grams was the queen.

Amazingly, the first emotion to surge to the surface was not shame, but a boiling anger. It hummed through her muscles, clenching her hands into fists. French tipped nails dug into her palms.

"You went into my bathroom?" she screamed. "What for?"

Grams sat ramrod straight, glaring at her in a way that threatened physical harm. "If you cleaned up the place once in a while, I wouldn't have to. Now I would like you to explain yourself. Sit down, please."

Ivanya threw herself onto the overstuffed sofa and put her head in her hands. Sobs wracked her tiny frame. "I don't have anything to say for myself, except that I'm scared. I didn't mean it, and I started out wanting it, but I changed my mind, b-but it was too late!" Tears jumped into her eyes and over the lower lids to commit suicide on her cheeks. She hazarded a glance at Grams. She had seen her grandmother angry before, but never like this. Her face had gone bone white, eyes blazing behind her glasses. The cheeks that were usually lined with wrinkles were pulled taut, making her face appear years younger. She hopped out of the rocking chair, the back of it slamming into the wall. Her normal leisurely steps were strong and purposeful as she stomped across the room and swung the closet door open. With one quick movement the shotgun was racked and ready to go.

"Who is it?" Grams snarled, sighting in the gun. Ivanya stayed silent, tears still streaming down her cheeks and grinding the toe of her boot into the rug. She felt like she was six years old and had broken a vase or something. She knew the disappointed look was only seconds away. Very soon, Ivanya would be exiled, never to return.

"I don't know," she whispered. "I never got his name."

Grams crumpled in on herself, shoulders hunching, knees buckling, hands shaking. She slid to the floor, the shotgun laying across her knees.

"I'm so sorry, Grams. I was drunk and stupid and—"

"No need to apologize, dear one. This is not your fault, don't ever think that." She seized the door jamb and used it to pull herself to her feet. Without a word, she shuffled into the kitchen, suddenly seeming very old and fragile. Ivanya followed her silently, afraid the slightest sound would shatter her grandmother.

Grams filled the kettle and placed it on the burner. As the flame whumped to life she turned to Ivanya, motioning for her to sit. Ivanya sat—Grams' expression left no room for argument. The steely gleam was back in her eye and she sat tall once more.

"Ivanya, I love you more than life and I want you to know that I don't blame you, but I need you to tell me everything that happened. Start to finish."

Her face flushed at the idea of explaining such details to Grams. "I'm not sure you'll think that way when you hear it, but here goes. It war right after Cole dumped me. I was feeling sorry for myself, so I went to Cy's to drown myself in whiskey."

"Cy McManus? He served you?"

For one terrifying moment, Ivanya thought Grams was going to leap from her chair and try for the shotgun again; Ivanya relaxed when she stayed put and motioned for her to go on. And after a moment's hesitation she did go on. And on. Through clenched teeth and a veil of tears, she told her grandmother everything. Grams blanched when told about the six shots of Jack she had enjoyed with the bartender. Ivanya assured her that she had a fake ID and Cy was not to blame. It was, after all, a very good one.

Originally, Ivanya had planned to leave out all of the crazy stuff, the stuff that could never happen in a million years, in the interest of keeping herself out of the looney bin. But once she started to speak, the verbal deluge kept coming, spilling from her mouth before her brain could even process the thoughts. There were no further interruptions from Grams, but her stony face filled with grief and sorrow, followed by a dawning horror that stormed her features. All of those emotions except the one she had expected—disbelief. No trace of that whatsoever.

26

"I'll make an appointment for tomorrow."

"For what?" Ivanya asked, even though she was pretty sure she already knew.

"The abortion," Grams replied, matter-of-factly. "This is going to ruin your life. I can't let that happen."

How could Ivanya tell her that she was sure it wouldn't work? That she already tried to end it? That she was still here to talk about it? She couldn't, that's how. Not at all.

"I can't do that, Grams," she said instead. "I don't believe in that."

Grams studied her hands, not meeting Ivanya's gaze. "Of course you don't, honey. I'm sorry. We'll find a way to deal with this."

A thunderous crash sounded from upstairs. Grams clapped a hand over her chest and Ivanya wondered briefly if she were having a heart attack. She heard the familiar sound of shoes thumping down the stairs and after a few seconds was rewarded with the vision of Abigail Kayne stepping into the kitchen.

"Vani! I almost died tripping over a pair of your shoes!"

"Maybe you should watch where you're going," Ivanya retorted. "You didn't hurt my shoes, did you?"

Abby rolled her eyes and fluffed up the front of her black tutu. She retied the strings of her lace corset and smoothed back black hair that was held in place by two silver barrettes topped with skulls. She ratcheted her gaze from Ivanya to Grams and back again, sighing speculatively.

"So she knows?" asked Abigail.

"Yes, *she* does," replied Grams, acidly. "Did you really think this was a secret you could keep?"

Abby sighed. "Is she grounded?"

"No she's not. Everything is fine. Why don't you girls go up and talk? Are you staying for supper?"

"Yes, please, Mrs. D. I also want to let you know that I didn't do this."

The corner of Grams' mouth perked up and she shook her head. "I'm glad to hear that, Miss Kayne. Skedaddle, girls."

They did not need to be told twice.

*****

Supper could wait. Irena waited for the girls to disappear upstairs before she rose, straightened her dress and began the arduous journey down to the cellar. Ivanya never came down here; she'd been afraid of the place since she was little, which suited Irena just fine.

She moved through the basement, expertly avoiding dusty crates, chairs, and defunct appliances until she reached the center of the room. The pull string was rough and frayed, she would have to replace it soon. The bare bulb flickered to life, bathing the room in a soft, yellow glow. Gossamer cobwebs hung from the rafters, almost close enough to brush the top of her head. She made her way to the north end where three bookcases stood against the wall. Old and dusty volumes packed the one on the left; everything from ancient cookbooks and canning manuals to hunting guides and encyclopedias. Things Ivanya would never be interested enough to look at if she did come down. The middle set of shelves contained mason jars of tomatoes, beets and green beans. The top two were dedicated to antique bottles and glass jars filled with herbs and medicinals. Some of these were ordinary: rosemary, thyme, basil, and parsley. Jasmine, angelica root, silverweed, licorice root, and slippery elm were more toward the back, as these were not used as often. Irena ignored all this, concentrating on the last set of shelves. These held an old sewing machine, miscellaneous vases, and a section of old work boots that had belonged to her husband. She braced her foot against the concrete wall, squeezed her fingers into the depression at the back of it, and heaved with everything she had. It swung out with a sound like cracking bones and scraped against the concrete floor.

When they first built this house, her husband, rest his soul, had created this hidden room for her as a place for her to work. He was the only one who ever knew for sure what she was, and he had loved her fiercely in spite of it. She stepped inside, again searching for the pull cord to the lights; in the windowless room it was much harder to find. After a few moments of reaching on her tiptoes, her fingers found the string, wound around it, and pulled. Dim light washed through the room, illuminating more shelves filled with glass vials and small wooden boxes. An altar stood in the center of the room, draped with a white cloth and dotted with tall pillar candles in the corners. An old red book lay on the white cloth. The first of two, this volume detailed the history of Irena's family—a history her granddaughter knew nothing about.

Irena opened it, carefully turning the thin, brittle pages until she found what she was looking for. She read the prophecy of the Ca'taal three times before closing the book and putting her face in her hands. Irena knew the prophecy specifying the birth of a special child would come to pass in her lifetime, but never did she imagine it would affect her so personally. Ivanya was the carrier of the vessel that would house the most malevolent spirit of all time. One that would wreak havoc on all of humanity. She couldn't let it happen. She had sworn two oaths: one to the Circle when she was but a girl...and one to Ivanya.

Chapter 4

People filled the sidewalk in the town square. Some bustled to work with paper cups in their hands; others milled around, typing quickly on handheld devices. Tarik walked among them, barely resisting the urge to knock a cellphone from their hands or trip one and send them sprawling to the ground. He did not worry about being noticed by these creatures; he would look like nothing more than heat rising from the pavement to them.

Tarik sniffed the air, taking in the scents of coffee and cologne. He dug deeper, searching for the undersmell. There it was, the musky scent of envy; the cinnamon tang of lust; the rosy aroma of love. But none of these were what he sought. He needed to find other scents that would lead to the target.

A woman pushing a stroller walked past him and the infant inside screamed. The sound spiked an icepick into his brain. Because infants and small children did not have the blinders that came with age, they were able to see him, even in mist form. Some of them screamed and cried, but others smiled and clapped their repulsive, chubby hands. He wondered about these ones; wondered if they were born into the darker parts of the world. Would they grow up to be evil? He made a mental note to find them in the future and see.

He moved quickly, darting around couples with linked hands and avoiding dogs, who could sense his presence with no difficulty. The smell of hot metal marked the manifestation of intense fear and strong magic. Old magic. Finally, after four days, he was on the right track. He followed the aroma out of the square and down a side street. He inhaled deeply as it sharpened and mingled with another one: despair. It smelled of damp leaves and rotting trees and stagnant water. Yes! This was it. This was the house where despair lived.

It was the yellow of mid-morning sunshine with white shutters framing the windows. Deep green ivy crawled the trellis by the porch, dotted with morning glories. It was a pretty manor and he hated it. He longed to crack it like a walnut and devour the meat inside, but that would have to wait. For now, he would watch and learn.

He observed from the boughs of a maple tree, catching glimpses of the residents from time to time. One was an old woman with gold and silver hair trailing in an intricate plait down her back. A pair of black spectacles perched halfway down her nose. Though she was old, there was an aura of strength that surrounded her.

The target, the one who smelled of fear and despair, was an adolescent female; slender, with long blonde hair and sharp feline features. She instantly interested him because under all of the delicious smells was one that was much more interesting. The scent of a parasite feeding on a host. Pregnant women exuded a specific blend of pheromones that were intoxicating. He was a little angry with himself for not catching it sooner.

He faded out and reappeared in Lykah's chamber. She was out, so Tarik made himself comfortable on her throne of bone and iron. Now that he had his legally and demonically binding contract, he didn't need to impress her anymore. In fact, he was curious to see what her 'wrath' looked like.

Some time later, Lykah sauntered into the chamber shrugging off her cloak before she was all the way inside. She froze mid-stride, eyes narrowing, hands clenching into fists.

"What do you think you're doing?"

"Waiting for you."

Her eyes were slits that threatened to flame. "There is a corridor outside where my people traditionally wait for an audience with me. In the future, I expect you to do the same."

Tarik smiled and ran his tongue over the tips of his pointed teeth. He stood, looking down at her with a predatory smile. "I am not of your people, and I am anything but traditional. I am here to give my first report."

She settled into the seat he had just vacated, leaning forward and steepling her fingers beneath her chin. Her brow ridge arched, "Well?"

"The target resides at 1342 Peachtree Lane. Surname Devereaux. Lives with an old woman who smells of magic." A soft growl escaped his lips as he remembered the scent. Delicious.

Anger colored Lykah's face. "Devereaux? Ivanya Devereaux?" She pounded fists against the armrests. "Of all the girls in the world, of course it would be this one! And now I know why the timeline is off!"

"What is next, Priestess? Do I proceed as planned or do we need to re-evaluate the mission?"

Lykah had to think for only a moment before, spitting through gritted teeth, "The old woman must die. Soon. Now." She stood and paced the room, robes swishing around her ankles.

"Yes," he hissed. "Some action."

She stood before him, some of her bravado returning. "Not so fast, Tarik. This cannot be accomplished with your usual…verve. It needs to look like natural causes. Or an accident. And Irena Devereaux is not someone to be trifled with. She is powerful, resourceful, and determined. And so are her friends."

34

Tarik nodded, filing the warning in the back of his mind, but not taking it too seriously. He had never been defeated and no human would change that.

"As you wish. Consider it done."

*****

The old woman gazed at him with sharp, blue eyes that were colored with disgust, but not nearly enough surprise. She had been expecting him, or something like him. She stood before him, not as a frightened old woman, but as a brave warrior. Her legs were parted, feet rooted resolutely to the ground. Courage emanated from her, the likes of which he hadn't seen in hundreds of years. And never before in a human.

A sudden wind whipped through the yard, raking the skeletal fingers of a nearby tree over his arm. His obsidian scales burned, oily ichor welling to the surface. The sensation was unpleasant but not terribly painful. He studied the tree for a moment before laughing to himself. Rowan, commonly used for protection by witches and other such ilk. If that was all she had up her sleeve, Tarik's job would be finished quickly.

"You do not belong here," she shouted in a voice as old as time. It was layered with power, the cadence foreign yet familiar. "Get thee gone!"

To his horror, Tarik felt his body wanting to obey her orders. His legs turned in the opposite direction and began to take tiny steps of their own accord. He ground sharp teeth against his lower lip, forcing his body to obey his own commands and not hers. Now he gazed at the woman with new eyes. He studied her as a worthy adversary instead of just prey.

Her jaw was set in a hard line, her blue eyes steely. Silver and gold strands of hair escaped from the long braid and whipped around her head on the strength of a sudden wind. A beaten leather satchel hung across her left shoulder. From it, she extracted a small glass vial and threw it at Tarik. It smashed against his face, scalding the meat of his cheek. He screamed in pain and rage, his eyes widening in disbelief. He raised his hand to the burning flesh, appalled at the sight of the brackish ooze on his palm. She had *hurt* him. No human had ever achieved such a feat.

He wanted to run over there, take her head in his hands, and crush her puny human skull until pinkish-gray brain matter spurted over his fingers. He would gaze into her eyes as he supped on her fear until sated.

The breeze caressed his black skin as he stripped off his cloak and tossed it onto the grass. Red markings wound their way up his torso, across his chest and up his neck like crimson ivy. He lowered his bald head, scraped his left foot twice against the ground like a bull and charged at her. His heavy form picked up speed as he hurtled toward her. Faster. Faster.

He realized something was wrong just in time to do absolutely nothing about it. He could not smell her. There was no olfactory sense at all, save for the air and trees. If he were blind, he would never have known she was there. That was when he ran into an invisible something; a wall he could not see, only feel. Every inch of his body seemed to flatten against it. Teeth cut into his cheek, washing his mouth in blood. He crumpled to the ground, every bone feeling as if it had been shattered.

A loud roar like thunder cracked the silence in the yard, a primal scream of pain. It took him a few seconds, but he managed to stand on shattered legs. He bit his lips against the screams that wanted to pour from his mouth, as his bones fused themselves back together. He concentrated on the woman, on her stony face. She had done this to him and he was going to make her pay. He bared his teeth and hissed at her, his forked tongue darting out to taste the air. With one taloned finger, he reached out to her. The invisible field around her crackled to life as he brushed it with his hand. It was not a wall exactly, but a thin bubble of blue energy.

"Get away from here," she cried, the bubble muffling her shouts. "I know what you are!"

A malicious laugh issued from his throat. She may have known of the supernatural—as the humans called it—but she knew nothing of him. He was unique, the only one of his kind. How he came to be was a mystery even to him.

"Your inferior human eyes have never feasted on one such as me," he spat. The woman moved backward as he stalked toward her, calling upon the power within him. The runes on his skin throbbed and burned, but this time the ache was welcome. It meant that his strength was increasing.

She chanted in a language he didn't understand, the words causing a ringing in his ears. No matter. He had been caught by surprise before, it would not happen again. His fingers received a shock as he pushed them against the bubble. He clenched his jaw against the pain and kept pushing. His fingers inched ever closer, closer, blisters bubbling his hand and up his arm. Just when he thought he could not bear the pain any longer, he broke through the field and stepped inside. Scents assailed him. An ancient aroma of cloves and rosemary filled the sanctum of the circle, a smell as old as the earth. It was constricting, oppressive; he couldn't breathe.

"Gypsy," he snarled, baring his teeth. And not just any gypsy, but one with strong magic, a high priestess of a sort. He encircled her wrists in an iron grip, not hard enough to bruise—he did need to make it appear accidental—but he was strong enough now that only minimal pressure was required. With her hands bound, the magic faltered and he could breathe again.

Pulling back his right hand, he allowed the power to spark on his claws. Blue arcs of electricity snapped at the air. Calmly, slowly, he moved the hand toward her. He relished the scent of fear that now saturated the woman. It drowned out the other, more unpleasant smells.

Tarik inhaled deeply from just below her ear, where the aroma was strongest. Her eyes widened as the electricity neared her chest. He touched her blouse and her body began to shake, each limb and extremity moving on its own. Her blue eyes were bright with pain. Tarik watched until those eyes saw no more; until he felt the last tendrils of life leaving the body. The whisper of her last breath one word: Ivanya.

Stage two, complete.

Chapter 5

When giving her report to the police later, Ivanya would not be able to recall exactly what had made her descend the stairs. It began as an uneasy feeling in her stomach that she mistook for hunger, but looking back, she would remember that it happened when the wind grabbed the shutters and thumped them against the siding. Her feet padded across the rug in the hallway and she gripped the bannister to walk down the stairs.

Food sounded awful, just the idea of putting something in her stomach made it roil in protest. But she needed to eat because dry heaves were truly horrible. A chill ran over her flesh as she paused at the back door like she always did and glanced out the window.

Her heart leaped into her throat and her hands shook as she grasped the knob and yanked open the door. Grams lay on the ground in a crumpled heap beside the rose bushes. Ivanya sprinted across the yard, her belly sloshing with bile, praying as she went. She wasn't at all sure if anyone was up there listening, but at this point it couldn't hurt.

Ivanya crashed down next to her grandmother, the ground rubbing painfully against her knees. It was impossible. No. More than impossible; unacceptable. The world turned because Grams was the axis that made it so. Without her, the planet would fly off course and crash into the sun. Grams was Ivanya's living anchor, without which she would be cast adrift. But Ivanya felt the stillness of the skin on her withered neck, cool to the touch despite the heat outside. She searched into the once vibrant eyes for any spark of life, but they were only opaque, unseeing orbs.

Grams was dead, in her heart of hearts she knew that, but her brain refused to accept it. Acceptance meant giving up and she wasn't ready to do that yet. Fingers laced together, one hand on top of the other, she began chest compressions. She hoped she was doing it right. During the CPR class in school, all of the techniques for the different age groups ran together.

One.

Two.

Three.

Four.

Five.

Ivanya pressed her lips to the cold mouth and a shiver wracked her body. Exhale. Grams' chest rose, then deflated and lay still.

There was no point in continuing, but she couldn't bring herself to stop until five minutes later. She dug the phone out of her pocket, dropping it twice before managing to dial 911. She spoke in hushed tones as if afraid to wake the woman on the ground. If only it were that easy. She would shriek at the top of her lungs if it meant that Grams could come back. But Grams was gone. Dead. There would be no last minute rescue, no happy ending. Just…gone. Dead.

Tears rolled down Ivanya's face as she curled up on the ground, laying her head on her grandmother's stone chest.

"Please," she whispered. "Don't leave me alone."

*****

Detective Corl cursed softly when the distress call came over the radio. He knew the address the call had originated from, knew the people involved. There was history there and it wasn't great. His partner, Kingston, raised an eyebrow. The question was unasked, but there all the same.

"I know the kid that lives at the address we're headed to right now. Busted her three times in the last year. Pranks mostly—stupid shit. Her and a friend hopped the fence at the bus garage and painted one of the buses pink. The whole thing."

Kingston smiled.

"Yeah, I thought it was funny, too. Problem was, the school board didn't. She wouldn't give up the friend, so the school pressed charges. Trespassing and vandalism. I had to take her in."

Thumbs down from Kingston.

"Next time I caught her drunk in the street, screaming at a traffic camera. Threw her in the tank for a few hours and took her home. Had to give her an MIP. She got probation and community service. The look on her grandma's face said she was getting more than that.

"And then, three weeks ago, she Saran wrapped my car. Again, funny, but not so much. You might say she hates my guts."

Corl finished Kingston's briefing on the Devereaux girl just as he pulled in the drive. He heaved his ample frame out of the driver's seat and slammed the door. It was hot out in the sun and sweat popped out on his brow.

Something caught the top right corner of his eye. On a ladder propped against the side of the house, a girl was making her way to the second story window. Corl caught Kingston's eye and placed his index finger vertically in front of his lips, the universal gesture for shut the fuck up. Slowly, he made his way across the yard until he reached the bottom of the ladder.

"Can I help you?" he called, using a rough tone he thought of as 'cop voice'.

In hindsight, Corl probably should have gone through the house and met the prowler inside. The ladder shook and he had to grab it quickly to keep it from falling down. He flashed his shield. "Care to come down from there, miss?"

The girl made quick time getting to solid ground.

"You almost frickin' killed me, idiot!" she yelled. She went on about how he was an incompetent piece of shit, but he was no longer hearing her; he was focused on her appearance. The kid seemed to put a lot of effort into making herself look weird, Corl surmised. She had a piercing in her left eyebrow, a stud under her bottom lip, six rings in each ear, and a swine ring in the septum of her nose. Her hair was short and black, smooth in front and spiked out in the back. Hues of pink and dark blue streaked the top of her head. The clothes, a dress made from blue and black colored bubble wrap, made her look like a creature from outer space. A belt of what seemed to be a thousand soda can tabs encircled her tiny waist. Thigh high leather boots completed the look.

"Or do you need me to call my dad?" She glared at him defiantly.

Corl shook his head to break his concentration. He hadn't heard a word she'd said, but he wouldn't let her know that. Cop voice again. "What did you think you were doing? Breaking and entering is against the law, young lady."

She rolled heavily lined eyes at him. "Puh-lease, I didn't break anything except for almost my damn neck, thanks to you. This is my friend's house, and that," she pointed to the open window, "is my personal door."

"Really. What's your name, kid?"

She shot him a snotty look that he would have loved to wipe off her face. "Abigail Kayne."

It was a good thing Corl was a veteran poker player, or his face would have given away his chagrin. Boy, had he just stepped in it. The Kayne family was the richest and the most influential in Watson. Hell, the hospital was named after Herbert Kayne, who financed its construction around a hundred years ago. They donated frequently to every high profile charity possible, often holding large gala events at their home. She looked a lot different than the pictures in the society pages. Not that he read the society pages.

As much as he wanted to, busting Abigail Kayne would be a career ender. He would be directing traffic for the rest of his life. Plus, he had no reason to if her story checked out.

"How good of friends are you with Ivanya Devereaux?"

"The best," she replied with pride.

"You better follow me, then. I might need your help."

As if it had been waiting for a cue, an ambulance pulled in behind Corl's car. Good deal. They'd be able to get the body out of there. In this heat it would start to stink soon.

"She's in the backyard, guys." They were a caravan led by Corl, then the Kayne girl (who was lobbing endless questions at him), followed by Kingston, the ME and the paramedics. They made their way down the cobblestone pathway that wound around the side of the house and into the backyard.

Cops don't cry. That was what Detective Corl chanted over and over in his head as he took in the scene before him. The old woman lay on the ground, her blonde and silver braid twisted above her head like some bizarre halo. Her eyes were open, staring at the sky, but seeing nothing. A small girl curled against the dead woman's side, eyes closed and tears glistening on her cheeks. She lay shivering in the heat, holding the cold, stiff form of her grandmother.

Corl stepped forward and squatted next to her. "Miss Devereaux, it's Detective Corl. It's time to get up."

The girl did not open her eyes, just snuggled closer to the dead woman.

46

Kingston nudged Abigail. When their eyes met, he nodded toward Ivanya. Slowly, taking deliberate steps, she moved to her friend's side and kneeled down.

"Vani, honey, come on. We need to let these people do their jobs." She gently pulled on Ivanya's arm, but the girl just held on tighter to the body beside her.

"No," she whimpered. "I c-can't. Grammy needs me." Her voice had taken on the high falsetto of a child, which frightened Abigail even more than the body on the ground.

By this time the medical examiner had come to kneel beside the body as well. He cast a meaningful look at Corl, who in turn, delivered the same look to Abigail. She gripped Ivanya just under the armpits and pulled her away from the dead woman. Ivanya thrashed and screamed, kicking and lashing out with her fingernails. Abigail heaved her backward as hard as she could and they both went sprawling toward the wooden swing next to the hydrangeas. She wrapped her arms around her friend, cooing softly as she brushed hair matted with sweat from Ivanya's forehead.

"What happened, sweetie?"

Ivanya didn't answer, the only sound she made was a high keening moan.

As the paramedics zipped up the body bag and placed it on a stretcher, all Corl could think was *cops don't cry.*

Chapter 6

It was like moving through quicksand with her eyes open. She could see shapes, but they all appeared to be brown and grainy, like an ancient sepia photograph. Was this what the world looked like now, without Grams?

Moving required more effort than she was capable of; just raising her head to look around exhausted her. She was no longer in the yard, but on the couch, wrapped in a handmade quilt. She still shivered, but they were much less severe than before. There were things that needed to be taken care of: the funeral home, life insurance, and notifications, but not just yet. For now, she was content to live in denial; in her version of reality.

A knock sounded at the door, one made from the side of a fist. Cop knock.

Abigail appeared out of nowhere and strode toward the door. Ivanya could hear her whisper yelling, though she couldn't make out the words. She must have lost, though, because she stalked back into the living room with Detective Douchebag and what must have been a new partner on her heels. The new guy was pretty cute. Model cute, with thick dark hair and big brown eyes. His neck was marked with a puckered white scar, but instead of detracting from his looks, it added an air of danger.

"They want to talk to you," Abby said, unnecessarily. Of course they did. There had been a dead body in the yard. The cops sat in wicker arm chairs across from her. Abby lifted Ivanya's feet, sat down and drew her friend's legs over her lap."

"Ms. Devereaux, we just need to ask you a few questions," said Corl, settling his ample weight deeper into the chair. It creaked in protest.

"What's his name?" Abigail purred. "Or should I just call him Detective Cutie?"

Ivanya kicked her in the thigh. Now was so not the time.

"This is Paul Kingston, a forensic psychologist that consults with the police department. He can't speak, but he's supposed to be some kind of genius. I haven't seen any evidence of that, though." Kingston shot Corl a dark look. "Now, Miss Devereaux. What were you doing prior to the discovery of the body?"

"She's *Grams,* not the *body.* At least call her Irena."

"Irena, then."

Ivanya was slightly mollified at that and felt the hectic flush fading from her cheeks. "I was cleaning the bathroom. Grams has been on my case all week." She clapped a hand over her mouth after realizing she had used the present tense. She smiled weakly. "She was always on my case about cleaning. She thought I was a slob."

"You are a slob, Vani," Abigail interjected, patting Ivanya's legs over the blanket. Ivanya gurgled an attempt at laughter that failed miserably.

Corl cleared his throat and she saw pity coloring his hazel eyes. He ran his left hand through his carefully disarranged spiky hair. "What happened next, Miss Devereaux?"

She glanced up apologetically. "I got hungry. I recently found out I was pregnant and my stomach was growling like crazy. I went downstairs to get something to eat. I-I saw her out the window." Tears streamed down her face.

"Do you need to stop?"

She continued as if he hadn't spoken. "I ran out there and I tried to do CPR, but it di-didn't work!" She sobbed openly now, hiccupping shallow breaths. Abigail reached for her hand and squeezed in an effort to calm her.

"Did Irena have a history of stroke or heart disease?"

"No. She was healthier than me."

Corl heaved himself out of the chair and straightened the lapels of is jacket. "That will be all for now, Miss Devereaux. Here's my card if there is anything you need. I'm sorry for your loss."

Abigail stood and walked them to the door, throwing an extra sashay into her step for Kingston's benefit.

Ivanya breathed deeply with O-shaped lips, tightening her abdomen on the exhale. The exercise was supposed to release chemicals in the brain that reduced stress. In: two, three, four. Out: two, three, four. She felt her body begin to calm down. She hadn't realized how badly she had been shaking until the tremors stopped. Her teeth ached from clenching her jaws so tight. There was a weight in her chest, though, and it showed no signs of disappearing just yet. Exhaustion weighed down all of her limbs and she was falling. Falling in the abyss of a dark life as an orphan.

*****

Corl dropped the file folder on his desk and contemplated the bottom drawer for a few seconds. Behind the hanging files lay a thermos filled to the brim with Johnny Walker. He longed to pull it out and take a deep swig. Not enough to get drunk, just enough to clear his head and let him think. But he refrained. He didn't know Kingston well enough to judge whether the kid would narc him out or not. Better to play it safe.

He sat down and opened the folder. Peggy Lofton. He had to testify about that case in the morning. It was a doozy. Peggy was diagnosed with schizophrenia when she was twenty-two years old. She frequently went off her meds. She turned to drugs for self-medication, mostly meth. She started stealing and dealing and Corl busted her more than once. She had a baby and named him Adam. She got clean for a while it seemed, went back on the meds. Then the voices came back. According to her, a 'smoky apparition' told her that he was going to steal her baby. She had to protect him. That's what she said. "I had to keep him safe. He's safe now." Corl had discovered the child wrapped in a baby blanket in the middle of a car lot. He was surrounded by a circle of salt and lavender. There was no question that she did it. Security tapes showed her placing the boy on the concrete and she confessed immediately upon entering the interrogation room. Though she had been advised of her rights, the defense was trying to get the confession thrown out on the grounds that due to her illness, Peggy did not understand the implications of what she was saying and should have had representation.

If the confession were suppressed, the argument could be made that she found the baby and did the elaborate ritual as a sort of funeral rite. She could get off. Where she needed to be was a hospital somewhere, so she could never hurt anyone again. She needed treatment, and she would not get that if she were found not guilty.

Corl sighed. He took a swig out of the thermos. Let them fire him. He was beyond caring right now. He had to get the image of Peggy Lofton and baby Adam out of his mind. And the image of Ivanya Devereaux clinging to her grandma's body. He just wanted to forget it all, if only for a while.

Kingston dropped another file folder on Corl's desk. Corl picked it up and perused the pages inside.

"The ME's report is back. COD was a massive cardiac event that ruptured the aorta. Death was within seconds. No foul play suspected."

Kingston nodded picking up the folder to read it for himself.

"Something isn't right," Corl mused. "I thought for sure something more was happening here. My spidey sense was tinglin' something awful."

He'd glared at Ivanya Devereaux as a suspect at the scene, which lasted all of two minutes. She didn't do it. Her grief was genuine. When he questioned her at the house she no longer looked suspicious, just broken, like a talking doll with shattered clockwork insides. And her words through chattering teeth had the ring of truth to them. But damned if he didn't think there was more to the story.

The ancient touch-tone phone on his desk began its shrill ring. He answered with the same gruff tone he always used.

"Corl here."

"John, its Jack." The ME. Great. The report wasn't complete, otherwise Jack wouldn't be calling him. "You told me to call if there was something hinky."

"Hinky, Jack, really? What is this, an episode of Scooby Doo?"

"That's jinkies," Jack replied, defensively. "Open the report to page four and you'll see what I mean. Hinky is the only word to describe it."

Corl snapped his fingers and pointed to the report in Kingston's hands. Kingston handed it over with a furrow of his brow.

"Got it. What's hinky?"

Jack cleared his pack a day throat. "The blood work on the decedent shows elevated levels of adrenaline and cortisol. Those are chemicals that produce the fight or flight response."

"And…"

"And it means she was scared, John. Scared to death."

Corl's mouth was suddenly dry. He needed another long pull off that thermos. He could feel this taste buds straining toward the drawer, his throat parched with need.

"What does that mean? Are you changing your ruling?"

"No, but you might want to take another look around."

As Corl hung up the phone, his brain quickly ran through the possibilities. It could still be natural causes, but it could also be…hinky.

*****

She woke the next morning to sunshine on her face and a gurgle in her belly. She barely made it off the couch and across the room before the gurgle became a gorge erupting from her mouth. Ivanya clutched a small wastebasket to her face and heaved up everything she had ever eaten. When it was over, she leaned against the wall feeling empty and exhausted. And hungry. No, famished. It was strange to go from vomiting to ravenous. Pregnancy was weird.

In the kitchen, she cracked eggs on the griddle and arranged bacon and sausage around them. The food sizzled applause as it cooked. When it was finished, she piled it on a plate, set it on the table and slid into a chair. She scrolled her social media while she happily stuffed her face.

Almost mindlessly, Ivanya speared a sausage on her fork and brought it to her mouth. Flavor exploded across her taste buds. It was the best sausage she had ever tasted. A sonnet could have been composed about it; she had half a mind to write one right then. She reached down to stab another piece, but the slippery thing avoided her utensil. She tore her eyes from her phone and gaped in horror at the plate. It was as if a miniature murder had taken place before her. The tasty victim had been cannibalized horribly; blood and grease seeped across the striking whiteness of the porcelain, mixing with yolk and tainting the thick egg whites.

Out of reflex, Ivanya flew from the chair and bolted to the sink, expecting to be violently ill. Strangely, she wasn't. In fact, it was all she could do not to return to the table and scarf the rest of the bleeding sausages down her throat. The idea revolted her on a basic human level, but that did not stop her from yearning for the bloody meat.

A sound in the doorway startled Ivanya, and she whipped her head toward the noise, a hand on her chest to keep her heart inside.

"Mornin', Vani," Abigail mumbled, oblivious to the fact that she had nearly caused a major cardiac event. She opened her eyes widely to make them wake up. "How are you?"

"Besides losing ten years off my life span, I'm ok. You spent the night?"

The 'duh' was unspoken but heavily implied. "Well, I wasn't going to leave you alone."

Ivanya poured Abigail a cup of coffee, watching her come alive by degrees as she drank it.

"Mmm. So good. Thank you." Abby tried in vain to smooth down her hair, which stood up in comical spikes reinforced by yesterday's hair gel. She muttered an expletive that sounded like bucket and turned to Ivanya. "Sit down, girly. We need to have a chat." Abigail patted the chair next to her.

Ivanya stood resolutely where she was, arms crossed defensively over her chest. She knew what was coming.

"What are we doing about the baby?" There it was. The loaded question she had no answer for.

"I'm working on it," Ivanya snapped.

Abigail scoffed. "No, you're not. You haven't done a single thing. You've known about this for three weeks now. Have you even made a doctor's appointment?"

"I will," Ivanya said, the words sounding more like a whine than a resolution. "I have to deal with Grams, then I'll take care of it. Okay?"

"And we have to go shopping," Abby squealed, clapping her hands like an excited toddler. "The baby needs things and you need things. We need a nursery. How long till we know the sex?"

"Abs, you're rambling." Ivanya sighed her irritation. "And you're way ahead of yourself. I'm giving the baby up. I'm not keeping it."

Abby's eyes blinked rapidly, trying to staunch the tears that had suddenly appeared. Ivanya knew then that Abigail wanted the baby and that giving it up would be difficult because she would fight for it every step of the way. It was as if their roles were reversed and Abigail had gotten the maternal instinct.

Well, tough cookies, said voice, cackling like the witch she was.

"Shut up, Susan," Ivanya whispered under her breath.

"What?"

"Nothing. Never mind. I'll call the doctor later this afternoon." That should be enough to placate Abigail for a while.

Ivanya turned to head into the living room.

"Vani!" Abby shouted. "Did you know this sausage is raw?"

Oh, she knew all too well.

Chapter 7

Tarik surveyed the funeral from the crest of a nearby hill. He stood in the shadow of a maple tree, reveling in the scents from the people below. The air was heavy with grief and unshed tears. Even from this distance he could almost taste the melancholy.

The target leaned against her friend, clasping her hand tightly. Tears fell unrestrained as people milled about, offering whispered condolences while they waited for the services to start. She nodded feebly and mumbled what were sure to be mangled thank you's, if she bothered to speak at all. The custom was strange to him. Everyone seemed to want to talk to the target and touch her arm or brush back her hair, but as soon as they said their piece they avoided her, as if grief were a disease that was catching.

Snippets of conversation wafted up on the breeze.

"That poor girl…"

"…heard she's pregnant."

"What is she going to do?"

"…just a baby herself…"

Some of these words were said with genuine concern, but others dripped with malicious derision.

After a few minutes, the crowd parted, making way for a man in a black suit. He seemed oblivious to the heat as he stood before the group and called them to order. Mourners and spectators alike formed a loose horseshoe around the honey colored coffin. Tarik sat enthralled as the human death ritual began.

First came the singing, which bored him tremendously. Then came a strange custom where a wreath of dying carnations was placed on the casket and the spectators each placed a long stemmed rose alongside it. Why honor the dead with flowers that must suffer the same fate? Wouldn't it be more meaningful to use live plants, as a way to triumph over death? Yet another reason that humans fascinated him.

The man in the suit was wearing a microphone, so his voice was rich and clear as he intoned, "We are here together today to celebrate the life and to mourn the passing of Irena Devereaux." There was a collective sniffle as he continued. "Irena was one of the most intelligent and interesting people I have ever had the chance to meet. Her knowledge spanned a multitude of subjects, but she enjoyed books, gardening, and cooking the most. And more than all of these things, she loved her granddaughter, Ivanya."

He was a great speaker, knowing just when to pause to generate maximum emotion from the crowd. "Irena is not gone, my dear. She is with you in the taste of an expertly cooked pot roast, in the laughter brought on by a dirty joke, and in the very blooms of the flowers she loved." Another pause to allow the onlookers to dab tears with kerchiefs and cast pitying glances at the target. "I now ask for anyone who has a memory of this wonderful woman to come up and share it so we can celebrate a beautiful soul that has left us too soon."

The friend extricated herself from the target, who sagged slightly but managed to remain standing. She moved to the front of the crowd wearing a simple black dress. There was no blue or pink in the dark hair that laid across her head in soft waves. When she spoke, no microphone was needed—Tarik could hear every delicious word.

"Mrs. D didn't like me much. She thought I was a bad influence on Vani and that we would get into trouble. I was and we did. But when my parents went out of town on business, there was always room in the house for me. When she made pecan pie, she would always save me a piece, because she knew it was my favorite and that I would be over at some point to eat it." The friend's voice was strong and steady, but tears were sliding down her face. "She gave me a home when I needed one and she gave me a sister. Thank you, Mrs. D."

More people stepped forward and regaled the assemblage with memories. A large woman with short red hair spoke about prize winning roses. A short, hunched over old man talked at length about a joke the old woman had told that had him in stitches. Apparently, no one thought she had it in her. Tarik had obviously seen a side of this woman that she hid from others. She was never more herself than in the hour of her death.

Eventually, the humans tired of trying to find sense in the senseless, to find reason where there was none, and began to disperse. That was when it got truly interesting. A loud grinding noise cut through the air and the casket began to sink slowly into the earth. Most did not pay much attention to this and continued moving toward the parking area. Until the target screamed. The long, piercing howl drilled directly into Tarik's brain, making him wince. He clapped his hands over his ears and inhaled deeply, tasting pure anguish on the air. The target ripped the wreath and the roses from the casket lid and threw them to the ground, not caring that thorns were scoring her palms. The scent of blood added yet another appetizer to the menu. Tarik was glad he had come.

The target beat on the lid of the box with small, bloody fists. She screamed at the body inside to come out right now and be with her. That she couldn't do this alone. There was more, but it was no longer words, just the garbled keening moans of the bereaved. The coffin didn't answer, the lid didn't open, it just continued its journey into the ground. She stood there for a moment, destroyed flowers strewn about her shoes

63

as it went deeper and deeper still. Spectators looked on in horror and awe as she stood on the edge of the hole and leaped inside.

There was more screaming, but it came from the people who had stayed. Some stood back in stunned silence, but one or two rushed forward to help. The machine ground to a halt as a large man reached into the maw of the earth and pulled the now supine form of the target from it. Her skirt was dirty and torn, her hair tangled, and she was utterly unconscious. It amazed Tarik how weak the girl was. At this rate, she would not survive long enough to fulfill the Priestess's prophecy. The man laid her on the grass and stroked her cheek, whispering words that Tarik could not hear. Sirens sounded in the distance and Tarik faded out to give his report.

*****

Lykah paced her chambers, too excited to sit down. The old witch was dead, the girl was with child, and Kabe was searching out the other items needed for the ritual. The daily reports from Tarik had been most satisfying, the girl was getting more and more isolated each day, which meant taking the child would be a simple task. In a few short months, the child would be born and the spirit of the Ca'taal housed in its body. Then, sweet power would be hers.

She frowned slightly. Tarik was a wild card, though. There was no question that he was the best demon for the job, but he was so unpredictable. He had a penchant for human watching; like a child with an ant farm, they seemed to hypnotize him. She hoped he would not develop an affinity for this human. That would be a catastrophe.

He was unique in every way. And beautiful. And ruthless. Everything that Lykah deemed important. His skin was black as night, laid over thick layers of ropy muscle. Crimson markings wound around every inch of him. Across his bald head, down his cheeks, over his neck and, she imagined, in all of the places covered by clothes. Just looking at him sent tingles of desire through her body. But she wouldn't give in to it, no matter how she wanted to.

That would be bad for business.

She sat on her throne and picked up a tattered scroll, holding it gingerly with two fingers on each side. The prophecy. The blueprint for the future. She read it again, anticipation burning through her.

Born with light the darkness grows

The one that sees, the one that knows

With no heart, but many souls

All seeing eyes, black as coal

In the light the power lies

The future hides behind the eyes

The war shall rage, cities burn

A hellish song, a dark nocturne

In the end, only one will stand

Light turns to dust, grains of sand

This was what she waited for, what all of these preparations were leading up to. As far as her people knew, the child would be a weapon to help in the war against humankind. That was only part of it. With the power of the Ca'taal, Lykah, High Priestess of the Trynok would hold dominion over all. Above and below. Every being would bow to her and grovel at her feet. The world would bathe in blood and fire, and Lykah would watch from her perch on high.

Chapter 8

The sausage incident had been sufficient motivation for Ivanya to finally make an appointment with a doctor. Her first thought was that the place looked fake, like one of those clapboard houses found on an artillery range. It resembled a real home on the outside, but once inside you began to notice things. The doctor's office was like that.

The lobby was painted a soft marbled pink with baby blue carpet on the floor. Eight by ten photographs of smiling mothers and children hung framed on the walls, but they looked to Ivanya to be the ones the frame had been purchased with. Comfort had not been on the mind of the person who had designed this room. The chairs were hard plastic, like those you would find in a classroom. But the thing that disturbed her the most was the plants.

An African violet occupied a terracotta pot on the table next to a perfectly fanned out array of magazines. These were dated years ago, but looked new; the covers were in mint condition and the spines were not cracked. The plant was dead. The leaves had taken on a sickly brown hue and the soil was dry and cracked, like sun baked black clay. Branches had snapped off the Fichus in the corner, its fronds also brown and parched. Dust caked the leaves.

That's what you get for picking the first doctor's office that you hear about, Susan whispered.

"Shut up," Ivanya retorted, her voice sounding flat and hollow in the empty room.

An assortment of kid's toys sat next to a line of smaller chairs. These were also in pristine condition. No crayon marked the play kitchen, though there was a collection of art supplies on a nearby table, and the rest of the toys were piled neatly in a crate.

The television mounted on the wall in the upper right corner was off. Unplugged.

She sat in one of those uncomfortable chairs, apprehension swirling around in her head. Just the idea of staying in this plant cemetery unnerved her. How could she have faith in a medical professional who allowed the office plants to perish?

Ivanya wanted very much to get up and rush out the door.

Get ahold of yourself, she chided. *You're being paranoid.*

Screw that, the voice said. *This place is creepy. There is something wrong here.*

Ivanya was about to heed Susan's advice when the door on the far side of the room opened and a nurse emerged, clipboard in hand.

"Miss Devereaux? The doctor will see you now." Her voice was rough and gritty and not in the least bit pleasant. "I'm Ruth, and I'm working with Dr. Hammond today."

They walked down the hall in relative silence, which made Ivanya uncomfortable.

"You should really get some artificial plants in your waiting room," she blurted out.

Ruth looked surprised and a little dismayed at the thought. "Why on earth would we do that?"

"Did you not notice that they are all dead?"

"I guess not."

Ivanya looked at her incredulously. This didn't make sense. The lobby was immaculate and someone must clean it every night. So how did someone so thorough miss the fact that the plants had died, probably a long time ago?

"I guess I just find it…unsettling," Ivanya said. "This place is supposed to be dedicated to keeping me healthy. You guys can't even keep the plants alive. What am I supposed to do with that?"

Ruth pursed her thin lips and motioned for Ivanya to step on the scale.

"One hundred and twenty eight pounds," she said through clenched teeth.

Chagrin burned in Ivanya's cheeks—she hadn't meant to be so offensive. She opened her mouth to apologize, but the other woman had already stalked halfway down the hall.

Ivanya followed the nurse into EXAM ROOM #1 and came to a dead stop two steps in. Were they kidding? This room was straight out of the seventies, when comfort was secondary. The stainless steel table glared at her under fluorescent lights, except where it was covered by the one-ply sheet of tissue paper. Cruel steel legs stuck out at the end of the table, each topped with a small cup. Stirrups.

All the walls were a cold white, with no pictures or diplomas adorning them. Black and white checkered tile covered the floor. Other surfaces in the room were composed of brushed stainless steel, heavily scratched. Various jars sat on the counter, holding things like cotton balls and tongue depressors.

"Sit, please."

Ivanya obeyed, raising an eyebrow at the nurse's tone.

Ruth wrapped a blood pressure cuff around Ivanya's bicep and pumped the bulb vigorously. The Velcro torture device tightened painfully, the veins in her arm rising from her skin. The pressure was enough to make her cry out, an expletive on the tip of her tongue.

Finally, the pressure relented. The blood returned to her fingertips; they tingled painfully.

"Change into the gown," Ruth snapped, "and Dr. Hammond will be in to see you shortly." She spun on her orthopedic shoes and marched from the room.

The gown was scratchy, like weak sandpaper, and the open back left her feeling exposed...and cold. Her butt sat on the chilly surface of the table and shivers coursed through her. If the doctor didn't come in soon her butt was going to become a glutesicle. There wasn't even a blanket to cover herself with. Her skin broke out in gooseflesh.

Shortly turned out to be a half hour. By this time she was ready to leave. Scratch that. Wishing she had never come. Her eyelids drooped for a moment, and when she opened them again, a white jacketed man sat on the stool next to her. He moved like a phantom; she had never even heard his footsteps.

"Hello, Ms. Devereaux; I'm Dr. Hammond. How are you?" His round cheeks jiggled a little when he pulled them into a smile.

"Good, I guess," she squeaked.

"And what can I do for you today?"

She pointed sarcastically to her slightly rounded stomach. "The baby is doing strange things to my body. Some smells are making me vomit, and smells that should make me vomit make me hungry instead. And my side hurts like hell."

"Well, let's take a look then." He smiled and gestured for her to lay down. He gently pressed on her abdomen. "How does that feel?"

She cussed under her breath.

He smiled in response. "I guess that answers that. What is the quality of the pain? Is it an aching, stabbing, cramping or throbbing?"

"Cramping."

"That's good. It's perfectly normal. In order to release an egg, the ovary must contract. Sometimes, especially in early pregnancy, the ovary still goes through the motion, though an egg is not released."

Well, you're not dying. That's good.

"Would you like to hear your baby's heartbeat?"

Ivanya nodded uncertainly and laid back on the table. Dr. Hammond placed a cloth over her hips and pulled the gown up, exposing the smooth skin of her midsection.

"Nurse, please get the gel for me."

She slapped it in to his hand without a word.

"Now, Miss Devereaux, this is going to be a little cold."

Without more preamble than that, he squirted a generous amount of it onto her stomach. She gasped, instinctively flinching away from the frigid substance. Dr. Hammond's eyes twinkled at her reaction. He plucked something off the counter that reminded her a portable CD player. Static filled the room when he flipped it on and placed a small microphone into the gel.

Until that moment, pregnancy had been an abstract concept to Ivanya. Sure, she knew there was a baby growing inside her, but visualizing herself as a mother had been impossible. It had not been real. That all changed the instant she heard the heartbeat. It sounded like a washing machine, a light swishing sound. Amazement bathed her in sudden warmth. There really was a person in there. A tiny little human being, with a heartbeat and maybe a few limbs. That heartbeat sealed her fate, there was no longer a choice. She needed this baby. The child had forged a connection in her that went deeper than the umbilical cord that sustained its life.

"Hmm."

"What? What's wrong?"

Dr. Hammond grabbed a tape measure and pulled it over Ivanya's stomach, just above the pelvic bone. "You're just a little larger than I expected. Hold on a minute. I'm going to do an ultrasound so we can see exactly what is going on here."

His tone sent a stab of fear through her heart. Was something wrong with the baby?

"No, Miss Devereaux, I don't think so. I'll need the ultrasound to confirm, but I believe you are further along that you think."

She hadn't realized she'd spoken aloud until the doctor answered her. He was still smiling. He must be jacked up on something—nobody smiled that much.

He left the room again, leaving Nurse Ruthless standing by the door wearing a scowl. The hostility radiating from the nurse made Ivanya's stomach roll around inside her. But before she had to think about it too much, Dr. Hammond came back in. The wheels of the cart he pushed squealed, the sound bouncing off the bare walls. It was laden with computer equipment and miscellaneous cords.

Again with the gel. Another microphone looking thing skated around on her belly. A grainy image in the shape of an upside down V appeared on the monitor. Varying degrees of gray swirled on the screen. Some of it moved so fast that it began to mess with her eyes.

"Ah…," he whispered. "Here we go."

Ivanya didn't really see anything; it was all movement and strange blurry shapes. How could anyone make sense of that?

"Okay," he said, as he moved the probe in a circular pattern. "There it is, the head. And see that? That is your baby's heart."

Her breath caught in her throat. It didn't really look like anything, but it moved quickly. It pumped back and forth, a tiny drum swathed in salt and pepper snow. That little heart was enough to stop her own. There was a certain impressionistic beauty to the image on the screen. Tears sprang to her eyes, blurring the picture further.

She had to peel her eyes away to calm down; she flitted them about the room instead and tried to slow her breathing. Her gaze lit upon the doctor's head. She hadn't noticed before that he was balding. His hair seemed greasy and an angry red rash patched his scalp, but that was not the worst of it. The hand that held the ultrasound probe was not covered by a glove. His nails were rough and each had a crescent moon of dirt underneath.

The desire to leave had grown, become a deep rooted need to be miles away from this place, from these people.

The voice shifted anxiously in Ivanya's underbrain. *Something is wrong.*

"Ruth, please prepare Miss Devereaux for her exam."

Ivanya jumped as if goosed by a cattle prod. Oh, she knew what he was referring to, and it was not going to happen. Even if Hammond washed his hands and put on gloves, the damage had already been done. She couldn't allow that hand to venture inside her; not even for a moment.

"I really don't have time for that right now." She used the hem of the gown to wipe the remnants of goop from her belly. "I have a birthing class at the hospital in about twenty minutes. Can we reschedule the pelvic please?" The lie rolled so smoothly off her tongue that she almost believed it herself.

Dr. Hammond meticulously returned all of the ultrasound instruments to the cart; he said nothing, Ruthless spoke for him.

"Miss Devereaux," she began, her sandpaper voice hardening the words. "There are some things that we need to look at if we are going to provide the level of care you need. You appear to be further along than you know." She was trying to sound nice. It wasn't working. "We have to make sure that everything is alright with the fetus."

Ivanya stood, not caring at that particular second that her ass was hanging out. Her prime objective was making it to the door. She stripped off the gown and let it fall to the floor. Her jeans and t-shirt sat folded on the chair next to the exam table. She snatched them up, pulling the pants up her legs. There was a little trouble getting them over her hips, but with a grunt she managed. Her shoes were under the chair. She bent to get them and all hell broke loose.

Bony fingers closed around her arm like a vise, hard enough to make her cry out.

Stop it, the voice said. *No one can hear you!*

She realized with dawning horror that her inner self was right. This appointment was in a partially deserted section of town; the buildings next to it had for sale signs in the windows.

And there were no people. No other patients, not a single squalling baby. That was odd, but not a cause for concern; maybe it was just a slow day. It was the lack of staff that should have alerted her to the wrongness of the situation. But it hadn't, and now she was going to suffer for being an idiot.

The nurse spun around, pinning her to the wall with a bony arm across her throat. "We're *going* to do this, Miss Devereaux."

"Like hell we are," Ivanya wheezed. She hiked a bare foot into Ruth's kneecap. The other woman yelped and reflexively reached for the insulted joint, freeing Ivanya's neck for a second. That was all she needed. Lowering her head, Ivanya pushed off the wall with one foot and rammed the nurse in the stomach. The woman flew back a few feet, hitting the floor with a solid thud. Ivanya didn't stop, not even to see if

Nurse Ruthless was getting up. About ten feet lay between her and the door. She had to get there.

Hammond stood in the doorway, seeming much bigger than he previously had. The rash on his scalp was more pronounced now and had spread to the sides of his face. Small patches of skin had begun to peel, revealing a layer of yellow pus beneath. Gone was the joviality from before. His expression was stormy, with all the fury of a hurricane.

She summoned every ounce of strength to the core of her being. She could feel it inside her, pulsing, growing, becoming something that she couldn't explain. Adrenaline buzzed through her veins, muscles throbbing as they hardened with the anticipation of what was to come. She welcomed the ache.

The doctor grunted as he lumbered forward, fists like giant mallets swinging for her head. Ivanya threw herself back and down to the floor before one of them could connect. Knowing that luck would only stay with her for so long, she darted between his legs and out into the hallway.

A scream of rage followed her down the corridor. Bangs and thuds sounded as the good doctor and his accomplice struggled to get out of EXAM ROOM #1.

Everything was black except for the point directly in front of her. The scenery didn't matter.

Nothing mattered except getting out of there alive. She ran faster than she thought she was capable of until, hallelujah! her palms pressed against the cool metal bar on the door and she spilled out of the building and into the sunshine.

Her silver Chevy truck was only a few feet away. She ran for it, fearing all that time that it would fade like a mirage. That fear did not abate until she pulled the door open, clambered into the seat and locked herself inside.

Minutes ticked by on the dashboard clock. Nobody burst from the office with teeth bared to take a bite of her flesh. Ivanya waited awhile longer before she turned the key and put the truck in gear. From the corner of her eye, she noticed the building. The place looked drastically different than when she had arrived. The concrete blocks were stained and cracked. Instead of panes of glass, the windows were filled with sheets of plywood. Burger wrappers and cigarette butts littered the sidewalk in front of the door.

It was as if no one had been in or out in years.

Chapter 9

Ivanya lay curled in bed, replaying the afternoon's events. The memories were more like smoky dreams in the process of dissipating, but she knew it had been real. So real. For some reason, this baby was special, and they, whoever *they* were, wanted it. Why? She had no idea. It was just a baby, what could it gain for anyone? Not for the first time that day, Ivanya thought of Grams. There were no tears this time, though, just a weird niggling feeling in her stomach.

When Ivanya had come clean about the baby, Grams' knee-jerk reaction had been to suggest an abortion. Grams, who had been staunchly pro-life up until then. Had she known something? Ivanya tried to put it out of her mind, but the thought lingered. It dug tentacles into her spine and sent cold waves of foreboding through her body. The answer was here, somewhere.

She took her time going downstairs, the heavy emptiness of the house pushing upon her lungs, bringing tears to her eyes. She stood in front of the basement door, trying to decide if she really needed to go down there. Grams had been in the basement often, especially in the weeks before her death. It was time Ivanya knew why.

The metal knob was cold against her hand as she twisted it and pushed in the same second, before her brain could stop the impulse. Only the top two steps were visible before the darkness swallowed the rest of them. Though she couldn't see it, she knew there was a pull cord within arm's reach. The problem was that it was within arm's reach from the second stair. The one on the edge of the abyss. She gulped and gingerly placed a foot on the top step. Her arm stretched out, fingers brushing against the string. It swung out of reach. Sighing heavily, her chest tight with fear, she took a step down and tried again. Pushing her terror of the dark and of the basement itself to the bottom of her belly, she reached out and caught the bastard string, yanking it hard. The cord chafed against her palm as the basement below appeared in the dim light.

She passed by ghostly shrouded furniture and stacks of old paint cans. On her left was an old steel washtub with a wringer and a pyramid of precariously stacked mason jars. To the right were Grams' shelves. Books about roses and container gardening were stacked neatly next to jars of homemade potpourri. Everything was conspicuously clean here. No dust on the jars of herbs and spices, some of which Ivanya had never heard of.

What the hell did she need wormwood for? Was there an absinthe still down here?

Ivanya continued browsing the strange boutique, picking up jars of roots and powders, opening wooden boxes that contained ornate fabrics and tools. There was something odd about the last set of shelves. It was pulled out from the wall just a bit. And from that crack, a sliver of wavering light.

Mystified, she pulled on the bookcase and it swung out easily. Behind it was a small room with shelves dug out of the stone walls, like a mausoleum or a tomb. And on an altar in the center was a lit candle.

It wasn't large, just a thin, white taper in a crystal candlestick, like the kind you might see on a dining room table. It was burned about halfway down. As she gazed transfixed at the flame, it went out with an audible poof of air. She should have been afraid, being plunged into sudden darkness, but she was not. A feeling like a soft, warm blanket surrounded her.

"Grams?" she whispered, not bothering to hide the hope in her voice. "Is that you?"

A soft glow illuminated a shelf behind the altar, and she moved forward to investigate. She didn't trip or bang her shins on anything. It was as if she had known this room her whole life. As she neared the glowing shelf, the light overhead snapped on. In front of her, taking pride of place on an embroidered square of white silk was a book, bound in worn red leather, an eye emblazoned on the cover in silver. She picked it up, knowing in her heart that this is where she would find understanding.

She sat at the small chess table and began to read. The first few pages contained beautiful drawings. A gothic cathedral under a sky teeming with birds. She could feel the movement behind the lines, practically hear the screeching of the crows. A bridge over a small stream was on the next page, detail so fine it could have been a photograph.

Soon she was engrossed in the tale of Lillian, a witch who had fallen in love with a priest named Michael. They had kept their union secret and he only visited her every few weeks at her cabin in the forest. She never ventured into town, as nature provided everything she needed.

Neither Father Michael nor Lillian foresaw the inevitable consequences of their union. She met him at the door, fear making her voice tremble.

"Michael," she whispered, touching his cheek with the palm of her hand.

"Yes, my love?" He kissed her lightly on the lips.

Getting lost in that kiss, in him, would be easy and she was tempted to let it happen. No! She could not. There was serious danger afoot. She had to tell him.

"I am with child," she said. Nausea soured her stomach. She did not know whether it was the normal sickness that came with impending motherhood, or whether it was born of nervousness that came from fear.

A mixture of surprise and unadulterated love colored his face. He glowed with exaltation. "Truly?"

She nodded, unable to speak. He leapt from his seat, folding her in a tender embrace. He ran a hand across her middle, a smile brightening his finely chiseled features.

"A child. I hope it is a daughter, as beautiful as you."

"You have no problem with this?" she asked, incredulously. "Does it not frighten you, the prospect of having our lives put into peril for this?"

Michael shook his head. "Now that I know of our child, the only thing that frightens me is not bringing her into this world. Anything else is secondary. I love you, Lillian. More than anything else in this life. This child is proof of that, a symbol of our devotion to each other. How could that frighten me?"

Lillian wanted to tell him he was being foolish, that this child was a danger to them both, but she could not move the words beyond her lips. The very moment she realized that her symptoms were that of pregnancy, she'd fallen in love with the child. It was a piece of

Michael. Keeping it would be unsafe, but being without it would be agony.

If it were known that Michael fathered a child, he would be excommunicated from the church and punished severely. Worse still, if it were known that the mother was a witch, they would all burn. At the thought, she could feel flames licking her feet. Smell the sweet aroma of her burning flesh. The screams would erupt from her throat, and once begun, would not cease until she was razed to ash.

Lillian tried to quell her emotions, to keep the fear at bay, but it was difficult when Michael was gone. His leaving had always been a necessary precaution, but now the stakes were higher, secrecy ever more important.

Her stomach grew quickly as the weeks passed. That sickness that should have calmed by now was even more violent. Each day she heaved the contents of every meal into the chamber pot. The larger she grew around the middle, the thinner her arms and legs became. Her silky, chestnut hair had faded to the dull color of mud. Weakness claimed her. Most days she was too ill to even get out of bed. Eating became difficult; there didn't seem to be enough room in her stomach for food. On his rare trips home, Michael fed her broth by spoon. He did this often and in small amounts to help her keep it down.

The only thing that kept her living was her power. She drew life from the trees and the soil. She breathed it on the wind. She leeched life from the trees and ferns, until, unable to sustain her any longer, they began to die. Leaves fell to the ground in dry piles, some skittering around on the matted brown grass like bits of parchment. Lillian tried not to think of what would happen if the life around her could no longer sustain her own.

She awoke to rays of sunlight poking through the knots in the wood. Like the air in a tropical climate, the heat oppressed her. Breathing took tremendous effort. But that was not what woke her. It was the perfect silence that had shook her from sleep. There was no sound. Not the rustling of branches as the wind danced through the trees, nor the sound of birds chirping as they fed their young. Nothing; the silence hurt her head and made her entire body shake.

She was paralyzed instantly by the sharp stabs of agony that attacked her torso. At first, she couldn't move, couldn't breathe, couldn't even scream. The pain in her stomach wracked through her, causing her body to flail uncontrollably. Up and down, up and down, so violently that it sent her sprawling to the floor. Her head banged on the thick wooden planks. A burning slit opened in her forehead. Blood flowed into her eyes, turning the world a dark red. The color matched the pain.

When the tremors wore off, she sat up and looked around, trying to make sense of what was happening. She gasped in horror at the pool of viscous liquid between her legs. Her water had broken; the baby was coming. Weakness consumed her. The edges of her vision clouded and black spots danced before her eyes. She tried to fortify herself by drawing from nature, but everything around her was either dead or too weak to be of use.

Intense pain and all of the blood on the floor pushed her to the realization that this was no longer a tough labor—it was now a battle for survival. If she did nothing to renew her life force she would perish. But more important was the blinding epiphany that if she died, the baby would die as well. The thought motivated her enough to bring her to her feet. She stumbled to the door, sinking her fingers into the recesses between the logs of the wall for stability. With weak arms, she pushed the door open. Light blinded her as she stumbled outside, the deafening silence broken only by her groans and unsure steps.

The breeze felt good on her hot skin. Goosebumps rose to the surface, the sweat on her chest becoming cold. Some of the strength returned to her body, making it easier to walk. The screams would come again, and sooner rather than later. The proximity to the village was too close; there was no chance she wouldn't be heard. For all she knew, her earlier cries of agony had already sent people into the woods to investigate.

The further she got from home, the easier it was to move. She called the elements to her, begging them to help her. To strengthen her enough to bring the baby into the world. She whispered an incantation in Latin. She didn't know what the translation of the words was, but she knew what the spell would do. Paralyzing her vocal cords would allow her to scream without giving away her location.

Unfortunately, there was no help for the pain. She could draw from nature to combat the blood loss, but it was still going to hurt. Gasping, she laid herself at the base of a willow tree, resting her head against its trunk. The grass was cool against her legs and she sighed in relief. It was short lived. The pain came again. Torturous agony ripped through her, tearing at her insides. Her nether parts flamed as the child's head began to push through. She thought that the spell for silence had been a stroke of genius, but if anything, it made her situation worse. Screaming did not bring the relief that it had before. With no sound, the effort was useless.

Lillian mouthed the reversal spell. To her complete horror, nothing happened. She couldn't believe that she had made such a novice mistake. A spell had to be spoken so it could be heard by those you were asking for help. If her mother were still alive she would have boxed her ears. Not only could she not call for help, she could not call to Michael when he came looking for her.

Cohesive thought was lost to her now. She thought in spirals of red and strings of expletives. The burning between her legs intensified as she pushed, the worthless screams tearing up her throat. She never felt pain such as this. A thousand razors cut into her flesh. Another soundless howl burst forth. There was a fullness within her. It built up, gained pressure, pulsing and throbbing, straining away from her while still inside. Then the dam broke with an audible pop and the child slid out of her. It was slick with blood and fluid, covered in a sheet of something like vellum. Tiny arms struggled, clawing at the sac that held it captive. Lillian leaned forward while scooting back, until her spine rested against the tree. She exhaled softly and blotted sweat from her brow with the sleeve of her gown.

Tearing open the sac was harder than it seemed it would be, but she managed to extract the baby. A girl. The most beautiful thing she had ever seen.

Michael found her in the forest, about a half mile from the house. She was a vision in disarray, a soft flush to her cheeks and an infant suckling her breast. She had never looked so beautiful.

"My love, are you all right?"

She sighed and nodded. She gestured him to come closer and handed him the child.

Michael gasped. She was perfect, beautiful in every way. A full head of raven hair, clear ivory skin, but the eyes, they were black as night. There were no whites, just a flat blackness that filled him with dread.

What had they done? How could he have gone through with this? By satisfying his own desires, he had made room for evil, and it had brought forth this...abomination. The God he loved so much was punishing them. But perhaps there was still solace to be had. Moving quickly, he turned and fled, clutching the baby to his chest when all he really wanted to do was throw it as far away from him as he could. But that would not do.

It took him some time to reach the church, but when he arrived he did not delay. Laying the thing on the altar, he covered its chest in holy water from the font. Smoke rose from its skin, accompanied by the sound of sizzling meat. He spoke in Latin, so quickly that the words were almost unintelligible. He asked his Father for forgiveness and made an oath to serve only him for the rest of his life. Then, from his back pocket he removed his knife and positioned it squarely above the abomination's heart. He muttered a prayer and plunged the blade through its chest. It screamed, an unearthly chorus of voices and squeals like a wounded cougar. Black blood and a fine mist escaped the hole where the blade had been.

Lillian appeared in the doorway, her eyes burning with hatred. She leapt at him, clawing at his face with hands like talons and maternal ferocity. His flesh burned as his skin was rended by her fingernails. Smoke billowed through the room, and it took a moment for him to realize the church was on fire. Outside, he could hear the chants for his death from the villagers who carried torches and weapons. Lillian scooped the baby from the altar and cradled its lifeless form to her breast, silent tears coursing down her cheeks. She didn't move from the spot or avert her gaze from the child, even when she started to burn.

Ivanya closed her eyes to absorb what she had just read. Whoever wrote it down had taken some creative license to be sure, but she believed every word. She couldn't explain why, and she knew she would never tell anyone, not even Abigail, but the truth of the words ran bone deep. There was more, a lot more, but there was no time for it now. She would come down another day and read the rest. Maybe it would shed some light on what was happening to her.

Chapter 10

Summer had begun to fade into early fall, and all of Watson was covered in a crispy quilt of leaves. And as the season changed, so too, did Ivanya. She was now about five months along and huge. Her belly could have been its own planet, a strange and new world. It was mapped with stretch marks and veins that composed the visage of rugged terrain.

Each aspect of pregnancy was a double edged sword. She was eager to meet her child, but she didn't look like herself anymore. With the added weight in her face and on her body, the reflection she saw in the mirror was unfamiliar. None of her clothes fit right either, but she finally had boobs and that feeling was fabulous. Never before had a shirt been too small in the chest. She sincerely hoped that the bosoms would stick around after the baby came.

Food was another thing that continued to baffle her. It was like she had reverse senses and the things that smelled terrible were actually what she should eat. If it smelled good, chances were that she would be eating something terrible. Just yesterday, she had grabbed the milk out of the fridge, so thirsty that she began to chug right out of the carton. It was not until the thick, soft chunks hit her tongue that she knew it was spoiled. As with the sausage incident, she was appalled and fully expected to throw up, but she had to make herself spit it out and throw the carton in the trash.

The worst change of all though, was the people around her. The neighbor ladies, especially that nosy assed Mina Gulleckson, all clucked their tongues and talked behind her back about how she was too young to have a baby. When she entered the grocery store or the gas station, conversations would cease. They would stare at her, some with mild curiosity in their eyes, others with outright hostility.

Even relationships with friends changed. At first, everything was exciting and you would discuss what kind of mom you would be; you'd come up with ideas for the kid's future and everything was great. It was when the belly grew that things got weird. They began to see pregnancy as some kind of flesh-eating parasite that they could catch just by being in the same room as the afflicted one. They stopped coming to visit, opting instead for the safer phone call option. But even those began to taper off after a few weeks and the pregnant person was left alone and frightened as their bodies betrayed them in the basest of ways.

Ivanya thought that Abigail would be the exception to this rule, but she hadn't been around in days. Hadn't even called.

As she was thinking about her, her cell phone rang. She didn't even look at the display, just answered it feeling sorry for herself.

"Hello?"

"How is my little piñata today?" It was Abigail, think of the devil, and she sounded especially chirpy.

"Piñata?"

Abigail laughed. "You are colorful and full of something fun!"

Ivanya screwed up her face. "How do you know it will be fun? I could be brewing a two-headed creature with a tail for all you know." She almost laughed in spite of herself; Abigail didn't know how close she was to the fear in Ivanya's heart.

"Well, then it will be unique. Listen, I need you to come over today. Around one-ish. I need to pick out my dress for the Chesterfield gala that my parents are hosting in November. *Mother* says that it has to be *classy* and *conservative.* In other words, not me. I need help." Abby sounded like she was going to hyperventilate.

Though Ivanya hadn't felt like a teenager for quite some time now, a bit of it came back to her. Suddenly, picking out a dress seemed like just the thing.

*****

At one o'clock sharp, Ivanya stood in front of the ornate Kayne mansion. The house really had no business being in Watson, Michigan; it would have looked more at home in Hollywood or Paris. Every house in town looked like a shack compared to this one. It was a hulking white structure three stories high, with balconies and patios galore. Pillars reminiscent of Roman bathhouses supported the large stone veranda. Knocking on the door was useless for a house this large. She rang the doorbell. The door was opened by the butler, yes butler, complete with tuxedo. Ivanya had the insane urge to dance like a penguin, but that would be tacky.

"Miss Devereaux," the tall man intoned. "Right this way."

He led her through the marble foyer, down a hallway and into a dining room that was bigger than her backyard.

"SURPRISE!" screamed a roomful of people.

A large banner that read IT'S A BABY hung over a table that could easily seat twenty-five people. Streamers of pink and white crepe paper twisted over the ceiling, stray strands trailing down the walls. The table itself was laden with intricately wrapped gifts of every size.

And people. She knew some of them, like Pennie Martin from sophomore English and Lindsay

95

Stoll, who had been her study partner in chemistry class. Even Candice Larson had come, even though she lived in New York now. They had been pretty close until Candice got a modeling contract junior year. Now the only time anyone saw her was on magazine covers. Ivanya was flattered that she flew all the way back home for a baby shower. Most of the other people were strangers to her, people Abigail knew from society soirees and such. Ladies that would have been offended if they weren't invited to a party at Kayne Manor, even if they didn't know the guest of honor.

Ivanya moved deeper into the room, accepting hugs of congratulations and kisses on cheeks. Hands reached out and rubbed her belly like she was a wish troll or a genie lamp. It was unnerving that people felt they had permission to touch her without asking. It was still her body, wasn't it?

Three banquet tables lined the west wall, laden with all manner of food. Thick slabs of watermelon, cantaloupe, and honeydew sat on a silver tray next to a bowl of fruit salad. There were subs on various breads, stuffed with meat and cheese. And pigs in blankets. Ivanya loved those damn things; she wondered how much arguing it took for Isobel to say yes to that menu item. There were eclairs and strawberry shortcake, brownies and fudge. A three tier cake with pink and blue icing stood on miniature pillars, housing a chocolate fountain beneath it. Written in an elegant script was *IT'S A BABY*!!!   That cake would have been more at home at a wedding reception than here.

Abigail ran to Ivanya's side, taking her by the arm and helping to ease her into a chair at the head of the table. There was an awkward moment when they had to pull the heavy chair out further to accommodate Ivanya's mammoth belly.

"Who are all these people?" she whispered to Abigail.

She laughed.   "Friends of friends."   She straightened her floral print dress, (no doubt a demand on Isobel's part) and addressed the crowd. "Now that our super adorable guest of honor is here...let the festivities begin!"

Much to Ivanya's surprise, she had a great time. Everyone gushed (and lied) about how good motherhood looked on her. How she seemed to be glowing. She wondered if Abby paid them off for their flattery. Whatever the case, Ivanya appreciated it.

Even Isobel seemed to be okay. She only glared in Ivanya's direction one time and a ghost of a smile actually appeared on her face when Abby had the bright idea to see how many sheets of toilet paper it would take to make it completely around Ivanya's midsection. Twenty. So much for the ego. Next, they had a contest to see how many safety pins a blindfolded person could sift from a bowl of rice in one minute. Ivanya won that one and received a pair of movie tickets and a gift card for snacks and drinks at the theater.

The gifts yielded everything from high end outfits and shoes to bottles and receiving blankets. Rattles, teething rings, and pacifiers. There was a beautiful dark cherry crib that could later be transformed into a toddler bed. All of the sheets and blankets were done in a lovely sage dragonfly pattern. The thing looked more comfortable than her own bed. From Isobel, there was a lacy bassinette with storage underneath. Candice gifted her with a heavy changing table that matched the crib perfectly. There was a bathtub and a car-seat/stroller combo with little elephants on it. Abigail bought seven tutus, all a different color and loaded with sparkles. Ivanya looked at Abby with confusion on her face.

"How do you know it's a girl?"

"I just bought these to put it out in the universe because I want a girl."

"Yeah, it's all about what you want. Dork."

"When are you going to learn that it has always been and will always be that way?"

Next came the diapers. So many diapers. They ranged from newborn to size six, which looked like they'd fit a toddler. There would barely be room for anything else in the baby's closet. Hell, it would take a truck to haul them away.

"Holy cow, I don't think I'll ever have to buy diapers," she said in awe.

The women that already had children laughed knowingly. "Oh, you'll need more. Babies poop a lot."

She didn't know what surprised her more: the fact that she would use all of these diapers and then some, or one of the most elegant people she had ever seen saying poop in front of people. Whichever the reason, Ivanya laughed hard and it felt great. It had been a while.

Even Spencer Kayne, the object of her obsession since she was thirteen put in an appearance. He was cuter than ever today, with his sandy brown hair flipped across his forehead. He looked like he could have just come from a GQ photo shoot as he strode toward her, a dark blue gift bag in hand. He leaned down close to her face and whispered congratulations in her ear. Chills coursed deliciously down her neck as his warm breath touched her skin. Every surface of her body was suddenly on fire. At that moment, she didn't care that she was as big as a house, she wanted to take him home.

An elbow from Abigail pulled her back to reality just in time to stop the moan that had formed on her lips from escaping.

"Um, thanks," she replied to him, if a little unevenly. Cautiously, she opened the bag and laughed as she pulled out a pair of the tiniest bunny slippers she had ever seen. He walked away to talk to his mother, which allowed the flush that settled over her skin to cool.

After all of the gifts had been opened and cake had been eaten, people began to straggle toward the door. Ivanya stood up, her butt tingling from sitting too long. She picked up a plate and headed to the kitchen when a voice behind her asked what she thought she was doing. Isobel's expression was cold and cloudy when Ivanya met her gaze.

"Just taking care of my dishes." Her eyes widened with confusion.

"We have people for that," Isobel snapped. Her expression was one of pure hate, layered with a measure of disgust. It was only there for a second, then her face shifted and she was once again herself. The corners of her mouth turned up. "This is your party, Ivanya. The guest of honor is not supposed to clean up after herself. You'll have plenty of messes to clean up when the baby comes."

Ivanya set the plate down. If it was that big of a deal...

Then she went to find Abigail. She was going to give her the ass kicking of a lifetime for leaving her alone with that woman. Isobel had never liked Ivanya; she didn't think that Ivanya's tax bracket made her a suitable companion for her children. The crush that Ivanya had tried so hard to keep camouflaged, never even speaking of it to Abigail, was all too obvious to Isobel. And the woman hated her for it.

Spencer was her pride and joy, the apple of her eye, and all of those other ridiculous clichés. It was obvious in the way she doted on him, and in the way that she pretty much ignored her step-daughter. There was a reason that Abigail chose to look and act the way that she did—classic second child syndrome.

Ivanya was not comfortable here and she wanted to go home. She had only been in this house a handful of times, and not for very long. Abigail preferred to hang out in Ivanya's room to her own. Where the hell was Abby? Ivanya didn't want to leave without saying goodbye. Her heels clicked against the marble floor as she wandered down the hall. She peeked into the living room where two old ladies sat on the sofa sipping champagne.

By the time she reached the top of the staircase her calves were on fire. She called for Abby, her voice bouncing off the walls and the marble busts that adorned small tables in the hallway. All the doors were identical, and closed. She approached the first one she came to with caution, softly rapped on the dark wood with her knuckles, and after receiving no answer, turned the cool brass knob.

Her heart caught in her chest as she beheld Spencer in the process of changing his shirt. Thick muscle coated his bones, writhing with each movement. Bronzed pectorals topped a perfect washboard stomach. Denim hugged a pair of the most fabulous buns on earth.

He turned around, completely unsurprised with a cocksure smile upon his lips.

"See something you like, Vani?"

Her skin burst into flame.

"I-I was just looking for Abby," she stammered.

Spencer strode toward her. With one hand, he reached over her shoulder, casually pushing the door closed. The soft snick of the latch startled her a little. Suddenly, he seemed too close. Too large. Too...*there.*

"Well, she isn't here. It's just you and me."

How many times had she dreamed of this moment? Of his face close enough to kiss? Of him realizing that he wanted her? And now that it was here, as was evident by the way his eyes burned into hers, she had turned into a gigantic chicken. The lust she felt was tainted by an overwhelming desire to flee.

The distance between them was barely enough to slide a sheet of paper into. His skin was just shy of touching her belly. She inhaled the musky scent of him as he traced her jawline with his index finger.

She closed her eyes, breathing becoming quick and shallow.

Lips brushed against hers, feather light, like the wings of a butterfly. Then they withdrew, leaving her weak and wishing for more.

"What the hell was that, Spencer?" Her head swam with giddiness as she forced out the words that just might make him rethink the whole wanting her thing. But she had to do it, had to know. "Why do you all of a sudden like me?"

"Why do you assume it's sudden?"

Ivanya straightened up and stepped back until her spine pressed against the wall. She asked him what the hell he was talking about.

"Have you not realized how gorgeous you are? You never had one of those awkward, gangly phases." He raked a hand through sandy hair. "I've been attracted to you for quite some time. I'm just a better actor than you are."

"I-I have to go." She fumbled with the knob and flung the door open.

"Wait," he said, blocking her exit with one muscular arm across the doorway. "Come to dinner with me. Tonight. I'll pick you up at eight?" The cockiness was gone now, replaced by uncertainty and a glimmer of hope.

She glanced pointedly at her stomach. "Pregnant, remember? Dating in this condition seems a little strange to me."

"Babies need to eat, too," he prodded.

Without a word, she nodded and left the room as fast as she could. She was still reeling from the unexpected kiss as she walked out to her car and drove home; her quest to find Abigail forgotten.

Chapter 11

Kingston stared at the computer screen, wishing the words would come. Usually he liked writing reports, found it soothing. Not today. Today he just sat there, contemplating the blank screen and wishing he were somewhere else. Like maybe with that black haired girl that called him Detective Cutie. She was nice.

He typed Peggy Lofton's name on the first line and hit enter. There. He was started. Competency evaluations were the worst. If the person was found not competent to stand trial in a case like this one, people tended to get upset. Most believed that child killers should go to prison or die to pay for their crime, not be remanded to a 'cushy' psychiatric facility. Little did these people know that some of those places make prison look like a tropical getaway. Peggy Lofton had failed her exam with flying colors. Her delusion was so engrained in her psyche that she truly believed the only way to save her son from evil was to kill him. There was no doubt in Kingston's mind that she had loved Adam. She had done the only thing she could do. She would go to a hospital and she would be there until she died, which could be soon given that Kingston had put her on suicide watch. Peggy wanted nothing more than to be reunited with her son.

He tried to type some more, but he couldn't make the words cooperate, so he shut the computer down and prepared to head home.

A deep shout filled with anguish tore through the silence of the station house.

"Help me, please," the shouter begged. "My wife is gone!"

Kingston sprinted to the front desk and beheld a broken man. His cheeks were splotchy and red beneath a patchy brown beard. His curly hair stood up in a haphazard fashion. But it was his eyes that drew Kingston forward. They were wide and brown like those on a cow, and in those eyes, behind the thick lashes, was a pain so profound that Kingston couldn't fathom the extent of it.

He stood by as Sherry Tate, the desk sergeant, helped him into a chair and gave him a bottle of water.

"What's your name, sir?"

"Benjamin Crane. My wife's name is Peyton." Tears filled his eyes. "I can't find her. She's gone."

Sherry patted Benjamin's arm reassuringly, but the compassion didn't reach her eyes. She knew as well as Kingston did that the spouse was always the first person to rule out. This could be an act, albeit a good one. She shot Kingston a meaningful look over the weeping man's shoulder. She extracted a small notepad from her shirt pocket and began to take notes. Meanwhile, Kingston reached into his jacket pocket and hit the button on his memo recorder.

"When was the last time you saw Peyton?" She was good at this, Kingston mused. She used the woman's name to humanize her in case her husband had something to do with the alleged disappearance.

"Last night when I left for work. I work midnights at the foundry. I came home this morning and she was gone."

"I see. Generally, we do not file missing reports until the person has been gone at least forty-eight hours. Have you tried to contact her friends and family?"

Quiet weeping became all out sobbing. "Forty-eight hours? Someone took my wife. What if she doesn't have forty-eight hours? I called everyone we know, no one has seen her."

Sherry pursed her lips. "What makes you believe that Peyton was abducted, Ben? May I call you Ben?"

He nodded absently at her question then furrowed his brown in concentration. "Her purse and her phone are still on the counter. I take the car to work, we only have the one."

"Any signs of a struggle? Like disturbed furniture or an open door? Broken windows?"

"No."

Sherry scribbled furiously on her notepad, rapidly firing questions at him.

"Is there a possibility that she left on her own? Were you having marital trouble?"

"No. We're so happy. We are expecting our first child. A girl. Her name is going to be Emma."

Alarm bells went off in Kingston's head. He heard Sherry ask if Ben knew of anyone that would want to harm his wife. Kingston didn't need to hear the reply to know that it was no. He hurried down the hall to Corl's office, barging in without knocking. Corl banged one of his desk drawers shut and jumped from his chair.

"You ever hear of knocking, kid? I'm working on something in here."

From the smell of it, he was working on getting drunk, but that wasn't important now. Kingston slapped the recorder on the desk and pushed play. Benjamin Crane's voice filled the room. Corl listened for a moment, then stopped the recorder.

"Let's check it out. What are you waiting for?" Corl popped a piece of gum in his mouth, put on his suit jacket and left the room, making his way to the front desk. Benjamin was seated in a plastic chair next to the desk, Sherry Tate still taking notes. Corl approached the man cautiously, as if he were a bear or a rhinoceros.

"Mr. Crane, I'm Detective Corl and this is Dr. Kingston." He reached out and shook the man's hand. "I understand your wife is missing and I would like to help. Would you like to talk in my office?"

The husband nodded, his eyes moist with gratitude. Corl hadn't bothered to see if the man was following, and he was halfway down the hall before Crane was out of his seat. Kingston followed, typing like a mad man on his phone. As Crane sank into one of the chairs opposite Corl's desk, Kingston sent the email he had been composing, with a list of questions he wanted to ask but couldn't. Corl would do the asking and Kingston would observe. He sat in the other chair and waited for his partner to begin.

Corl steepled his fingers beneath his doughy chin and made brief eye contact with Crane before consulting the email.

"What does Peyton look like? Do you have a picture?"

Crane's hands shook as he slid a photo from his wallet across the desk. She was a pretty girl, probably mid-twenties, with honey colored hair and expressive blue eyes.

"She has blonde hair, like wheat. Blue eyes. She has a good tan right now because we've been doing a lot of yard work. Five-six. One fifty-five or so." Kingston noticed that Crane had continued to use the present tense when speaking of his wife. Sometimes guilty people messed that up; talked about the victim in the past tense by mistake. Those were the things that Kingston was trained to look for.

"She's beautiful," Corl said. "And you guys are expecting a baby? When is it due?"

"December twenty-second."

"So she's…"

"About seven months in."

"Has Peyton been acting strangely in the recent weeks, Mr. Crane?"

Benjamin scoffed, a little bitterly, Kingston thought. "Besides wanting pickles with vanilla ice cream and eating liver and onions for supper every night, no. She's pretty emotional, but that's normal with pregnancy, right?"

Kingston and Corl nodded simultaneously.

"Ok," Corl said. "Might there be a friend she went to visit or a family emergency? Maybe she forgot her phone when she left?"

"That thing is usually glued to her hand. She does a lot on social media because she doesn't go out much. She wouldn't have forgotten it."

Corl continued asking the prescribed questions, like was the marriage happy, had there been infidelity on either side, and what was their last argument about? Kingston gauged Crane's reactions. So far there was no hint of deception or evidence of guilt.

"What was your wife wearing when you last saw her?" Corl started with his own questions now that Kingston's were out of the way.

"One of my t-shirts; blue, I think. And a pair of grey shorts. She was getting ready for bed." He sniffled at the thought, fresh moisture in his eyes.

"Have you noticed anything in the neighborhood? Like a car you didn't recognize hanging around? Anything like that?"

Crane shook his head, mutely.

"Ok. We would like to come look at your house and see if there may be a clue as to where she went. Or with whom. Will that be alright?" Corl narrowed his eyes almost imperceptibly. Even if it wasn't alright, it was going to happen.

A brief flash of anger clouded Crane's face. "You're still acting like she left on her own free will. I'm telling you she didn't. She wouldn't do that. But come look around. Maybe you can find something that convinces you that someone took my wife."

*****

111

The Cranes lived in a brown double wide in the park off Walnut. The place was old, but well kept. It looked like it had been power-washed recently, and the white trim was newly painted. The large deck was surrounded on all sides by hewn log flower boxes containing carnations, lilies, and crisp white roses. There was a wooden swing set out in the yard, next to a newly built sandbox. Looked like they were getting everything ready for their little girl.

The house was dead silent when they walked in and sadness hung on the air. Kingston wanted to loosen his tie so he could breathe. Corl asked Crane to remain on the deck until they finished looking around.

The living room was pristine. No newspapers on the coffee table, no cups by the couch. The floor was vacuumed in neat lines. Two sets of footprints disturbed the carpet. Kingston assumed they belonged to Peyton and her husband, but he knew Corl would double check that. For all his shortcomings, he was smart as a whip and a good cop. He could make connections where no one else saw them.

Corl took pictures of the footprints on his phone and moved into the kitchen, which was just as clean. The floor was mopped with a citrus detergent and no dirty dishes were in the sink. The curtains above the sink were open, the window looking out on the clothesline out back. As Crane had reported, Peyton's purse, keys and cellphone were on the island next to a four-slice toaster. Something wet on the counter caught Kingston's eye and he leaned in closer. It looked almost like leftover moisture from a sponge or damp cloth, but it seemed oily. He bent down and smelled the substance; it was an alkaline odor he couldn't quite place. He snapped his fingers to get Corl's attention and waved him over. Corl smelled whatever it was.

"Hinky," he said, under his breath. He saw the question in Kingston's eyes. "Something the ME said."

He took what looked like a manicure kit from his pocket and withdrew a Q-tip and a small paper envelope. He swabbed the smear, sealed the Q-tip in the envelope and placed it all back in his pocket. He would have the lab analyze it later.

They continued through the house. The bathroom smelled strongly of disinfectant and bleach. There were no streaks on the mirror, no smears of toothpaste in the basin. The trashcan had a new lavender scented liner in it. Kingston opened the medicine cabinet and whistled. Not at the contents, which were perfectly innocuous bathroom items, but the manner in which they were kept. The entire house could pass a white glove test, but the medicine cabinet was over the top. All the tweezers and nail clippers on the bottom shelf were arranged by size and spaced a half inch apart. The vitamins and analgesics were also arranged this way, but the labels were also perfectly faced out. There was not a speck of dust on the bottles or the shelves. This indicated a rather severe case of OCD. From the look of the husband, obsessive compulsive disorder was not something he struggled with. It must have been the wife.

The next room was the nursery. It was done in a pale lilac with a blue border that had baby animals on it. The mobile over the crib had dangling animals on it: an elephant, a lion, a bear and a hippo. Baby toys and books were filed neatly on waist high shelving units.

"Well, that's weird," Corl said, breaking the silence in the room. "Where's the diaper bag? Maybe they have it in the car in case she goes into labor?"

Kingston shrugged. Although if the diaper bag was missing it would pose some very interesting questions.

Corl picked up a stuffed giraffe, squeezed it a little and replaced it exactly as it had been. They continued looking through the house, but didn't find anything of interest. Once back in the car, after assuring Mr. Crane that they were actively searching for his wife, Corl turned to Kingston.

"Do you think he has anything to do with this?" he asked.

Kingston thought about it for a moment, then shook his head.

"Why not, it's usually the spouse. Statistically."

Kingston put his fists side by side, then moved them down in a snapping motion.

"Yeah, he seems broken, but what if it's an act, or he feels guilty?"

It was his gut, but Kingston didn't know the charades that would make Corl understand that. Finally, he patted his stomach.

"Oh, you have a gut feeling. I can respect that." Kingston looked over to see if Corl was poking fun at him, but he wasn't. He seemed genuinely satisfied with the answer.

"Okay. So Crane's clean. Where does that leave us?" Kingston didn't try to answer, he knew Corl was just trying to work it out in his head. "So there are no signs of a struggle, which means she left on her own or was coerced. Maybe someone used a ruse?"

Kingston nodded, thinking there were only a few reasons that Peyton Crane would have left the house that late at night. He guessed it was something to do with the baby.

"So we're going to pull phone logs and get a warrant for her laptop. Anything else?"

Kingston shook his head. He sensed the disappearance of Peyton Crane would not have a happy ending.

115

Chapter 12

The target had changed, the entire atmosphere charged with energy. She was *happy*. It made her smell different and Tarik didn't like it. Ever since she returned from wherever she had gone, it was as if a tornado had been released in the house. He watched in fascination, moving from one window to the next to watch the insanity reign.

Human women were creatures he would never understand. Hidden in a tall tree with a perfect view of her bedroom, he watched as she laid out shiny instruments, of which the only practical use would have been torture.

It started out innocently enough. First, she pulled a brush through her long blonde hair, repeating the process until the strands were soft and shiny. That was the end of the normal.

The target picked up a small metallic thing shaped like a v, leaned toward the mirror (he loved that thing, he could see everything), and turned it toward her face. She brought it closer and closer until the metal points touched the skin above her eyeball.

"Yessss," Tarik hissed. He waited in anticipation for her to jam the thing into her eye.

He was disappointed.

Instead, she gripped a tiny hair and with a quick tug, yanked it out of her forehead. She winced, tears springing into her eyes. What in blazes was she doing? As if that weren't strange enough, the idiot human did it again and again, yipping in pain each time.

She touched a finger to a cylindrical device plugged into the wall and immediately pulled it back. She cursed as she blew on the finger. He didn't understand this ritual until he saw the small red welt on the tip of her finger. The instrument was hot, it had burned her. Served her right for engaging in these ludicrous, albeit interesting, behaviors. Separating a section of hair from the rest, she twirled it around the cylinder, holding it close to her scalp for ten seconds. When she released it, a long ringlet fell down past her shoulder. She repeated the process until all of her hair was curly.

Next, she opened a potion vial and began to slather a beige colored liquid on her face. It sank into her skin as she rubbed. Tarik waited for the effects of it to manifest; perhaps her face would turn green or she would become invisible. Nothing. Her skin looked a little smoother, but that was it. All of this was to alter her appearance. He could barely contain his disappointment. He slunk away into the night to collect more of the ritual elements Lykah had chosen.

*****

Ivanya was waiting on the porch when Spencer pulled up in his black Audi. He presented her with a potted purple orchid.

"You look beautiful, Vani. I like the curls." He looked at the ground almost shyly.

Her heart sped up. He thought she was beautiful! "Thanks," she said, absently twirling one of the ringlets around her finger. "It took forever."

Spencer smiled, crookedly. "You did all that for me? I'm flattered."

Ivanya snorted. "Don't be. I did it for me." She waddled around the car and he offered an arm to help her inside. She had to move the seat back in order to fit.

"Are you okay? Do you want to take your truck?"

She thought of all the McDonald's wrappers and empty soda bottles on the floorboards and grimaced. "No, I'm good. Where are we going?"

"I thought we'd have dinner on the boat tonight. It's all set."

"You afraid to be seen with me in public?"

"Absolutely not. You're ravishing. I want you all to myself."

The car wound through deserted streets toward the marina. Spencer's boat was lit up with twinkle lights and there were flowers everywhere. Roses and lilies, daisies and orchids of every conceivable shade. It looked like he bought the entire contents of Mrs. Gridley's shop. He led her up the slip and onto the deck, helping her into a cast iron chair at a small bistro table. Chilling in a silver ice bucket was a bottle of champagne.

"Champagne?"

"Sparkling cider, actually." He smiled again, completely disarming her. Usually he was a moody guy, snobby on his best day. There was no trace of that here.

"You really have thought of everything," she mused.

The salad arrived first, served by the same butler that had answered the door at her baby shower. It was delicious and she devoured it quickly. Spencer watched her with a half-smile on his lips.

"Sorry," she said, blotting her lips with a linen napkin. "Did I gross you out?"

"Of course not. I'm actually kind of impressed. Most of the girls I date are so dainty and barely eat anything. They frequently waste food that I pay quite a bit for. It's not about the money. It's just nice to see someone enjoy a meal for once."

She laughed. "Just wait till you see what I do to the main course."

They drank the cider from champagne flutes and talked. Spencer would be attending college in three months for marine biology. He was particularly interested in shark behavior and hoped to be able to create a protocol that would stop shark attacks on humans in the future. Ivanya felt out of place to say the least. She had no plans for the future besides having this baby and maybe fitting into a bikini next summer. There would be no college for her right now, and she wouldn't be swimming with sharks. Not the ones in the ocean anyway.

No excitement for you, the voice jeered.

Shut up, she thought back. *I built toes today. That's all the excitement I need.*

"So you think you're having a girl. Have you picked out a name?"

"I'm tossing a few things at the wall, but so far nothing has stuck." She chewed on her bottom lip. "I want to name her after Grams in some way, so I might go with Irena, but I don't know. I need to find something that other kids can't find a way to make fun of."

He laughed a little. "You know, Spencer would work for a little girl."

Her eyes widened as she shook her head. "Could you imagine the gossip if I did that? Mina Gulleckson would publish that you're the father in her stupid blog and your mother's head would explode."

"Someone would write about you?" Doubt was written all over his face.

"Do you ever read the 'Watson Watcher'?"

"Can't say that I have."

"Well, Mina is my next door neighbor, so I feature prominently in the 'Watcher'. The whole town knew I was pregnant almost as soon as I did. She must go through my trash. She started a pool to see who the father was. There are fifty-eight bidders so far." Ivanya's lip curled in disgust. "She used to use the blog to start trouble with Grams, but now I'm her whipping boy.

"But enough about that. I'm curious about something."

"What's that?"

"Why did you ask me out?" She was almost afraid to hear the answer. "What changed?"

He was silent for a long moment. "You did."

Ivanya raised her eyebrows, her heart pattering in quick time.

"You were always beautiful, but now you're...real. You have a sense of purpose now. A maturity about you. You're not that giggly girl anymore. You're a young woman."

Ivanya was minutely flattered and more than a little offended by his statement. "So, I wasn't good enough before, but I'm good enough now? Are you certain it's not the very obvious fact that I put out? Is that what changed?" An angry flush crept up her neck and bloomed like roses on her cheeks. Of course, he wasn't interested in her. She had been stupid to let her guard down and come here.

Distaste colored his features and his voice deepened with bitterness. "Wow. Thank you for thinking so little of me. Maybe I was wrong about you, after all. Maybe you never did grow up. You're certainly acting like a little girl right now."

"How dare you!"

"If the shoe fits, Vani, lace it up."

"I can't lace them up," she shouted. "My feet are too fat."

Thunderstruck silence followed. Then they both roared with laughter.

"Is that true?" Spencer asked, between fits of mirth.

She wiped tears from the corners of her eyes. "I'm not just wearing flip-flops because it's warm out. They're the only things that fit."

"Do you feel better?"

She found that she did. "What's for dessert? I got my heart set on chocolate cake."

*****

Abigail was waiting on the steps when Ivanya returned. She leaned her elbows on the top step, not bothering to hide her surprise (and mild disgust) when Spencer placed a tender kiss on Ivanya's lips. He sped out of the driveway and Ivanya approached Abigail.

"You should wash your mouth out, Vani. It's very possible that he has cooties." Abigail made a face.

"I had a nice time."

"But I was waiting for you. The truck dropped off all your gifts and I had them piled into the living room because you weren't here to tell me what to do with them. We need to work on the nursery."

"I'm sorry to have kept you waiting, Ms. Kayne. Heaven forbid I should enjoy myself for an evening with someone other than you."

"Whoa. Snappy. Those hormones are no joke." Abigail shot her a wry smile.

"You bring out the worst in me," Ivanya muttered, crankily.

"That's a lie. You would be so bored without me."

Ivanya sighed, heavily. "Yeah, I'd be bored. And it would be blissfully quiet for once." She stared off into the distance, as if seriously contemplating such a future.

"Enough," Abigail declared. "Let's just admit you can't live without me and get down to business. We have a nursery to build."

They walked into the house and Ivanya gasped. Every available surface in the living room had been covered. The couch, chairs, and all the tables were overflowing with gift bags bursting tissue paper from the top. Boxes were stacked neatly from the doorway to the wall at the front of the room. There was only a small path to walk on, everything else was occupied by some baby item or another. The gifts seemed to have multiplied.

"I may have done some more shopping," Abby said, a sheepish grin on her face.

Damn it, Susan said. *It's going to be a long night.*

She didn't see the black shadow settle into the maple tree as she began moving the bags.

Chapter 12

Tarik had watched her for weeks, watched her belly grow heavy with child and her breasts swell with the means to feed it. He saw each stage of the supposed miracle and decided that women were masochists. Why else would they insist on doing this to themselves? They allowed parasites to feed on their bodies, letting life drain from them to sustain the leech. For what? To put another screaming mouth to feed in a world that was overflowing with them already?

But the thing that boggled his mind, the thing he couldn't understand no matter how hard he tried, was how they could like it. Women went out of their way to do this to themselves. The only explanation he could think of was this: human women were lunatics.

That theory had been validated on many occasions. The target spent ludicrous amounts of money on the child. Clothes, shoes, toys. Yesterday, the friend had brought over a literal truckload of stuff for the leech. He watched in fascination as they wrestled with the thick wooden slats of the crib. The target read aloud from the instruction booklet, something about inserting slat B into slot G. The friend, who was now sweaty and flushed, short hair in her eyes, stomped over to the target and ripped the booklet out of her hands. She balled it up, tossed it to the ground and stomped on it. The target laughed as she picked it up and tried to smooth it out. They finally got the crib together, but after seeing the process, Tarik thought he would probably opt for a pre-built version.

Then came the bright blue plastic tub with inclined seat for bathing the infant. A basket with a soft, white lining was next. It puzzled him at first until he realized it was another bed. Two beds. The very idea incensed him. Why should this...half person be entitled to double the luxury of a complete one? Yet another logical fallacy of the human race.

After the shelves were up and the small things placed upon them, the friend left and the target sank into a rocking chair, absently rubbing her stomach and humming. He pictured the parasite inside, pulsating its fat, white body like a carnivorous slug as it fed on its mother. Not much made the large demon squeamish, but the thought of a throbbing leech feasting on his flesh made him almost physically ill. A shiver ran up his spine.

He turned away from the window, now thoroughly disgusted. From the corner of his eye, he detected a movement from the neighboring house. He turned his head just in time to see a curtain shift back into place. The fat, nosy human may not have seen him from the cover of the maple tree he hid in, but there was only one way to be sure. With a smile on his face and excitement burning in his veins, he left the target and snuck under cover to the house next door.

Tonight, there would be blood.

127

*****

Things were getting weird around here, Corl reflected, as he shoved the new half-pint of Scotch behind some files and closed the desk drawer. The station was mostly empty this time of night, just the regular crew of uniforms running the desk and the lock-ups downstairs. Everyone else had gone home. Corl had just ran in a few drunks and then he was heading home as well.

The industrial park in Watson was prime real estate for all manner of addicts and the occasional hooker. There was not a week that went by that someone wasn't busted for some kind of business down there. Even if it was just open intox on one of those new substances that were sweeping the market. While the drugs were technically legal, given that they were invented after the laws, so new ones had to be written, being publicly intoxicated was still against the law. Corl exploited this loophole often, dropping hoods in the drunk tank to sleep off the effects of whatever they happened to be on at the time. These drugs were sometimes worse than the illicit ones. He considered it his sworn duty to get these people off the streets before they hurt someone.

The phone rang.

"'Lo?"

"Detective Corl?"

128

"Yeah, it's me." He had to work at keeping the slur from appearing in his voice.

"This is Officer Kara Davis." Ah, he remembered Davis. He had thought about asking her out once upon a time, but he was a good deal older than her. Not that he cared, but she might. And her dad definitely would, him being the chief of police and all.

He shook his head, trying to dislodge the drunken images appearing behind his eyes. "What can I do for you, Officer Davis?"

"I was called to do a welfare check by one Edgar Townsend. His neighbor was supposed to meet him for bingo at the VFW, but she never showed up. He was concerned. I arrived at the address with Ryder and, well, you better get down here sir."

"Davis, I'm tired. I've been rounding up trash all goddamn day and I need to get some sleep. Just work the scene and present me with your findings in the morning." He really was tired and the last thing he wanted to do was hold hands with a pair of rookies.

"Look, Detective. The chief told me to call you in; you can talk to him if you like, he's here with me. I can pass him the phone." She let the threat hang on the air. "He said you and your partner are the closest thing we have to a homicide unit, so how about you come down here and do your damn job?"

She barked the address just before hanging up on him. God, he needed to stop stepping in the shit with people. It was happening with alarming frequency these days.

Wishing he were doing anything else, he picked up the phone and punched in Kingston's number. He picked up on the first ring.

"Meet me out front in ten minutes," Corl growled and slammed the receiver back in the cradle.

The Chief was on the porch at 1326 Peachtree Lane, his face drawn and pasty.

"It's bad in there guys," he said, drawing in a ragged breath. He wiped some sweat from his forehead with a blue handkerchief. "I have never seen anything like it. I want daily reports of your progress and you work on nothing else until this is solved. Expect some overtime boys."

Corl turned to head into the house.

"Detective?" Corl twisted around and faced the Chief again. "Next time you get a call out, you get your ass down here. Understood? I don't care if you need a nap or not."

Corl nodded, fists clenched to his sides as he turned away and stepped inside. The narrow hallway was congested with uniforms hugging the walls. All of them wore the same expression on their faces: a mixture of disgust, anger, and fear. Every officer in the department must have been in this house. He threw a casual elbow into the ribs of a guy from traffic, partly because he was in the way, but mostly because the man had the nerve to give him a parking ticket the week before. Not his particular brand of revenge, but under the circumstances he would take it.

Cole Ryder stood at the entrance to the kitchen looking positively green. His throat worked as if he were going to puke all over the crime scene. Fucking rookie. Corl pulled a paper lunch bag from his jacket pocket and handed it to Ryder.

"You are not gonna puke in my crime scene. Get the fuck outside."

Kingston gave Corl a dirty look as Ryder shoved his way down the hall to the front door, the bag clutched to his face.

"What?" Corl asked, innocently. "Kid's gonna contaminate something. Had to get him out. If he can't handle the job, he should find a new one. Some people have no business working in law enforcement, *partner*." He smiled as Kingston flipped him the bird.

Corl cupped his hands around his mouth. "Attention! All non-essential personnel need to leave the scene. Stop with Chuck in the driveway to have your footprints taken, because not a single one of you

131

are wearing the booties that I put on at the door. Look at this guy." He pointed to Kingston's feet. "He's not even a cop and he's following protocol better than you people. Davis and Ryder, talk to the man that made the call. Townsend? See what you get out of him. Hall and Parker, take the houses on this side of the street. Monroe? We need to notify next of kin, find out who they are and get it done."

The kitchen looked as if it were painted by Jackson Pollack during a red period. Blood was everywhere, spattering the ceiling and streaking down the walls in long red sheets. Arterial spray. A humongous torso with stumps where the arms, legs, and head should have been, lay in the middle of the floor surrounded by an ocean of blood. A coil of intestines that looked disturbingly like spaghetti spilled out of the cavity of the stomach.

"Vic's name is Mina Gulleckson."

Corl whirled on Davis. "Jesus Christ, you're like a fucking cat! Don't do that!"

She smiled widely, her blue eyes crinkling in the corners, clearly pleased with herself. She tucked a red curl back under her cap and handed Corl a pair of latex gloves. "Some detective you are. With those years under your belt and you still let me get the drop on you? You're slipping, sir." She offered a pair of gloves to Kingston as well.

132

Corl snapped them on and pulled his cell phone out of his pocket. He hated the damn thing, but he hated charades more. Kingston not being able to talk was a pain in the ass and Corl didn't think he had any business working with the cops, but apparently the kid was some kind of genius when it came to homicide investigations. It was someone's sick idea of a joke to partner him with Corl; probably trying to force him to retire. Well, it wasn't going to work. Because he had no patience for Kingston's gestures, he relied on text messages to communicate with him. It was one-way, Kingston could hear just fine.

The coppery scent of blood was on the air, thick and cloying. Corl moved toward the body, captivated. He squatted next to it, completely taken in. The body— he couldn't think of it as a person—had been slashed from throat to groin, the edges of the gash rough and ragged. Thick white ribs gleamed through the gore, but the cavity they protected was empty.

The phone vibrated in his hand.

Check the abdomen, it read.

"I was getting to that," Corl snarled. He had to concentrate to keep the nausea at bay. Drawing a pen from his pocket, he gently moved the tangle of intestines aside. Nestled in there, looking as if it could have been sleeping, lay a tiny Chihuahua with a broken neck.

"Holy shit." This bastard was sick. Seriously batshit.

And that wasn't the end of it. He ignored the vibration of the phone as he walked slowly around the rest of the kitchen. Never had he seen something this gruesome; he would bet money that nobody had. The victim's head, eyes bulging, mouth frozen in the midst of a scream, sat on a silver platter in the center of the table. Her large legs, fat sagging and shiny knobs of bone peeking from the tops had been discarded under the table.

Another vibration. He checked it this time.

It's like a performance. A stage setting. The legs weren't important to his vision.

Corl moved on. Blood spotted the window over the sink, tiny puddles collecting on the sill. More blood spattered dishes in a nearby rack. One large arm stood straight up out of the sink. Gravity had worked on the cold flesh, pulling it down into a large lump about four inches above the elbow. It was jammed into the drain up to the wrist. The gore streaking the windows had come from the killer trying to feed the arm into the garbage disposal.

So what did he do with the organs and the other arm?

"I have no idea." Corl turned to the crime scene guys that had just come in the back door. "Your

134

mission is to find the missing body parts. I want no stone left unturned, literally. Search toilets, wastebaskets, even the potted plants, for God's sake. We'll be next door helping with the canvas."

I've seen a lot in my life. Never anything like that, Kingston typed as he followed his partner across the lawn.

"Some of those famous insights would come in handy right about now, genius."

I'll let you know if I figure anything out. Did you see whose house is next door?

"Where do you think we're going? That girl hates us, but she might have seen something."

You. She hates you.

Corl flipped off Kingston and continued across the lawn.

*****

Tarik watched from his perch on the roof, nothing more than a shadow against the chimney. They scurried like rats, admiring his handiwork. Not that they would be able to appreciate it—human consciousness could not possibly comprehend the artistic sensibilities that he had put on display in that kitchen.

He had eaten his fill of the fat, nosy woman. Her meat was succulent and juicy, if a little on the greasy side. Tarik did not overindulge. Keeping his physique was a necessary part of employment. Also, humans tended to give him indigestion if he ate too much. The right arm, liver, spleen and lungs provided a four-course meal, followed by her enlarged heart for dessert.

Apparently, the police were searching the grounds for the missing items now. They would never find them, though. Not a trace. He had devoured each muscle of the arm, leaving only bones. These, he discarded in the industrial park where the homeless and the drug addled lived. Even if found, it was unlikely that they would be reported to the authorities.

Two of the officers were crossing the lawn now, on their way to the target's house. He thought of engaging them, as the larger one was deliciously doused in rage. As soon as the thought crossed his mind, the skinnier man with the small, black device in his hands looked over to the roof where Tarik sat. He knew the man couldn't see him, but he also knew that sight was not the most important sense in any being. There was another mind beneath consciousness, where all else was experienced and stored. This was the sense the man used now.

A car door slammed below. He jumped slightly at the sound, mentally chastising himself for this pitifully human reaction. Ah, the friend was here. The policemen moved more quickly across the lawn, the skinny one looking around every few feet, trying to define the source of the chill that was crawling across his scalp. Tarik settled in to watch.

This could be fun.

Chapter 14

She dreamed of priests and witches. Of the spirit of evil on the wind above a burning church. It traveled for a long time, drawing strength and power from nature, as its mother had done. Bodies of cattle and horses littered fields of ruined crops. Stiffened forms of birds lay next to well-trodden paths near overturned and broken wagons.

A girl of about four approached the black, misty cloud and held out a chubby hand. Tendrils of smoky mist curled around her, invading her mouth, eyes and nostrils. Soon it was gone and in the place of the little blonde girl was a raven haired beauty in early adolescence, with pale skin and black eyes. She walked alone for a long while in bare feet over stones and burning earth, before she was joined by six acolytes with eyes as black as hers.

Ivanya woke with a start as the front door banged open and Abigail tromped into the room, followed by Detective Douchebag and his partner. Ivanya scrambled up, quickly folding the blanket she'd been using and placing it on the back of the couch.

Corl and Kingston sat on the couch where she had just been, while she perched in Grams' rocking chair. Abigail folded herself on the floor at Ivanya's feet making googly eyes at Kingston.

"Miss Devereaux," Corl began. "Have you been here all night?"

"Yeah. I fell asleep around nine, I think. I wasn't feeling good." She cradled a protective arm over her belly as she asked why they wanted to know.

"Did you hear anything from next door? Banging or yelling? Any kind of disturbance around ten? Maybe something you sort of heard in your sleep?"

She pointed mutely to her phone on the end table, with earbuds plugged into the jack. "I was listening to music on that. I didn't hear anything until you guys came busting in here." She looked down at Abby. "What are you doing over here at one a.m.?"

"Club was boring. Came to see what you were doing."

"We don't have a club, we have bars. It was boring because it's Tuesday and sensible people are in bed. Like me. I was asleep. Thanks for wrecking that for me."

Corl cleared his throat impatiently. Ivanya and Abigail turned to him.

"How well did you know Mina Gulleckson?"

"Mina's a nosy b-"

"Wait!" Abigail shouted, holding up a hand to shut Ivanya up. "What do you mean by did?"

"Excuse me?"

"You know what I mean," said Abigail. "Why are you talking about her in the past tense?"

The universal expression for 'oh shit' crossed Corl's face. He recovered quickly. "I'm afraid Mrs. Gulleckson was murdered in her home between ten and eleven pm. We are questioning all the neighbors." He smiled a predatory grin. "Now, Miss Devereaux. What were you saying about my victim?"

Ivanya's face had gone ashen and her eyes bulged from their sockets. "Mina's dead?"

Kingston caught her eye and nodded solemnly.

"Ok. I think she's a bitch, but I was happy to ignore her or talk about her behind her back like she does to me. I would have tp'd her house or put bologna on her car. I-I didn't kill her!"

Corl glared at her for a few seconds before softening. "I'm mainly looking for motive. Unless you're the Incredible Hulk, I don't think you did this. Especially in your…condition." He checked his phone. "Did Mrs. Gulleckson have a habit of upsetting people?"

Abigail laughed bitterly. "Do you read the Watson Watcher, Detective?"

Kingston's face was the picture of befuddlement, but Corl's eyes were bright as he pounded a fist on his knee. "I knew I had heard the name before! I read her blog sometimes, but didn't make the connection! You know they have a pool going on who-"

"Yeah, I know," Ivanya snapped.

"So you see what she means? If you go by people she pissed off, then you'd have to interview the entire town." Abigail favored Kingston with an appreciative look. "Except you. I've never see you in the Watcher."

Corl snorted. "You have to have a life in order to create gossip. He doesn't have one."

"I'll help him give them something to talk about." She licked her lips lavisciously as she leered at him. Ivanya kicked her in the shoulder.

"You're being more inappropriate than usual, Abs. Knock it off." The beginnings of a migraine throbbed in Ivanya's temples.

"Can't help it. He's yummy."

Ivanya turned back to Corl. "Mr. and Mrs. Stephens are getting a divorce because Mina wrote about him getting frisky with Cathy Sullivan at the DMV." She brushed a stray hair away from her mouth. "And Marty Clark lost his job at UPS because it got around that he was keeping things that fell off the truck, if you know what I mean. You should read back issues of the Watcher, there might be something there."

Kingston typed quickly on his cell phone and Corl's vibrated in response. Ivanya was instantly irritated. They were questioning her in connection to a murder and they were texting each other in her living room? What the hell?

"Am I boring you?" Ivanya asked, sweetly, venom in her voice.

"Sorry about that. My partner was talking to me."

"Your partner isn't this guy?" she asked, pointing at Kingston.

Corl grunted in exasperation. He hated telling this story. And he always had to do the telling because Kingston had the luxury of not being able to talk. He nodded to Kingston. "You might as well show her, so we can get back to business."

Kingston pulled the collar of his shirt to the side, revealing a puckered white scar, about four inches long and a half inch wide. She wanted to get closer, to investigate it herself. Being a bit of an expert in cutting, she was curious.

"He used to interview patients at the psych ward in a hospital in Chicago. The last one managed to get his pen away from him and jabbed it right into his neck. Kid almost bled to death. They managed to save his life, but his vocal chords were pretty shredded." Corl sighed as if he were the most put upon person alive. "So we converse via text because I hate charades."

"So, what was his question?"

"He wanted to know if you were okay. You're looking a little…under the weather."

She felt under the weather. The baby was smashing around on her insides like a pinball machine, she had to pee, and she was so exhausted she could barely keep her eyes open. "I'm just tired. And worried. Am I safe here?"

"There will be units around for a while, canvassing the neighborhood and the crime scene boys will be next door. You will be safe here. But if you are too worried to sleep, I can call in a voucher for the Holiday Inn for you."

Corl was uncharacteristically kind today. Maybe there was something disarming about a terrified pregnant woman practically passing out in a chair.

"We'll be right next door most of the night." He rose and handed her a card with his number and Kingston's on it. "Call us if you need anything, or if you have a feeling that something isn't right."

As they moved toward the door, Abigail jumped up and followed closely behind Kingston.

"I like that you can't talk. No one will hear you scream when I finally get my hands on you." She said this closely to his ear. Ivanya could see the shiver work its way up his neck, followed by a flush of red. Abigail was going to get herself arrested for sexual harassment if she didn't watch it. Sometimes Ivanya felt more like her mother than her friend.

"Thank you, Detective." Ivanya shook Corl's hand. Maybe it was time to bury the hatchet with him. He was only doing his job all those times he arrested her. Now that she was going to be a parent, she understood it a little better. There were times when she could have died had he not intervened. She would want someone to do that for her daughter.

She locked the door behind them and laid back down on the couch, too tired to climb the stairs. Abby sat in the rocking chair, a steely glint in her eyes. "I'll take first watch. Get some sleep, Vani."

*****

Ivanya woke to a wave of nausea and Abigail staring at her from the rocking chair. Dark circles perched under her eyes, some of it from smeared eyeliner and running mascara. Had she been crying?

"Morning," Ivanya croaked, the coughed a little to clear the frog from her throat. "Have you been up all night?"

Abigail nodded. "Couldn't sleep."

Something was odd here. It was decidedly un-Abigail to just sit quietly. She was vivacious and full of life, always on full blast. And she didn't have a mute button. Or a pause. Seeing her like this was enough to wake Ivanya the rest of the way up.

"So what are you doing?"

"Worrying," Abigail replied, her voice thick with emotion.

"You never worry. You always leave that to me." Ivanya grabbed a sleeve of crackers off the coffee table and popped one into her mouth. Stale, lovely. She grimaced as she chewed the thing and felt the mass go down her throat as she swallowed. "What are you worrying about?"

It was like a cork had been pulled from her friend. She sucked in a deep breath and spewed words all over the living room.

"You! I'm worried about you. There was a damn murder next door and you are here all alone. What if the killer comes here?" Abigail huffed in gasps of air, her cheeks red and lips trembling. "Even if we take the crazed murderer out of the equation, there are still things to worry about. You're like seven months along—what if you go into labor or something?"

Her reply was automatic. "I would call 9-1-1 or drive myself to the hospital. What's really going on here?" Ivanya felt like she was prospecting for gold, trying to find the vein of emotion that was underneath all the bluster.

Abby shoved her phone in Ivanya's face. She took it wordlessly, at first not comprehending what she was seeing. The image was of a full colored flyer stapled to a power pole downtown. In the background were more power poles displaying the same flyer. MISSING, it said in bold capital letters. PEYTON CRANE. Beneath the words was a picture of a beautiful woman with blonde hair and blue eyes, with perfectly tanned skin, and a sizeable baby bump. LAST SEEN AUGUST 27TH AT 10:30 PM. The words 'please call with any information' and a local phone number were at the bottom of the page.

"Someone is missing. She is pregnant and you're worried the same thing will happen to me." Ivanya breathed, shakily. She couldn't say that this didn't change things for her. Suddenly, the house seemed too big, with too many possible avenues of ingress. A determined person could get in if they wanted to. Someone could slip the lock on the front door with a credit card if they wanted to, it wasn't that hard. She would have to remember to engage the

146

deadbolt before bed each night. Maybe even during the day. Crap.

"So what do we do about it?" Ivanya asked Abby, keeping her eyes pointed at the floor.

"Well, I could move in."

Ivanya chuckled. "Yeah. Leave your mansion with maid and butler for this house? Where you would have to do your own laundry and cooking and cleaning? Why would you leave all that?"

The expression of hurt that crossed Abigail's face was heartbreaking. Her eyes had filled with tears, the lip trembling again. "Wow. Ok. My best friend thinks I'm so shallow that I would put a butler over her life. Glad to know where I stand." Abigail shot up out of the chair so fast the back of it clunked against the wall with a resounding thud. She snatched her purse from the coffee table and headed toward the door, her boots clicking fast against the hardwood.

"Abs, wait," Ivanya cried. Only in retrospect did the sound of her words dawn on her. She'd been bitchy and hadn't given Abigail the benefit of the doubt. Some friend she was. Ivanya launched herself off the couch and almost biffed it when her feet got caught in the blanket. By the time she'd extricated herself from the blanket, the door had already slammed shut and Abigail's car had peeled out of the driveway.

She could smell the sour scent of roasted rubber on the pavement.

What did you just do? The voice asked.

"Messed up," Ivanya whispered back. "Big time."

Chapter 15

They hauled in everyone that had suffered a major loss as a result of Mina Gulleckson's slander. Corl bulldozed his way through the interrogations, slamming fists on the table and glaring at people in an effort to intimidate them. Dwayne Fisher, Carlie McCrae and Timothy Weston were all getting divorces as a result of infidelity that had been exposed by 'The Watcher'. Colin Martin had been recently brought up on charges for maintaining a meth lab. They all made good suspects, except none of them had the physicality to do what had been done. Kingston thought that maybe they had worked together, but the relatively clean crime scene did not support the multiple perpetrator theory. There had been only one set of shoe impressions and those were a size fifteen. None of these people had feet that big.

To be honest, Kingston was having a hard time concentrating on the Gulleckson case. His mind kept going back to Peyton Crane, who might still be alive. The keys and the phone on the table bothered him more than a little. Social media butterflies did not just forget their phones. He'd been mining her accounts when he wasn't working the murder and from what he could tell, Peyton and Ben had a good marriage and were over the moon about the baby.

She posted everything. The nursery when it was in progress, the swing set, even her living room after a good cleaning. Disturbing. Her page was like a blueprint for an intruder—they would know exactly where to go. And he did believe there was an intruder. Or someone with a very convincing ruse.

What could have convinced Peyton Crane to leave her house in the middle of the night? If he could figure that out, they might be able to find her. Kingston rubbed his temples in a circular motion with his index and middle fingers. He was missing something. Something important. If he was capable of yelling, he would have done it then. Corl barged into Kingston's office, the door slamming against the wall with a loud crash. "Got another missing girl. This one's pregnant, too."

Kingston was up and following Corl out the door in one smooth movement. As they loaded into Corl's beat up sedan, he gave Kingston the rundown.

"Lisa Sanchez, 22, single. She lives with her mom, Veronica Sanchez. She came home from work and Lisa was gone." He locked eyes with Kingston as he pulled back the shifter. "Paul. We got blood."

*****

Veronica Sanchez was an absolute wreck, shaking and sobbing near the front door as Davis jotted her statement on her pocket notepad. Corl stepped up onto the porch, introducing himself and Kingston. He grabbed two pairs of paper booties from the box Ryder held out and handed one to Kingston.

"We're going to look around, Ms. Sanchez. Is that alright?"

The haggard woman nodded mid-sob, stepping aside to let them pass. The living room was a mess, but it was hard to tell if it was due to poor housekeeping or a struggle. The baby swing in the corner was heaped with unfolded laundry, and cracker crumbs littered the carpet in front of the beige couch. There it was. It wasn't much blood, a couple drops on the edge of the beveled glass coffee table, but any amount was too much in a missing person case.

"Just a few drops, maybe from a nose? There's one on the carpet here, too." Corl pointed to the drop, almost invisible on the green carpet. He waved over Douglas from crime scene to get pictures and take a swab. "If we're lucky, it won't be her blood. Maybe she got a piece of him."

Check out the locks, Kingston texted. *They are pretty security conscious here. How would an intruder get past that?*

"No damage to the door. Except…wait a second. We got another drop of blood here."

Douglas ran over, snapped a photo and took a swab of this drop as well. Then he melted into the background like some kind of wraith, waiting for the next time he was called upon.

Corl stepped outside to speak to Ms. Sanchez. "Veronica? Did you have to use your key to get inside?"

"I always use my key. It's a habit. Lisa usually has the door locked because of that good for nothing ex-boyfriend of hers." She drew in a ragged breath, fresh tears popping into her eyes. "That's why I thought everything was okay at first. Because the door was locked."

Corl thanked Veronica and went back in the house.

How is that possible?

"The kidnapper locked up afterward? Have you ever seen that before?"

No. Generally abductors are in a hurry. Once they have who they need, they get out. They don't clean up, don't lock doors.

"Her phone's still here. Car's here. Keys are gone."

Douglas interrupted Corl's thought. "Got something here, Detective." He held up a swab and pointed to a spot on the coffee table.

Kingston squatted down to inspect the table where the drops of blood had spattered the glass. Next to the crimson spots was a smear of goo. Kingston had seen this before. It was the same snail slime found in Peyton Crane's home.

Snail slime. Like the Crane case.

"Well, now we know they are connected. That looks good on paper." Corl paced around the living room and ran a hand through his already messy hair. "So what would make Lisa open the door? If she was worried about an ex, I think it would have been locked."

Maybe someone knocked asking for help. Or to use the phone.

"Ok. That's good. Or maybe they were dressed as a serviceman of some kind. I'd open the door if someone said gas leak. Anyway, she opens the door to see what they need, but something doesn't feel right so she tries to close it. They push the door, hard, and it hits her in the face, which is where the blood on the door comes from."

She runs to the couch, shedding blood drops on the way, and stepping on the crackers.

"Why would she go to the couch? Why not toward the back door?"

If her subconscious sees the couch as a safe place, she may have ran there. It's the same reason people go to their bed when they are afraid or upset. It's a safe place. It may not make sense, but sometimes it happens.

"Or she was going past the couch when they caught her. Seems a little more likely to me."

The squealing of tires and loud shouts cut Corl off. He moved quickly out the door and down the steps, meeting the pretty brunette in the driveway just as she was exiting her vehicle. Three uniforms, shoulder to shoulder like a string of paper dolls blocked access to the porch.

"Get back in the car, Maureen," Corl said, gruffly, his jaw set in a hard line.

"You have a statement for me, John?" Maureen pulled her red lips into a sweet smile.

"Yeah. No comment."

She sighed. "You don't have to like that I'm covering this, John. But you do have to deal with it. How about a little professional courtesy?"

"Ok. I can be professional. You ready?" She fumbled a black recorder out of her jacket pocket. Corl's eyes narrowed and he seemed to grow in size, making himself big like he were confronting a bear instead of a small reporter in red. "I cannot comment

154

on an ongoing investigation with the media. However, Chief Davis will be holding a press conference at three p.m. in front of the stationhouse. You may direct all your inquiries to him at that time."

Kingston watched his partner turn his back on the reporter and stalk back across the yard to the porch. He ushered Veronica Sanchez into the house.

"Maureen Anderson with the Sentinel is outside. She is going to want a statement from you. I strongly suggest waiting until the press conference when the TV station will be there. Your statement will then have a straight line to the abductor, who will probably be watching. We will be able to coach you with words and phrases that will speak to whoever has your daughter."

Mrs. Sanchez nodded quietly. "I'll wait."

Corl's phone buzzed as he moved toward the kitchen.

History?

"Don't want to talk about it, kid."

You know the reporter. Personally. Not a question, just an observation.

When was the divorce?

"Three years ago. Now will you shut up?" He chuckled a little when he realized what he'd said. Kingston smiled as well.

Evidence was bagged, photos snapped and Kara Davis was just putting her pad back into her shirt pocket after finishing with Veronica's statement.

"Do you need a ride to the precinct?" Corl asked.

Veronica shook her head. "I'll drive myself. I want to be able to leave when I want."

"We can take you home when you're ready."

Steel replaced the tears in Veronica's eyes. "I won't be coming home. I'll be looking for my daughter."

Chapter 16

The woman cried while she spoke to the camera, begging for the return of her daughter and unborn grandchild. Her hands shook as she read from a crinkled piece of lined stationary.

"I want to speak to the person who has my daughter, Lisa. Thank you for keeping her and the baby safe. But we would like her to come home now to get the medical care she needs. She has a blood pressure condition that needs to be monitored closely. I know that you don't want to hurt Lisa, so please let her come home. Thank you."

Tears fell down Ivanya's face as she watched the woman fall apart at the podium. She couldn't imagine the pain that woman was enduring, having the thing she cherished most ripped away from her. The worst part must be the not knowing; the stories that your brain makes up could sometimes be worse than reality. How would she feel if her daughter was taken to endure some unnamed fate? She had a feeling that the woman on TV had just shown her how she would handle it.

Ivanya waddled down to the basement and sat in the rocking chair with the book.

The Ca'taal named itself and to this day it is unknown what, if any significance the name holds. It is only known that the Ca'taal is powerful and ruthless in its pursuits. It sought to punish for the loss of its earthly body and for the demise of its mother. In its guise as the girl, Agnes, it vowed to take away the world's children by turning them evil. These children were treated well and served as an army for the monster, offering protection from those who meant it harm. Of these, there were six that the Ca'taal held most dear. These were given special powers, taken from the Ca'taal herself. Rowan was given the power to slow time. Peter could summon lightning, which caused much destruction during combat. The power to create darkness went to Adele and Martha could throw fire. Daniel caused rage in others and Charlotte could change form. When physically linked to Agnes by hand, they were all powerful and nearly undefeatable.

They destroyed villages by the dozens, slaughtered men and women, the guilty and the innocent. Skies were dark with smoke and ash that fell like snow. The Ca'taal's army grew twentyfold, and then more. Children could be seen from miles away, marching down dirt paths toward their next conquest. The villagers saw them coming, but not in enough time to stop the inevitable. The children descended upon hamlets and towns like a plague of locusts, razing both with equal ferocity.

Finally, after the death toll had reached a number that defied definition, communities from all over the world began to band together. People from all walks of life, thieves and healers, clergymen of all faiths, alchemists and warriors, united in a common goal—to end the Ca'taal's reign of terror. They were known as the Circle of the Ca'taal. They waited at a hidden location for Agnes and her army to attack another village. As much as they wished they could interfere, they had to wait until the siege was complete and the army was sated before they could move forward with their plan. Though the loss of life was terrible, it would be the last time.

A high priestess entered first, followed closely by the most talented potion maker in the Circle, though she happened to be only nine years old. The Ca'taal slept in the same area as her Six, their hands linked as a measure of protection while they rested. A potion was thrown, one that could be absorbed through the skin, and it sprinkled upon the sleeping forms of the Six. She approached quickly and removed Rowan's hand from Charlotte's, trusting the potion to keep them asleep. The link was broken. They were vulnerable. Warriors set upon them with sword and dagger, rending the Six with a fevered fury.

The Ca'taal fought through the potion and awoke, but it was too late. Her Six were dead and she was tied with enchanted ropes. She was dragged to the center of the village and tied to the pyre that she had constructed herself. Agnes screamed as they lit it and her skin began to bubble and blister as the flames licked her. The Circle began to chant in the languages of their individual faiths. The Ca'taal emitted a glow *that had nothing to do with the fire. Her soul raised from her body, the red of rust and old blood, until it dissipated into the night air. It had been banished to the Land of the Dead and there it would remain.*

It would return someday, far into the future, but they would be prepared to fight her again, and would perhaps have the knowledge to finally destroy her.

Ivanya read the prophecy that followed, about a special child meant to serve as a vessel for the Ca'taal, and instantly knew what her grandmother had known. It was about her. Bitterness swept over her, followed by a searing flash of anger. Anger that Grams had understood what this pregnancy meant and had chosen to keep Ivanya in the dark about it. It was pure chance that Ivanya had found the hidden room to begin with.

Or maybe it wasn't. Maybe Grams had reached through the veil to guide Ivanya through this. She chose to believe that was the case. Ivanya put the history book in her striped tote bag, along with a medallion engraved with a Celtic knot, and a wooden box carved with the same design. The box contained stones, herbs and amulets that had been passed down for generations through the Circle. She also threw in glass vials of various colored liquids. She had no idea what they were for, but felt that she might need them. This was the last time she would visit Grams' inner sanctum for a while. Her belly was getting too big and she had a hard time seeing where to place her feet on the stairs. Coupled with the excruciating pain in her back and abdomen, any trek to the basement held the potential for disaster. Ivanya had even opted to stay in Grams' room on the ground floor until after the baby for safety's sake.

The front door banged open just as Ivanya was making her way through the kitchen. The crash of the heavy oak door smashing into the wall was followed by a series of loud thumps on the hardwood.

"I am armed," Ivanya called out as her heart pounded painfully against her sternum. "Leave my home now, while you still can."

"Armed with what?" a familiar voice shouted back. "Those humongous bazongas, while impressive, hardly constitute weapons."

Abigail stood in front of the open door, surrounded by bags and suitcases. She was a vision in fishnets, knee-high combat boots and a camouflage mini-dress. Ivanya was so happy to see her that a silent tear slipped down her cheek.

"Oh, my God, I am so sorry," Ivanya half screamed as she rushed forward to embrace her friend. "I'm sorry I hurt your feelings. Of course, you can move in!"

"Puh-leeze, I knew it was just the hormones talking. They always push your bitch button. The baby makes it worse, but it's nothing I can't handle." Abigail gently extricated herself from Ivanya's iron grip. "Now where am I putting my stuff?"

"You can have my room. I'm staying down here for now. Stairs are hard."

*****

The next few days were spent getting Abigail settled in and trying not to slap her around a little. She was such a doting auntie that she was driving Ivanya completely nuts. Abigail cooked (ordered) so much food that Ivanya felt like she was being fattened up for slaughter. Then, she would stand sentry over Ivanya while she ate, demanding she clean her plate, as she stared her down with a matronly gaze. She would practically shove prenatal vitamins down Ivanya's throat each morning, nausea be damned.

But there were good things, too, like the herbal teas and amazing foot-rubs and heartfelt words of encouragement. She wondered if this was what it was like to have a wife.

Through the next six weeks, four more women went missing—all pregnant. Ivanya thought of them often, wondering what the abductor would want with them. There had been no ransom demands or extortion of the families. And, thankfully, there had been no bodies yet, so there was still hope.

"Maybe it's some sort of black market adoption ring," Abigail murmured.

"Maybe," Ivanya agreed, trying to shrug off the eerie feeling that Abigail could read her mind. It didn't happen often, but enough for Ivanya to wonder. She'd asked Abigail before how she was able to respond to her very thoughts and she just shrugged it off, saying that she couldn't read minds, she just knew her well enough to guess. Ivanya left it alone after that.

"You think their kids are being harvested?"

"Absolutely."

"Eew."

"And yours would fetch a pretty penny, so don't get kidnapped."

Ivanya rolled her eyes. "I'll do my best," she quipped.

Chapter 17

Pictures floated behind his eyes as he waited for the target to wake. The Chihuahua nestled snugly in the tentacles of intestine, his neck lolling unnaturally to one side. The arm sticking out of the sink, shiny bone peeping through the fat. The women for the ritual, eyes widened in terror.

The emotions each woman had felt, the fear, the anger, the sadness that they may never see their families again, made him thirst for more. He was growing impatient as he waited for the time to be right. The target promised to be a treat to his senses and he wanted to take her. To hear her screams as he exercised the Priestess' will. The ingredients had been gathered, he was merely waiting on the moon.

The curtains moved slightly in the front window. Just a tremor before they were spread wide to let the sun in. The target's friend stared into the yard with a worried crinkle in her forehead. She scanned the yard, eyes darting back and forth. There was an almost military quality to her gaze, as if she were a general engaged in a threat assessment. No, not almost. Exactly like that. The sun glinted off the barrel of the shotgun she carried. There was no fear in this woman, just determination and an animal ferocity in her gaze, not unlike that of the old woman. This girl could be a problem.

"What the hell are you doing?!" came a scream from deeper inside the house. "Put that damned thing away!"

"Um, protecting you? From the crazed killer slash pregnant people stealer?" The friend rolled her eyes.

"You think you're going to protect me with that?" The target was still shouting at volume. "You're more likely to shoot me yourself."

"I'll have you know," the girl huffed indignantly, "that I am an expert markswoman."

"Really."

"Yes. Duck hunting."

"You hunt ducks." The target was skeptical.

"Well, on Nintendo…"

"That's it! Put that thing down before you blow a hole in the ceiling."

They went on like that for a few minutes, the friend extolling her prowess in this duck hunting, while the target pleaded with her to relinquish the weapon. After a much heated debate, she finally did. Tarik breathed a sigh of relief. The gun would not kill him, but bullets hurt.

Tarik felt a tingle on the back of his neck, then a sharp jab, like a hypodermic needle in the base of his brain. The Priestess was calling, and judging from the strength of the signal, it was urgent.

*****

Kingston sat in the bullpen with Davis and Ryder, going over the little bit of evidence recovered in the Gulleckson murder. They were retreading the same ground here and everyone knew it. It was disheartening and frustrating, but sometimes that was just the way of things. His mind wandered as he half listened to Ryder's rhythmic voice.

"I mean the whole thing was weird, but the slime on the edge of the sink is like something out of the X-Files," Ryder was saying, causing Kingston's thoughts to snap back to the conversation at hand. He texted Ryder.

Slime?

"Yeah. Specifically, slime from a common garden snail. Just trace amounts, but it was there."

There was slime at the homes of the missing girls. Kingston didn't like that one bit. The connection was something they could use, but it was also a bad thing. It showed that the abductor had a capacity for cruelty that was almost inhuman. There was a very real possibility that some, if not all, of the women were dead. Another thought teased his consciousness, but before he could latch onto it, shouts sounded out front, followed by hitching gasps. He could see her leaning

166

on the front desk for support as she begged for help in a gravelly, tortured voice. It was none other than Peyton Crane, and she looked like hell.

Ryder was on his feet and striding toward the door with Davis and Kingston close behind, when Peyton seemed to wilt and crumpled to the floor.

"Call a bus!" Ryder barked, as he burst through the door. Kara Davis squatted on the floor next to Peyton, two fingers laid against her neck, searching for a pulse. She nodded to Kingston when she found it. He pulled a chair away from the wall and helped a dizzy Peyton Crane into the seat.

Corl thundered down the hall from his office. "What's all the—Mrs. Crane." His voice lowered to an almost fatherly cadence. "We've been looking for you. Can you talk? Are you all right?"

"Can I," she swallowed hard, "get a cup of coffee? I need to warm up. I'm so cold."

Davis scurried to the break room while Kingston, recognizing the symptoms of shock, went to the supply closet for a blanket. Davis and Kingston made it back at the same time. He draped the blanket around Peyton's shoulders. She closed her hands around the warm paper cup, inhaling the steam into her nostrils. She shivered violently, drops of hot liquid spattering her hand, but she didn't seem to notice. "Thank you," she whispered.

"Can you tell us what happened to you, Mrs. Crane?" The fatherly tone was still in Corl's voice. "We could go into the break room where it's a little quieter, while we wait for the ambulance."

She nodded and they got moving, Corl in front next to Peyton, a steadying hand in the small of her back. Kingston trailed behind them, marveling at the change that had come over his partner. Ryder and Davis brought up the rear, both on cell phones. Davis with dispatch to get an ETA for the ambulance, and Ryder with Ben Crane, giving him the good news and asking him to come down.

Peyton settled gingerly into a hard, plastic chair, holding an arm over her stomach.

"We were all in a room," she began, her voice rough and shaking. She picked at a hangnail on the index finger of her right hand.

"The other women were with you?"

"Yeah, there were six of us at the end, but at the beginning it was just me. They were talking about another one."

"Can you tell us where you were? Anything that can help us find the others?"

She ran a hand through her grimy hair. "I don't know. They came to the door asking to use the phone because they had a flat tire. I took the security chain

168

off and, and I don't remember what happened after that. I woke up in a hospital bed in a place made of concrete, like a warehouse or a bunker or something. I was held down with restraints on my wrists. I wasn't there alone for long." She took a long sip of coffee, grimacing at the bitter taste. Her face puckered with distaste, but she went in for another sip. "Before I knew it, there were six of us. A nurse and a doctor brought some guy in to look at us. They checked our vitals, did ultrasounds to check on the babies. Like we were for sale. We kind of were, but they wanted the babies, not us.

"That awful nurse came to check on us every night. She didn't want any of us going into labor, so when someone got close, their bed was wheeled out of the room. We never saw them again."

She began to cry, rocking back and forth in the chair. "When my contractions started, I tried to hide it. I bit back screams and suffered in silence." She shivered and drew the blanket more tightly around her shoulders. "Nurse Ruth saw the spike on the monitor I was strapped to and had me moved. Orderlies rushed my bed down the hall, tightening the restraints to the point of numbness." She smiled, but there was no joy in it. Bitterness saturated the room. Kingston had the urge to cover his nose, as if it were a noxious gas, but he suppressed it. Peyton's voice was ragged with tears and fatigue, the volume barely above a whisper.

"I always thought that having my baby would be the best part of my life. Painful, sure, but worth it. And instead of my prize, I got this." She struggled to her feet against Corl's protests. Her trembling hands grasped the bottom of the green scrub top she wore and hoisted it to just below her rib cage. Her stomach looked like Frankenstein's monster. The cut was a large U-shape just above the pelvic girdle. It had been stitched together with aged cat-gut, and not carefully. The wound puckered, a brownish mixture of blood and pus seeping out around the sutures.

Corl pushed back from the table shouting, "Where the fuck is that bus?" as he ran down the hallway.

Kingston helped her back into the chair and handed her a glass of water. She drank greedily until it was gone, but continued toying with the glass as she spoke.

"They didn't use any kind of anesthetic. I felt everything. The incision as they carved me up. I felt it when they widened the cavity with their hands. No gloves. All I could think about was my baby getting some kind of disease from their dirty hands.

"When I woke up, I was alone, everyone was gone. I put on this pair of scrubs and searched for signs of my baby, but there was nothing. I walked for a long time. Thank God they salt the sidewalks; all I had on my feet were these." She lifted her feet, displaying a pair of soft yellow socks with rubber smiley faces on the bottom.

Corl burst back into the room as Peyton put her soggy feet back on the floor. "Ambulance is here, Mrs. Crane. Your husband is out there as well. Let's get you loaded up."

She followed him to the door, where two paramedics waited with a lowered gurney. She turned to Corl. "There is another one. Somewhere. Someone is going to lose a baby. They weren't done."

Corl met Kingston's eyes, communicating one thought with no words: Ivanya Devereaux.

Chapter 18

Ivanya never spent much time thinking about the future; she was more of a let the chips fall where they may kind of girl, but she found herself doing precisely that. A weight of anticipation was in the air; not heavy, but definitely noticeable. Something was coming—something big.

In six short weeks, Ivanya would be a mother. She knew that she counted as one now, but it was different. Soon, she would be holding a tiny, perfect child in her arms. She dreamed of it almost every night, but they were somewhat disappointing. They were filled with love and light and peace, but she never saw the baby. Not one single feature. When she looked upon it, she simply saw a bright light in the darkness, like a beacon guiding her home. The only thing she knew for sure was that her child was a girl. Though there was no test that had confirmed it for her, she knew deep in her bones that it was a daughter.

Today, she thought of the big things: first steps, first word, and first day of school. Graduation, marriage, grandkids. She could see the life they would have together unfolding behind her eyes; all of it filled with wonder and grace. But she saw the little things, too, and with amazing clarity. Ivanya rocking her daughter to sleep in the nursery, the scent of baby shampoo and lotion wafting in her face...later, reading 'Green Eggs and Ham', the little girl's happiness when

Ivanya used a funny voice…in the kitchen on Christmas Eve baking cookies for Santa. Ivanya dots a dab of flour on Vetra's nose.

Vetra.

The name had come out of nowhere, slamming into her brain and putting all other thoughts out of her head. It was perfect and instantly right. She lovingly caressed her belly.

"Vetra Irena Devereaux," she cooed. "Is that your name?"

Her belly gurgled, and though it could have been gas, it felt like an answer.

She sat for a while, enjoying the silence, disturbed only by the soft creak of the rocking chair and the occasional settling of the foundation. Abigail had gone for brunch with her parents, so Ivanya was left with only her ruminations for company. That, and the mother of all cravings for an apple fritter. She salivated at the idea and rubbed her belly the way she did whenever she thought of, or talked about, food.

She stood up and began dressing for the eight inches of snow that had fallen over the last few days. A cramp coursed through her belly as she bent over to tie her boots. She breathed through it and resumed her task. Contractions. They'd been happening sporadically all morning.

Nothing to worry about yet, the voice said.

"I know," she muttered.   On went the fluffy white parka with fur trim around the hood and the soft woolen scarf Grams had knitted for her the year before. She pulled a matching hat with a poof on the top over her head and snatched her purse off the table.   She dug through it like a mole through dirt, but came up with no keys.   Where the hell were they?

Ivanya rushed through the house, glancing at tables and plunging her hands between couch cushions. Nothing.   She looked under chairs and shook out blankets.   Again, nothing.   Whatever.   The bakery wasn't that far away.   She could hoof it.   It never once crossed her mind to wait or to text Abby to bring home one of the delicious pastries.   She simply walked out the front door, shutting it firmly behind her.

The air was brisk, with a sharp wind that stung her face, but she didn't care.   All she could think about was the apple fritter she would soon be chewing on. Three blocks and it would be hers.

*****

Tarik almost laughed as he watched her.   Snow kicked over the tops of her boots and sprayed out beside her in white tufts.   A fierce red blush painted her cheeks as she waddled down the side of the road.   He followed closely, drawing in her scent.   He did not like her smell today.   The sweet, cloying scent of joy was

174

nauseating—he preferred the pungent aroma of despair. It was a good thing he would be changing her state of mind soon. For layered beneath the happiness was another smell; the one he had been waiting for these last months. The checkered flag, so to speak.

He would soon get his fill of gypsy blood.

*****

In retrospect, fleeing down an alley when she realized she was being followed was not the smartest thing that Ivanya Devereaux had ever done. She hadn't heard any footsteps, just the quick snap of a twig behind her and somewhere to the left. Whoever was behind her had been trying their damnedest to move with stealth, which was the very thing that tipped her off. No one with good intentions would need to be that quiet.

And she wasn't stupid. She knew about the missing women—she just never thought it would happen to her.

Not looking back, she pumped her legs as hard as she could, her thighs burning, knees pounding into her distended belly. The whole thing was like something out of a horror movie; that's why she should have seen it coming. The blonde with the big boobs always falls, giving the villain just enough time to catch up. Sure enough, just as she turned the corner into the mouth of the alley, her boots found an icy patch in the snow and she spun out. With the last vestiges of her balance, she threw herself sideways, landing painfully on her left arm. Her head bounced off a dumpster with a dull clang. Disoriented, she lifted her head, opened her eyes and screamed.

There was no definition for the creature that stood over her. At around seven feet tall, it towered over her. It was black, like a shard of obsidian inlaid with ruby markings. The symbols were not in a language she understood; Ivanya doubted there was a single person on Earth who could make sense of them. Crimson eyes flashed in deep sockets as it gazed down at her. A thin forked tongue darted out, tasting the air. The thing's lips were peeled back over a row of sharply pointed teeth.

"Ahh," it hissed, little flecks of spittle spurting from between those horrible teeth. "I've been waiting for this for a long time. Please scream. I like the way it tastes."

Weight crushed her legs as it hunched down. A high-pitched howl ripped from her throat when her thigh bone snapped. The creature gazed into her face, leaning ever closer, until she could smell the desiccated meat on its breath. Its hateful tongue darted out again, sliming up the side of her face. The skin on her cheek crawled as the saliva soaked into her skin.

Long talons glimmered darkly in the light from an overcast sky, flashing toward her face. White heat

176

seared down her neck, over her chest and across her stomach. Her skin opened like a fault line, rocky cliffs of flesh and bits of down from her coat standing tall over a river of blood. The screams ripped from her body, coming from the very depths of her soul.

Roaring laughter reverberated off every surface in the alley. Crimson roses bloomed in the snow as the thing played in her blood, rubbing it over skin that appeared to be composed of millions of tiny scales. The pain clouded her vision, the scene becoming a kaleidoscope of red, squelching noises, and agony. The being stabbed its talons into the soft flesh again and again. Perfect dots of rouge spattered the dumpster and held their shape for just a moment before morphing into streaks of gore.

Blood flowed harder now, flying from her in long, wet sheets. The thing must have nicked an artery. She'd been afraid before; there were many things in life that scared her, but she never knew true fear until now. Not for herself, she was pretty sure there was no help for her—she'd lost too much blood for that. No, this was bigger, bone deep and paralyzing. Only profound love could bring forth such a reaction: the gut-wrenching terror for someone else. This fear was new, a many tentacled beast that wrapped its limbs around her insides, turning everything cold.

The horror was confirmed a few minutes later when, along with the agony, she felt a curious pulling sensation. The weight lifted from her legs as the creature pulled the child from inside her. Blackness invaded the edges of her vision and she was horrified to realize that she was seconds from passing out. Taking a deep breath, Ivanya used every ounce of strength she could muster to ball her hand into a fist. Then, wincing in anticipation of a pain that promised to be truly harrowing, she slammed the fist as hard as she could into her broken leg. Fireworks exploded in her brain, her lungs bursting with air she could not expel. But it worked. The darkness retreated, but vowed to return later.

"Aww," the thing sneered. "It's a girl."

"Vetra," Ivanya groaned. She held out her weak, trembling arms, praying that this was all a nightmare and that the creature, or demon, would deposit the squalling child into her arms.

This was no dream. Though it had a surreal, nightmarish quality to it, it was real. Crazy as it seemed, she was being mauled by a hideous monster. And worse still, her daughter was being abducted before she was ever born.

It began to turn away, but thought better of it and faced her again. The baby wriggled in the crook of its arm; she shrieked in rage and punched at the air with tiny fists. Apparently, the child was a fighter.

"I need one more thing from you."

What more could it possibly want? There was nothing left to take.

Clutching her daughter tightly in the hollow of his elbow, not unlike a football, the creature's other hand slashed out once more. Strangely enough, it didn't hurt. That was probably something to worry about, but Ivanya couldn't find enough in her to care. The chunk of flesh it had torn from her chest was jammed into a pocket of its cloak.

"Thank you for dinner, woman. Gypsy has always been my favorite." With that, the thing began to fade into nothingness. Its body became wispy tendrils of smoke, growing fainter and fainter until all that remained was a pair of crimson eyes. Those faded as well, and she was left alone.

As promised, the darkness returned, but Ivanya made no effort to fight it off this time. She cared for nothing anymore. All she wanted was for it to be over. Calmly, she surrendered. The darkness swaddled her in its cocoon. She no longer felt the cold or the pain. But she could still hear, though none of the words made sense.

The voice was far away, as if the woman were speaking from of other side of a thick, glass wall. She spoke with an accent, Southern with a dash of French.

"I already called an ambulance, Smitty. You're not listenin' to me. Shut your cakehole and open the ears God gave you." A vein of anger stretched through her voice. "What I've been tryin' to tell you is that you need to meet the ambulance when it gets there. This child needs your help and I think she need mine, too. I'll meet you there."

Silence.

"I'm not gonna tell you. You'll see it all when we get there. You got to see it for yourself or you won't believe it. And I need you to believe it. No other doctors get close to this girl for now."

A small beep sounded as the woman disconnected the call. Then, warm skin touched hers. Large, meaty fingers interlaced with her own and a soft palm caressed the top of her head.

Peace settled over Ivanya as she drifted away.

Chapter 19

Tarik entered the underground temple, the infant held in the folds of his cloak. The others crowded around him to get a look at the child they had all been waiting for. They regarded it like a precious jewel or a queen. Something to be revered. He didn't see what all the fuss was about. Human younglings were mewling, slobbering, disgusting things. One of the women arrived at his elbow, her hands held out for the child. Tarik was happy to be rid of the thing.

The putrid stench, however, did not move away when the little parasite did. He sniffed until he found the source of the stink. It was him. The little parasite shat on him. He searched his clothing until he found the offending garment and gasped in horror. A large, wet, black stain was embedded into the fabric of his cloak. It had the consistency of tar and smelled as if all the waste on Earth had been dumped on his clothes. Even if he washed it a thousand times, that horrible odor would still linger. Tarik almost wished for a priest—his cloak was in dire need of holy water.

He growled furiously as he stripped off the cloak and tossed it into a nearby fire. It erupted into a knee-high pillar of flames. Apparently, human waste was a highly flammable substance.

Tarik, wanting to be as far away from the parasite as possible, moved into the ceremonial chamber. It was all but empty. The cavern was a church of sorts, though not the kind you would find altar boys in. Simple wooden pews made from charred logs dotted the floor in a loose circular formation. Standing on tall, wrought iron stands were fat, black candles that dripped waxy tears into uneven pools on the dirt floor. In the center was a pedestal draped with a black cloth. Six silver basins surrounded it, forming a six-pointed star. Outside the star a table waited, stacked neatly with clay bowls, a mortar and pestle, and a silver knife with an obsidian handle. Tools of the trade. He settled in the front row and waited for the ritual to begin.

Female Stinger demons entered the chamber from behind a black curtain. Six of them. They all wore black ceremonial robes that drifted just above the ground. All but the backs, which were lifted about six inches by long, segmented tails. Their scaly skin was prismatic, rippling color with each movement. Their faces were oddly feline, the eyes changing hue above the high cheekbones. Tarik was enthralled by their beauty, but knew never to get too close. Stingers were notorious for the potent venom they carried in their tails. They could release it at will and were quick to anger. One sting could potentially kill even the most capable adversary.

He watched in fascination as they laid small bundles into the shallow basins. The blankets were removed, revealing squalling and writhing human younglings. The Stingers began coating the infants with something like a marinade that smelled of cloves and sulfur. It was divine and made Tarik a little hungry.

People, to use the term loosely, filed into the pews, chattering excitedly to each other. Tarik gave them a stern look, but they just ignored him. This made him want to rip their heads off their shoulders, but that would not be tolerated in this place. Instead, he memorized their faces, planning to meet them outside after the ritual.

A discordant tune filled the chamber as Lykah entered from a corridor on the left side of the stage, her hands in the air and a brilliant smile on her face. The silver ceremonial gown glowed in the candlelight, her plasticine skin shining in the darkness. She placed the parasite that had shit all over his clothes on the altar. Its face bore ancient runes in the language of the Trynok drawn on its skin in blood.

"This is a glorious day for the Trynok." Lykah's voice tinkled like bells. "We have followed the prophecy and it has led us here, to this moment. The weapon forged tonight will aid us in the coming battles. No longer will we need to hide in dark corners. The world will be ours for the taking." She bowed her head, her voice trembling with power.

"The souls of the innocent

Will combine to create

183

A vessel for vengeance

And darkness and hate

When six become one

Its will shall be done…"

With a nod from Lykah, the Stingers poised their tails over the basins where the infants lay. With a flick, the tails descended up the infants, easing into the soft skin like needles. The barbs constricted and released again and again, like the body of a snake digesting a mouse. A series of muffled popping sounds echoed off the walls as the suckers pulled out.

Next, the Stingers raised their razor sharp appendages over the one on the altar in the center of the star. There was a pause, pregnant with anticipation, before the barbs plunged down into the child's chest. The infant thrashed, screaming in agony for endless minutes before it fell silent, as the six souls settled into their new home. A brilliant blue light washed over it.

It became a ball of energy that grew large with every second. The sheer power was oppressive, cloying, making it difficult for Tarik to draw a breath. He looked around, no one else seemed to be having any trouble. He pulled the collar of his shirt away from his neck. Pressure built around the parasite until, suddenly, it burst into a wave of azure light. The pulse was so strong that it knocked Tarik slightly backward, almost spilling him to the floor. The baby glowed for a moment, whimpered softly and then...silence.

That is, until Tarik started screaming. Pressure collected in his head, behind his eyes, filling his ears. He clapped his hands over his skull, squeezing with his palms to keep it from blowing apart. Blue light invaded his eyes, even though they were clamped shut in agony. It seemed to be coming from inside his head, piercing his brain like a thousand knives at once. He screamed until his voice went hoarse and all that came out was a choked whisper. There was a burning on his wrist but he barely noticed. That pain was nothing compared to this. Finally, the pain began to ebb off, the blue light faded and he was able to open his heavy eyes. He looked at his wrist, which held the lingering ghosts of pain and beheld a brand of three horizontal lines.

Every eye in the house was upon him, wide and unblinking. Lykah approached him, a strange smile on her face. "What a surprise."

"Priestess, what happened to me?" He had to choke out the words.

"Bringing the child to us seems to have held an unforeseen consequence."

He briefly remembered the bloody retrieval. The forked tongue darted from his mouth, remembering the taste of the mother's blood, while he wondered if it had been worth it. He was beginning to think it had not.

Lykah gazed at him thoughtfully, her head tilted slightly to the side. "And what do you feel for it, I wonder?"

"I don't understand the question," he muttered.

"Do you, or could you in the future, ever like the child or even…love it?" she asked, sharply.

Tarik's face contorted with disgust. "The only thing I feel in its presence is hatred. Killing it would be my exquisite pleasure."

"Hatred is good, Tarik." She paused to meet the eyes of the others. "Tarik will serve as the child's Guardian!" she exclaimed. A roar of applause nearly deafened him.

The thing's Guardian! He wanted nothing to do with it. He had done the job he'd been hired to do, and now he wanted to move on. Be allowed to do what he wanted, when he wanted. Not sitting here, being tortured by a job he hated.

"With respect, Priestess, choose another. I want no part of this."

Anger flared in Lykah's eyes. "I did not choose you. You volunteered for the post the moment you touched her. You will be her Guardian. Protect her. Train her."

"I do not-"

"This is not negotiable. You were chosen. The only way out of this is death. And when that time comes, it will be your flesh she feasts upon."

This disturbed him more than anything else. More than he didn't want to die, he was disgusted by the idea of the little human parasite feeding on him. Bringing him into its wretched little body. So, apparently, it was either rear the maggot...or be devoured by it. Reluctantly, he consented, hating his life more than at any previous moment.

Chapter 20

The call from Linda had done nothing to prepare Dr. Hayden Smith. And when the patient was wheeled into the operating room, he knew that no amount of warning would have done any good. Nurses Mary and Polly counted to three and heaved the sheet under the girl onto the operating table. They buzzed around the room, gathering supplies like worker bees.

Smitty approached the patient with trepidation, acknowledging that he needed to see the extent of the injuries, but also knowing that the very sight of them would change him forever. The first thing he noticed was her beauty. Though her skin was pale from blood loss, he could imagine her with creamy peach skin and a rosy glow on her cheeks. Soft, blonde hair fanned out on the table, just a shade darker than the white linen sheet. He once again imagined her without the sticky blood making the ends stringy. She looked as if she could have been Sleeping Beauty; she belonged in a fairy tale, not an operating room. With two fingers, Smitty peeled apart the lids of her left eye, revealing a brilliant green iris. Unfortunately, the pupil was non-reactive to light.

The face was the only part of her that was untouched by violence. A cursory examination revealed four deep lacerations to the neck, slashes that traced the lines of her body. The stark white of the clavicle showed through the blood, deep crevices carved into the bone. The gashes were not so much cuts as tears in the flesh. Muscle was torn away from frayed tendons, some chunks of it missing. Three ribs on the left side had been snapped like twigs and the breast on that side had been severed. To his horror, those were the least grievous of the wounds. The ragged slashes traveled down the ribcage and through the soft flesh of the abdomen, terminating in a bloody hole just above the pelvic girdle. He continued the examination, noticing that the splintered end of her femur poked through the skin on her thigh. Once he fixed the bleeding, he would need to send her to Dr. Hardwick for that. She was the best orthopedic surgeon in the hospital.

"What is her name?" he asked, his voice cracking on the last word.

Silence greeted him.

"What is her name?" he growled, angrily. Nurse Polly jumped.

"Um, Ivanya. Ivanya Devereaux," she stammered, after consulting the chart.

Smitty ran a hand over the girl's forehead. "Wait, Devereaux? As in Irena Devereaux?" He could have kicked himself for not recognizing her. She was like a mirror image of Irena when she was younger. He should have seen it. Maybe he hadn't wanted to. "Ivanya? Can you hear me?"

No response, not that he expected one. The truth of the matter was that it would be a bald faced miracle if she survived. The blood loss alone should have killed her long before now. He suspected that the cold had slowed the blood flow enough to save her life.

"Ivanya, I am going to save you, but I need your help. I need you to hold on for me." Smitty always took the time to get to know his patients, so to speak. This was instrumental to his process, even if time was a non-existent concept in some cases. It reminded him that the patient was more than that. It kept him human.

Just as he held his gloved hand out for the scalpel, the doors to the room burst open. In stepped Linda, Big Mama Linda to her friends, though Smitty refused to call her that. She wore a pair of maroon scrubs that strained against her large body like a sausage casing. Her usual halo of kinky black hair was pinned down under a light blue surgical cap.

"I know you're not thinking of doing this without me."

Nurse Mary stepped forward. "You need to leave; Dr. Smith is about to begin an operation." Though Mary was a good foot shorter than Linda, she was still imposing.

"I am a registered nurse," Linda began, but Mary cut her off.

"A registered nurse that does not work at this hospital. You are a liability. Just being in this room leaves us vulnerable to a lawsuit."

"Then call me a damned consultant and get out of my way." The big woman's eyes were stormy and left no room for an argument. Smitty stepped between them, arms splayed out like a referee.

"We do not have time for this. Both of you to your corners. We need all the help we can get." With that, Smitty approached the table.

"Scalpel," he said, holding out his gloved hand. At first, there was no movement, then two of them crossed his palm. "Knock it off, you two. There is no room in my OR for your pettiness. If you can't do your jobs, you need to get the hell out."

Nurse Mary was taken aback by his attitude. Never had Dr. Smith spoken to her with such venom in his voice.

Ignoring everything else, Smitty explored the hole in the girl's abdomen. Large chunks of flesh were missing. Extensive reconstructive work would need to be done. Most of the uterus was missing, shredded beyond repair. A ropy strand of umbilical cord was still connected to the tissue, the end severed neatly by a sharp implement.

"No baby. Is this what you meant on the phone, Linda?"

The big woman nodded, her coffee eyes large and round. That worried Smitty. Big Mama Linda was a lot of things, but rarely was she afraid. "And more," she breathed, her voice slightly muffled by the surgical mask, "If I'm right."

Just the slightest traces of placenta remained, but as he felt around inside, he realized there was something there besides the muscle. With the scalpel, he sliced into the tissue, dropped the implement into Polly's waiting hands and used his own to widen the slit.

"Impossible," he whispered. There was not a name for this type of physiology. As far as Smitty knew, he was discovering it for the first time. The girl's uterus was segmented like the atria of the heart; divided into two compartments. And inside, shielded by the thin amniotic membrane, lay another baby. Smitty once again took up the scalpel and cut into the sac. He extracted the child, handing it off quickly to Mary, barely registering the fact that it was a boy before he went back to work. In seconds, the child cried out, and Smitty knew that it was unharmed.

After snipping the Fallopian tubes, he knotted them and allowed Linda to cauterize the ends. Smitty sliced the tissue that held the uterus in place and lifted the organ out. It landed in a stainless steel bowl with a meaty thud; he looked forward to studying it later. Now that the uterus was out, there was more skin for him to work with. He would have enough to close her up. He checked nearby blood vessels to ensure they were intact before he excised the rough edges of the hole and began to suture it closed.

He checked the stomach, which had miraculously escaped the carnage unscathed. The carotid artery had not even been nicked, though given the severity of the lacerations, it should have been severed. One more thing to check on before he finished sewing her up and left the rest to fate. He had noticed a cut in the liver and needed to check and see if a lobe needed removing.

"Suction."

Linda obliged, running the metal tube over the area, clearing the blood out of the way to give him a better look. Nothing. Not a trace of the gash he had seen earlier. He searched the entire organ, thinking that he must have been mistaken about the location. It was nowhere. It had been there. He would not have made a mistake of that magnitude. It had simply vanished.

"It's gone. The laceration is gone."

A squeak escaped from Linda, a sound like an exclamation of excitement and sorrow. "I was right. It's startin'."

He finished the arduous task of stitching all the cuts, which took hundreds of sutures, then released her to the care of Dr. Hardwick for the leg.

Smitty turned toward the adjoining room, where the nurses had taken the baby. Again, Mary and Linda were bickering, this time over who would hold the child.

"Girl, you need to let go right now."

"What are you going to do? Sit on me?"

Polly, who stood next to the door, head bobbing like she was at a tennis match, was surprised that such a thing came out of Mary's mouth. She was even more surprised at Linda's reaction. Her eyes immediately darkened, a brewing storm of anger. As quickly as it came, it passed, and a radiant smile lit her face.

"You know, that's not a bad idea. You wouldn't last ten seconds under my biscuits, girl. Now grow up and let me show Smitty what I was talking about."

"Actually," Smitty said, tersely. "You two need to leave. I need to examine this child and Linda needs a moment to explain her behavior." He turned to Linda. "Give him to me."

Nurse Mary cracked a smile as she followed Polly out the door. The idea of Dr. Smith reprimanding the other woman was too delicious.

Linda waited until the other nurses left before she handed over the infant without a single comment.

That was a feat in and of itself, as she was rarely without something to say.

Pulling the blanket aside, Smitty looked at tiny fingers and toes (ten of each), creamy skin without a single flaw, and something else. Something that didn't make a bit of sense. Another discovery that modern medicine has never seen. The boy's tummy was perfectly flat. The place where the belly button should have been was flush with the rest of his skin. No indentation or discoloration. Now that he thought of it, he hadn't needed to cut a cord when he removed the child from the womb. The umbilical cord was what delivered blood, oxygen and nutrients to the fetus. Without it, the fetus would never make it to term. Would never have become anything at all.

Smitty felt like he were in the Twilight Zone, where everything was wrong and nothing made sense. Physiology that had never before existed, giving way to a child that defied all laws of science and creation.

"Are you ready to listen to me, Smitty?"

"You know something about this?"

She leaned forward and inhaled, pleading to him with her eyes. "You are one of the few people who know who I am, Smitty." He began to object, but she waved him off. "Whether you choose to believe it or not. You know what I believe and that I believe it with my whole heart. So you listen good when I tell you that it's startin'."

"What is starting?" Smitty asked, not sure he wanted to hear the answer.

"The battle for Earth. Armageddon. Whatever you want to call it. And this boy is part of it, so is the child that's missing. And that girl and me and maybe even you. So buck up, because you're about to get a big wake up call. I'll be explainin' in detail when the girl wakes up, so be sure you're listening, or get out while you can." She thought for a moment. "You'll be lettin' me take the baby, Smitty."

She had to be insane, he thought. There was no way he could let her take a baby that did not belong to her out of this hospital. Legal would have his ass, and he was fairly confident he would not do well in prison. "I can't let you take that child, Linda. You know that. It's against policy and the law."

She glared in Smitty's face. "You spent all them years in college and you still ain't got no damn sense. This child is Irena's great-grandson. We need to protect him. If anyone finds out about this baby, whoever attacked that poor girl could come back to finish her off. You don't want that on your head."

"Even if I agreed with this, Linda, the other girls already saw the baby. They won't be able to keep quiet about this."

She smiled with all of her teeth and in that moment, Smitty saw her as Big Mama Linda. Her body shook like Santa as she laughed so hard that tears squirted out of her eyes. When she could finally speak again, she said, "They're probably in your office, eating those delicious cookies that *someone* left on your desk. That cranky nurse of yours will be there; she wouldn't pass up the chance to grill you about what you said to me. She's probably hoping you called the law."

Mystified, Smitty handed her the baby and passed through the doors to the OR, turned left down the hall and slowly turned the knob to his office. Adorable, like the baby in the other room, was the only word in Smitty's vocabulary that could describe the scene before him, even if it were not what he had been expecting. Not that he'd known what to expect—with Linda, there was no normal.

Nurse Mary slouched in Smitty's chair, her head lolling against the head cushion. Her mouth hung open and a soft snore issued from the back of her throat. Small crumbs of chocolate chip cookie dotted her shirt. Polly's head rested against the desk, a thin line of drool trailing over his desk calendar. A crumbling cookie was clutched in her hand.

Linda was washing the surgical implements when Smitty returned to the OR. Her face glowed with mirth.

"What did you do to them? Cast some of your voodoo mojo on them?" he asked, sarcasm like molasses dripping in his voice.

"Nope, I didn't use any of my mojo, as you call it—I used some of yours." She paused, presumably for dramatic effect. "I roofied them!" she cackled, loudly.

Smitty didn't ask where she got the Rohypnol; there were some things that he did not need or want to know. But he could see the wisdom in her actions. Rohypnol brought on dizziness and unconsciousness, as well as amnesia. It was perfect. The drug was ingested so soon after the discovery of the child, odds were that they would not remember it had taken place.

He smiled. "You're a genius."

"And don't you forget it."

Moments later, Mama Linda left the hospital, carrying her coat over her arm. No one noticed that every few steps, it moved.

Chapter 21

Abby returned home from a particularly grueling luncheon at the country club with her parents to an empty house.

"Vani," she called, her voice echoing off the walls. "Where are you, my little piñata?"

Nothing. The house was empty. It was a little disheveled, but nothing out of the ordinary. The couch cushions were askew and there was a blanket on the floor. It looked like she went out—her boots and coat were gone. She thought, not for the first time, that she would like to get a little dog that would come running when she came home, jump at her legs and kiss her face. Someone who would be happy to see her. Not that Vani wasn't good enough, but she had enough on her plate without having to worry about Abigail. Abby liked to think of herself as tough, and she was, but sometimes her hard shell faltered and unease managed to seep through the cracks.

A knock at the door made her jump. Cops. Their knocks were distinctive—and annoying. She put her eye to the peephole. Holy crap! It was that hot one. Detective Douchebag's consultant. Abigail breathed on her hand and held it in front of her nose to check her breath. Good. Looking down, she saw something that needed attending to. She tugged the bottom of her V-neck tee and pushed up on her boobs until a fair amount of cleavage was visible. There. Now she was ready for company.

In her excitement, she swung the heavy door open so hard that it smacked into the wall, the knob pushing a dent into the paneling. Whoops. Ivanya was going to have a fit.

"Dr. Kingston, what a nice surprise," Abigail purred, draping herself provocatively against the doorway. "What's the matter? Cat got your tongue?"

Kingston pulled his tie away from his throat as he looked at her, as if the temperature had suddenly increased fifty degrees. He shook his head and typed quickly on his phone. He thrust it impatiently at Abigail.

"Ooh…are we sexting?"

A stern look from Kingston.

I need to see Ivanya right away!!!

"Easy on the exclamations, guy. Vani isn't here."

Do you know where she went?

"No, sometimes she just flakes out and takes off, usually to get food." Abigail frowned a little, a crease appearing between her eyebrows.

Where would she go?

Abigail didn't know, but a pit of unease was eating at her stomach. Something was wrong. She could feel it all around her now, and could see the signs on Kingston's face.

"I don't know which place she would hit first, but I'm going with you."

He shook his head, but she stopped him with a glare.

"Obviously, something is the matter and if it concerns my best friend, then you have a navigator. Deal with it."

Once in the car, he handed her the case file he had spent the last few months building. It contained everything that had been happening. Details on the murder of Mina Gulleckson and things about the missing girls. Giving the file to Abigail Kayne made the sinking feeling in the pit of his stomach grow more pronounced. The girl was not a cop, or an attorney, or even a person who could shed light on anything in there. He could lose his job for letting her even touch it. But she was connected to Ivanya Devereaux and therefore, Kingston believed she was connected to this case. Plus, his condition made it impossible for him to tell her what was going on and drive at the same time.

Abigail read quickly, eyes scanning each sentence with growing horror. The conclusion he had drawn seemed tentative at best, but definitely thought provoking. If any of the stuff in this file was real, the only safe people would be the ones who didn't live in Watson.

"Is Vani in trouble?" she asked, the crease deepening between her brows.

Kingston tapped the side of his head with two fingers and nodded, meaning *I think so.*

Abigail did not need any further incentive. She quickly unbuckled her seat belt (the irony that she was breaking the law in a cop car was not lost on her), rolled down the passenger side window, and stuck her head out into the wintry air. She called her friend's name into the night, knowing that the odds of getting a response were slim, but unable to stop herself. It was the only thing she could think of to do and she was not the kind to sit around passively.

She wondered where Ivanya was, hoping that she was safe somewhere, maybe gorging herself on blueberry pancakes at the Flapjack House, or vomiting them up in their bathroom. But Abigail had serious doubts as to whether this was the case. From Kingston's notes, she knew that he thought whatever danger was going to befall her friend would be happening today. There wasn't much of today left.

If everything turned out to be okay, Abigail was putting a tracking chip on her friend. She couldn't handle this aimless searching and the not knowing. She smacked herself in the forehead, feeling like the world's biggest idiot. Kingston looked at her with a raised eyebrow, but she was already in action. She tapped the screen of her phone and brought up the *Find My Device* app. From the menu, she selected Ivanya's phone and waited for the map to load. Ivanya had lost the thing twice before, so Abigail had downloaded the app to locate it. There it was, the glowing green dot that would lead them to her friend.

"She's over by Hawthorne. Take a left here." Kingston cautiously took the turn, his hands at ten and two, guiding the wheel. Abigail was disappointed; she'd been hoping for squealing tires and a six foot plume of snow spraying the sidewalk.

She called Ivanya's name out the window as loud as she could, drawing stares from the few people who were out walking. They looked at her like she had lost her mind. In a way she had, she was mad with worry.

She saw the lights when they were still halfway down the block, blue and red strobing against the snow. Her heart sank to the floor and tears filled her eyes. Kingston pulled up next to a cruiser and Abigail threw her door open, nearly spilling out into the snow. She ran toward the crime scene tape that reminded her of some bizarre velvet rope designed to keep out undesirables from a high end club. She knew in some latent part of her underbrain that Ivanya had been selected to attend.

Corl approached her, holding a clear plastic bag containing Ivanya's cell phone. "Stay back, Miss Kayne."

"Is she in there? Is Vani down there?"

He shook his head. "No, she's not. We just got word that she was taken to the hospital in critical condition. We're still trying to piece together what happened, but it looks like she was attacked." He locked eyes with Kingston over her shoulder. "We've got slime."

"Slime?" Abigail asked, eyes wide with confusion. Then she remembered the case file. "Like the missing girls. And Mina."

Corl's face flushed instantly, hues of red on his cheeks with his forehead turning a deep plum. "How do you know about that?"

Kingston looked at the ground, suddenly interested in a clump of dirty snow near the toe of his shoe.

"You gave her the fucking file? You know, I accept that you can't talk, but I can't work with you if you're going to be stupid. You could get us both fired." He glanced at Abigail and back to Kingston. "And did you think about her? About her knowing what could be

204

happening to her friend? There is only so much that a victim's family needs to know; only so much they can handle."

Corl was so busy yelling at Kingston, that neither of them noticed when Abigail stepped away, drifting over to the tape. Blood was everywhere. Thick puddles of it carved holes in the snow, growing crusty around the edges where it had begun to freeze. Snowflakes skated on the surface, like carefree children that did not know there was a monster lurking beneath the lake.

Spatter patterns spackled a large green dumpster that smelled like a mixture of Chinese food and raw sewage. There was so much of it. It painted the back wall of the Bluebird Café, right next to the heavy door that employees snuck out of to smoke. Cigarette butts poked out of the top of a snow covered bucket like some weird porcupine.

A hand landed on her shoulder and she jumped, her heart slamming into her throat. She whipped around quickly, fist clenched and ready to throw a punch. It was just Corl, but she had the urge to throw the punch anyway. She needed to hit something, anything. He placed an arm around her shoulders and gently turned her away from the grisly scene.

"Come on, Miss Kayne. You don't need to see this. You need to see her. Alive. You should be at the hospital." His voice was uncharacteristically gentle, with a low timbre that was instantly calming. "We'll drive you there right now."

Without a word, Abigail let him guide her away and pack her into the car. It would be all right. It had to be.

*****

The hospital was bustling as Abigail entered through the automatic doors, flanked by Corl and Kingston. She couldn't contain herself any longer. She was so close. She broke into a run, skidding to a stop with her hands braced against the information desk.

"Ivanya Devereaux. Where is she?" Abigail huffed.

The gentleman behind the desk was about forty-five, with light brown hair gone grey at the temples. Wire rimmed glasses perched on the bridge of a nearly perfect nose.

"Your relationship to the patient?"

"Best friend."

He favored her with a sympathetic smile. "Miss, I'm sorry, but the law prevents me from giving any information about a patient to anyone without a familial relation. I can't even legally confirm or deny that she is here."

She was sick of people telling her that she shouldn't know anything. It was getting old and she didn't have time for it. "Look. Greg, is it? Ivanya has no family. I am her friend and roommate. There is no one else."

"I'm sorry. I can't."

Corl and Kingston approached the desk, both pulling ID's from jacket pockets.

"Is there a problem here?" Corl asked, authority ringing in his voice.

"I was just explaining to the young lady here that we can only release information to next of kin."

"Well, for all intents and purposes, she is next of kin. And we are the investigating officers in Miss Devereaux's case. I need you to page her attending physician."

"Right away, sir," Greg said, as he began tapping keys on his computer. He picked up the phone and hit the intercom button, paging in a professional baritone, "Dr. Smith to the chapel, please. Dr. Smith to the chapel." He caught the horror-stricken expression on Abigail's face. "Everything is okay. She is stable for now. The chapel is just a quiet place to talk."

Abigail's blood pressure decreased marginally as she strode down the hallway. She stood in front of the door with the stained glass window, the portal to the dark world beyond. After a moment, she opened the door and entered. She walked slowly to the front of the room, where a bank of candles flickered next to a covered podium. Abigail lit a candle and said a quick prayer. She was surprised and touched when Corl and Kingston did the same.

The chapel door opened, bathing the dim room in fluorescent light from the hallway. The doctor entered, his white coat wrinkled as if he'd slept in it. His hair was slightly mussed, like he had continuously raked fingers through it in frustration.

"Officers. I'm Dr. Hayden Smith."

"I'm Detective Corl. This is Dr. Kingston. PhD, not MD. And this is the victim's roommate and friend, Abigail Kayne." In answer to the doctor's raised eyebrow, Corl replied, "Yes. That Abigail Kayne." He settled into a pew, crossed his right leg over his left and balanced a notepad on his knee. He looked at the others expectantly, until they, too, settled onto the hard wooden seats.

"What can you tell us, Doc?"

Smitty explained the extent of Ivanya's injuries: the lacerations over the majority of her torso requiring hundreds of stitches, the partial hysterectomy, and the missing breast. Abigail started strong, but was crying by the second item, and nearly hyperventilating by the third.

"She is in a coma right now, which is actually a good thing. It will allow her body to begin the healing process without having to consciously feel the pain." He thrummed his fingers anxiously against his knee. "Now, on to the bad news."

Abigail cut him off. "The bad news? You mean that was the *good* news?"

Smitty grimaced. "I'm afraid so."

Sympathetic pain crossed Kingston's face; real pain slashed across Abigail's.

"Oh my God, the baby! Where is the baby?" It was not a question so much as a demand.

"Officer," Smitty began. "You may want to write this down."

Corl nodded, flipping to a new page in his notebook.

"The damage to the uterus was severe; in fact, it was utterly destroyed. The umbilical cord was severed." He swallowed a thick lump down his throat. "The baby was gone."

Kingston's face turned white, even though he had expected as much. Then, Abigail did something that Kingston thought she was too strong to be capable of, but which was entirely justified in this situation.

She fainted.

Chapter 22

Pale blue stars fell from the sky, breaking into a cascade of crystal shards that rained down on the earth. Ivanya like this place. It was beautiful and peaceful and busy. Things happened all around her, things that others would find extraordinary. She regarded them as commonplace, strange and wonderful things happened here all the time. And there was no pain here. She didn't know why that was an important factor, but it was.

Time moved strangely in this place. A moment could stretch out forever, or it could speed up and days would pass by. At least, she thought so. She tried not to think too much about it. It gave her an unpleasant feeling in the pit of her stomach.

This day was one of those stretching moment days. She seemed to float through a golden field of wheat. The tops of the wheat caressed her legs and tickled the skin on her arms. With splayed fingers, she tickled it back as the grass massaged the bottoms of her feet. Off to the right, a deer bounded through the field. It stopped, its big, brown eyes staring into hers before it disappeared into the forest, its white tail bobbing up and down.

She twirled in the meadow, her floral print dress spinning out around her. Before long, she made it to the lake. She walked out onto the rickety dock, where a gingham blanket and a wicker picnic basket waited for her. The sun baked on her face and shoulders as she uncorked a bottle of Moscato and poured some into a long stemmed glass. She sipped the wine and watched the ducks bob for food on the surface of the water. A green headed mallard regarded her curiously, then darted its head into the water. Ivanya watched them for a while, absently chewing on a dinner roll. She ripped it into pieces and tossed them into the lake, the ducks approaching the treats in a tight V formation. With some unseen cue, the ducks stopped their advance, all looking at her, before they spread their wings and took flight, the pieces of dinner roll still floating near the dock. The sound of beating wings was nearly deafening as they flew over her head, the rubbery foot of one almost touching her hair.

Suddenly, the sky grew dark. Rain pelted Ivanya's upturned face as she watched the clouds boil. An arthritic finger of lightning cracked across the sky, drowning everything in a bright, white light. The once lush trees were now the color of bleached bone. They jutted from newly diseased weeds, skeletal sentries preparing for battle.

Ivanya ran. Her haven had never behaved this way before. The terror thrummed through her muscles, and though her lungs burned, she did not stop. The rain came harder now. It fell in long sheets that seemed to have no end. The dress had plastered itself to her body, a linen skin. The sharp points of her breasts were dark brown through the fabric. In any other situation, she would have been embarrassed. The wet dress was more revealing than her naked skin would have been.

In the distance stood the dim outline of a cottage. Most of it was obscured by the rain—not that she cared. She didn't give a damn how old it was or even if there were rats inside. All she wanted was a roof over her head to protect her from the raging storm. She ran as fast as she could with the dress constricting her legs. Jagged rocks cut at her feet, but she kept moving through the pain. Through the field, up the splintery porch steps (she got a pretty good sized sliver in her heel), and crashed through the creaky door, slamming it behind her. She leaned against it, struggling to catch her breath. Her heart beat solidly against her ribcage, threatening to break the thin bones. Not so much falling as dripping down the door, she sat heavily on the floor.

This was wrong. All wrong. The storm had scared her right down to her bones. Strange things happened in this place, but it had never turned on her before. This was her place, her sanctuary. She was supposed to be safe here. It was becoming painfully clear that today that had changed. Bad Things were lurking. They didn't have names or faces that she could see, but they lurked just the same. Waiting for a chance to devour her.

Groaning with the effort, she forced her sore legs to rise. The place was dim, but not dark, so she decided to look around for a place to hide from the Bad Things. She would just cower there until the storm was over. When her world was normal again she would leave.

The floorboards creaked with every step. Ivanya had the crawly sensation that the Bad Things were listening to her every move with bated breath, waiting for the opportunity to descend upon her. She tried to move slower and step softer, but the floor seemed to squeak louder, so she abandoned the idea.

Paint peeled off the walls of what had once been a living room in strips; some of it crumbled on the floor, a dull yellow pile of dust. Thick cobwebs hung from everything: door jambs, window sills, picture frames, and light fixtures. The drapes were so caked in dust that she couldn't discern their natural color. The windows were dirty to the point of looking soaped over. Nothing outside could be seen, except the bent and wiggly ghosts of what could have been trees.

Off to the left was a staircase, which she stared at dumbly for about thirty seconds. Everything in this house was filthy, except the steps. The dark cherry wood of the bannister gleamed as if it had just been polished. The steps themselves were clean and free of dust, the hunter green runner newly vacuumed. Her feet moved to a silent rhythm, carrying her upstairs. At the top of the stairs, a thought occurred to her...she couldn't remember her feet actually touching the floor.

A small table sat against the wall and on top of it was a pile of clothes. She peeled off the dress; it came loose with a sucking sound as it pulled over her head. The pair of jeans and hooded sweatshirt fit like clothes she had at home. Scratch that. They were the clothes she had at home. There was a small frayed hole where the right back pocket hooked into the seat of the pants and the entire left knee was blown out. They were the most comfortable pair she owned.

She hadn't realized she was shaking until the warm clothes were on and the tremors abated. She donned a pair of combat style boots and started exploring the rest of the second floor. More disrepair. The same peeling paint, a missing doorknob here and there, a hole in the wall the size of a fist. Rooms lined the long hallway, but she ignored those. There was a door at the end, open just a crack. It sparkled as if imbued with diamonds. There was no choice involved; the door was open and she had to go in.

It was a little like stepping out of a space shuttle onto the moon. Astronauts had an academic idea of what the moon would be like, but did not truly understand it until they were hopping craters. Ivanya had been in rooms like this before, but this one struck her as odd, and a little...creepy. For no particular reason, she found herself on the precipice of a scream.

It was a normal nursery. The blue walls were dotted with mint green dragonflies that had intricate patterns like cracked glass on the wings. A rocking chair stood in the corner, a blanket draped over the arm and *Goodnight Moon* laying in the seat. It was like someone had put it aside to run an errand and would return soon.

Me, she thought, and shivered.

She moved toward the white crib, her hand outstretched. Her fingers shook violently.

This is the Bad Thing...right here...waiting for me.

She didn't understand how the Bad Thing could be a stationary piece of furniture, but it was. Or something to do with it, anyway. Slowly, trembling with fear, she touched the smooth white wood with the tips of her fingers. A grief she could not name washed over her, followed by a tidal wave of fear. In that moment, she knew everything had changed. This place, her world, would never be a sanctuary again. It had become, instead, the smithing shop where nightmares were forged.

(Baby! My baby!!)

Slashes of pain shot across her midsection. A scream built in her throat. It gained pressure, but stayed there, choking her. Her head bobbed back and forth, from one item to the next. A pink blanket. A blue blanket. Teddy bears. The mobile with zoo animals hanging from it like strange fish.

(Vetra...)

Her legs gave out and she fell to the floor in a trembling heap. Flashes of images shot through her head like lightning. The fatness of her belly. The assaults on her bladder. She had watched the baby move within her, flipping around in what might have been a uterine gymnastics competition. She remembered it all. She was a mother.

Vetra's mother.

This place had been nice, her refuge from the horrible event that had broken her. She had needed the magic it provided to heal her mind. But no longer.

What she needed was not here.

(she might not be here she might not be anywhere she might be dead just stay here where it's safe stay here stay here)

It broke free, the scream that had stoppered her throat, exploding into the room. There were no words, just a primitive shriek that bounced off the walls. She screamed until there was nothing left inside of her, and then lay still.

Seconds later, the walls fell down.

*****

This must be Hell, she thought upon waking. The lights were fluorescent torture burning her eyes. Over starched sheets lay across her and plastic snakes fed on her arms. Every muscle and bone in her body ached. Even her hair hurt, a thing she had never thought was possible.

She squinted in concentration, her bottom lip jutting out into a little pout. There had been nausea and pain, a wrenching agony that drowned the world. Memories assailed her, ramming her brain and pummeling at her heart. Blackness, all-encompassing darkness swathed her in a thick blanket; she couldn't breathe and found she didn't want to. The baby was gone. The creature, that smoky…thing, had taken her daughter. And the cruel joke was that she should be dead, and wasn't.

Ivanya screamed then, ripping the oxygen cannula from her nose. She howled like a wolf at the moon. She was feral in her grief, mourning with no words, contorting her fingers into claws and raking them across her face. Abigail jumped from a nearby chair where she had been sleeping and pulled Ivanya's hands to her sides. Ivanya struggled, but her muscles were weak, so she was no match for Abigail.

218

"I need help in here!" Abigail screamed. A nurse and two orderlies burst through the door. Seeing the result of Ivanya's frenzied self-mutilation, they leapt into action. One orderly grabbed her left wrist, yanking it away from Abigail. The other man hooked leather restraints to the bedrails. She fought as her hands were inserted through them and the leather straps pulled tight. Her foot lashed out, striking the first orderly directly in the crotch. He dropped to his knees, hands clasped to his front. His face was a ghastly shade of white with a tinge of green, and his eyes rolled back into their hollows, the lids fluttering epileptically. The nurse approached and caught Ivanya's ankle as she kicked again. The nurse quickly looped the strip around her ankle and tightened it down.

The physical pain was nothing compared to the mental agony. She wanted to die; willed it, prayed for it. This really was Hell, for her prayers were not heard. Her stupid heart kept beating, traitor lungs still drew breath. The screams died out, her throat raw and coppery tasting, but the sobs kept coming. She wanted to fold in on herself, to become smaller and smaller until she withered away, but she was restrained in a lop-sided spread eagle position, with her nearly shattered leg in traction. Apparently, grief wasn't meant to be comfortable.

"I'm sorry about this," the nurse whispered. "The doctor will be here to speak to you in a few

219

minutes." She followed the orderlies, one looking a little sick, out the door.

Ivanya turned her head to meet Abigail's eyes. Silently, she begged her friend to explain.

"Are you going to behave yourself if I loosen the restraints?"

Ivanya nodded innocently. She was over the urge to hurt herself for the moment. Now she just wanted to run. Which was what she would do the second she was freed. Abigail nodded back, but made no move to undo the straps. *She knows me too well,* Ivanya thought, bitterly.

"You've been hurt really bad, Vani." Abigail gulped before continuing. "You've been in a coma for a week. We weren't sure you were going to pull through. It's a miracle."

Miracle, ha! This was no miracle. The miracle would have been a swift death followed by heaven with her family. Not this sea of pain and sadness. She wanted her daughter, her little Vetra, not the emptiness. She wanted to hold her child in her arms, kiss the top of her head and sing lullabies while rocking in a chair. But that future had been ripped away from her by some nightmarish entity and now she was in limbo waiting for the other shoe to drop.

When the doctor entered the room, she listened to what he had to say with one ear, but her mind was on other things. The features of the fiend, the smells, and its powers, all saved to her memory bank for further examination later. Her ears heard Dr. Smith say the words 'partially eviscerated' and 'hysterectomy' and 'permanent scarring'. She filed those phrases away, too; just more things to thank the creature for. And the hatred. She balled some of that up as well; it would come in handy when she hunted the thing down and killed it.

A feeling had stolen over her, an emotion that she was not familiar with, but she grabbed it with both hands because it made the grief seem smaller. It was a rage like none she had ever known, so potent it was almost peaceful. With the presence of this new feeling, compartmentalizing her thoughts became easier. It was as if her mind were a computer with files for everything. The Vetra file was locked deep within the circuits, secured with an administrator password that she wished she could forget. The Creature file, however, was bulging with information.

"When can I go home?" she asked, voice still raspy and raw, but with a determined edge to it.

Dr. Smith was taken aback by her question. "Ms. Devereaux, you have just come out of a coma. You are lucky to be alive. Your vitals need monitoring and arrangements must be made for home care. You will be unable to walk until the leg heals, and your dressings will need to be changed each day. These are not tasks you can perform yourself."

"Am I going to die the second I walk out of here?" She couldn't keep the sarcasm out of her voice.

"Well, seeing as how you aren't leaving, I suppose the answer is no."

"You can't keep me here against my will," she cried out. She did not want to spend one more second in this bed, hooked to these machines that never shut up. The pain was beginning to return; it dug its sharp tentacles into her head, threatening to make a permanent home there.

"I have the responsibility to treat you in the hospital until you are able to survive on your own." He met her eyes, challenging her to disagree. "Your leg will not come out of traction for a few more days. Then we have to perform a psych eval to ensure you are not a danger to yourself or others. We'll re-evaluate then."

"So you need to see if I'm crazy after all this, huh? Bring it on."

Chapter 22

A soft knock sounded on the door and Nurse Mary poked her head in the room.

"Ivanya?"

"Come in," Ivanya croaked, her voice mangled by the tears she was all too close to shedding. Her moods were so volatile, she went from pissed to tears and back again faster than the rest of her could keep up.

The nurse entered the room and approached Ivanya's bed, followed by the handsome Dr. Kingston and the annoying Detective Douchebag. Mary took Ivanya's hand, careful not to jostle the IV setup in her elbow.

"Ivanya, these men would like to talk to you about what happened. They would have come sooner, but Dr. Smith would not allow them to question you while your condition was still critical." Turning to the officers, she said, "You can ask her what you need to, but do not upset her. If she wants to stop, you will stop. I'll not have you setting back her recovery."

She placed the call button on Ivanya's stomach, gave her a meaningful look and strode from the room. Abigail had remained silent through the exchange, but she smiled at Kingston and nodded respectfully at Corl. What the hell was going on? The last Ivanya knew, Detective Douchebag was the enemy.

Corl cleared his throat. "Ms. Devereaux. We need to talk to you about the attack. We'll try to keep it brief."

"Okay." The word came out tiny and weak. She wanted to sound sure and strong and was a little irritated she didn't.

They pulled up chairs to the bed rail and sat down, each withdrawing a notebook from an inside jacket pocket.

"Normally, I would ask the questions and wait for your answers, but I think I'm just going to let you tell it from the beginning in your own way. That sound good?"

Ivanya nodded, but didn't start talking right away. She had not spoken of the incident with anyone, even Abigail. What would be the best way to handle this? Tell the truth and have them think her a lunatic, or lie and maybe get out of the hospital a little faster? Decisions, decisions. She opted for the truth. Screw it, maybe she was crazy.

"Do either of you have kids?"

They both shook their heads.

"Spend any time around pregnant women?"

Corl shook his head again, but Kingston nodded enthusiastically. He scribbled in his notebook and showed the page to Ivanya.

My sisters.

"So you know about cravings." She breathed in through her nose and out through her mouth in an effort to center herself before she began dredging up the painful memories. "When you're pregnant, sometimes you want a certain food. It becomes a need. You need that pickle. Or that piece of cake. For me, it was an apple fritter from the Bluebird. I needed that donut. I couldn't think about anything else. So I went to get one."

"Why didn't you text me?" Abigail asked. "I would have brought you one."

Ivanya rolled her eyes. "Because I couldn't wait. I needed it right then. But I couldn't find my stupid keys, so I walked. It was only a few blocks." She drew in another deep breath, this one more ragged than the others. "I felt him before I saw him. There was this oppressive quality to the air, a suspense almost, like something was waiting for me. Then I heard the twig snap. The more I think about it, the more I think that he stepped on it on purpose. To scare me. I didn't even look back. I ran as fast as I could. But he got me just before I got to the bakery."

No one said anything, but Abigail looked suitably horrified, with wide eyes and her mouth parted in a small 'o'.

"His claws went right through my coat and into my skin—"

"Wait. Claws?"

"Yes, Abigail. Claws. Long and black and sharp."

"People don't have claws, Vani."

"Nope. They sure don't. I never said it was a person."

They all looked at her skeptically, all squinted eyes and a distasteful downturn of lips. They didn't believe her. Of course not. Who would? The knowledge that no rational person could possibly swallow her tale did little to assuage the anger boiling in her head.

"So, an animal, then," Corl asked, trying to rationalize her words.

"More like a humanoid lizard thing. It was black with red markings all over it." Flashes of memories hit her as she struggled to speak. "It had a forked tongue that kept flicking at me and some kind of slime dripped from its teeth. It burned when it touched my skin."

At the mention of slime, recognition stole into the eyes of Corl and Kingston. They were coming around, closer to believing her than previously. "Slime. Like drool? Or thicker, like a snail?"

"Like a snail, thick and ropy, a little thinner than the kind everyone is buying for their kids these days."

"Vani," Abigail began, tears in her eyes. "Monsters are not real. Not the way you're telling it. There was no creature. Your brain is playing tricks on you to protect you from what really happened."

That was it. She broke. It felt good if she was honest with herself. The rage she had been feeling for the last few days finally had a target. "I saw it, Abs. I saw the thing leering at me like I was the most delicious thing he'd ever seen. He told me he looked forward to tasting me because I was scared. That Gypsy was his favorite. I don't know what it meant, but I know he played in my blood like a kid in a fucking mud puddle. I know that he slashed me up like Freddy Krueger. How do you explain that? A normal dude with tattoos and four knives? And what about when his markings started to glow like a neon sign? What about that?"

"Vani—"

"No. You don't get to do that. You will never convince me my head made this shit up. And fuck any of you that feel the same. I don't need you to believe me. I *know* what happened." Ivanya deflated. She felt like she had aged ten years during the span of the conversation. Her eyelids began to droop and the rage that had been so potent before had dissipated, leaving only a profound sadness in its wake. "I need you guys to leave. I'm tired."

Chapter 23

After two weeks and a particularly grueling psychiatric evaluation, Ivanya was released. Even though it was freezing and her butt was numb from sitting on the cold, concrete bench, she was happy to be out of the hospital. She could have waited for Abigail inside, but being inside those walls for even one more second would have driven her loony.

A red Jeep Wrangler jumped the curb and lurched to a stop in front of her. Abigail hopped out, her cheeks pink with excitement, the ball on the top of her beanie bouncing with each movement. She looked happy, and Ivanya felt a stab of envy that quickly turned to anger. How dare she look all chirpy and cheery when all Ivanya could feel was the thin layer of numbness that sheathed her pain?

Abigail bounced up to Ivanya and plopped onto the bench next to her. "How's the pain today, Vani?"

"I'll fucking live," she muttered, sourly.

"That's good."

"If you say so." Ivanya did not look at Abigail, concentrating instead on the blades of dead grass that poked up out of a tiny mound of dirty snow, so she was completely taken by surprise when Abby's mittened hand knocked her upside the head.

"Knock it off, Vani." Abigail glared at Ivanya with the closest thing to rage she had ever witnessed in her friend. "I get that you're hurting, but you need to quit that shit or you can walk your gimpy ass the five miles home. You need to understand that you are not the only one effected here, and if that sounds cold and heartless then I'm sorry. I lost her, too, you know. I had big plans for that kid. I'm grieving too." At this point, tears cut paths through Abigail's make-up. "So, let's pretend this is about me for a second, okay? You ever talk about taking my best friend away from me again and you won't have to worry about doing it yourself. I will take you out with my bare hands. Got me?"

Too flabbergasted to speak, Ivanya nodded, her eyes round and bright. This was new behavior for Abigail. Perhaps, Ivanya was not the only one changed by this tragedy.

The look on Abigail's face calmed until the planes of her face were smooth and the wrinkles born of rage had disappeared. Only her friend remained.

"Okay, then. Let's go."

Abigail draped an arm around Ivanya's shoulders and shepherded her toward the Jeep. Ivanya wasn't sure why she thought getting in the car would be an easy task, but she was disappointed. Finally, after four minutes of repositioning in the hope that at last she would be able to scramble into the seat and take a breath, Abigail placed the palms of her hands firmly on Ivanya's butt and shoved with everything she had, bracing her feet against the curb for leverage. Ivanya practically flew into the cab, landing halfway across the center console. Abigail helped situate her in the seat, tucked her broken leg into the foot well and gently closed the door. Ivanya reclined the seat and leaned back, breathing heavily. Abigail tossed the crutches in the back before climbing into the driver's seat.

The Jeep maneuvered through the snow covered streets carefully and Abigail observed all traffic laws, which was a new and shocking thing. She usually drove like the devil was on her ass, and the glove box was full of tickets that proved it. Ivanya was not at all sure that she liked this new, subdued version of her friend. Part of Abigail Kayne's charm was the way she approached life with an almost inappropriate fervor, treating even tragedy as if it were a stand-up comedy bit. Seriousness was just not in her repertoire of talents. At least, it never used to be.

*****

As Abigail drove down Birch Street, a weird feeling crawled up the back of her neck. It was not unpleasant, but it grew stronger the closer she got to home. Suddenly, her foot stomped down on the brake pedal and the Jeep lurched to a halt. Ivanya flew forward, the seatbelt tightening against her body, and she cried out in pain.

"What the hell?" Ivanya shouted, but Abigail couldn't answer. She had no idea what the hell. All she knew was that her limbs were not obeying commands, because she had had no intention of stopping. Almost as if compelled by some unseen force, she hastily jammed the shifter into park and pulled the keys from the ignition.

"We have to go in there. Now."

"The occult shop? What in the world for?"

"I…I don't know. But we have to. We need something in there. It's important."

Groaning, Ivanya unbuckled the seatbelt and began the arduous process of extracting herself from the vehicle. Abigail couldn't hear what she was saying, but she was sure it was full of expletives. But she couldn't worry about that now. She floated toward the shop, millions of tiny fingers in her head beckoning her closer. Closer.

The shop was beautiful in some intangible way that she could not quite put her finger on. The façade was just that of your run of the mill, every day business; it was the feeling she got while looking at it that was arresting. Joy seemed to be embedded in each stone. Silent echoes of laughter teased her mind as she grabbed the knob and pulled open the door.

"It's about ti—", a silky Southern voice began. "Wait a minute...I wasn't expecting *you*. Who are you?"

Abigail couldn't speak, she just stared at the large black woman wearing a floral print muumuu and a tie-dyed ribbon in her puff of natural hair. The woman glared at her with piercing brown eyes that seemed to see into the depths of her soul, to see things within her that Abigail had not known existed. A balloon of anger swelled within Abigail at the intrusion and she opened her mouth to spew forth accusations of rudeness, when the soft, uneven shuffle of feet interrupted her.

Ivanya stood to the left and slightly behind Abigail, her shoulders held at awkward angles because of the crutches stuffed under her armpits. She stared at the woman with something like contempt before turning to Abigail and asking what they were doing there.

"There she is!" the woman cackled, happily. "We've been waiting for you. Well, sit down, girl. You look like you're about to keel over."

"Who else is here? You said we." Ivanya's eyes flitted around the shop, searching for the other party.

The old woman gave her a cryptic smile. "Soon. We have to talk first. There's things that need

to be figured out before you meet my special friend."
She turned to Abigail. "Who might you be?"

"Abigail Kayne." Her voice was clipped,
dripping with irritation. Since their arrival in the shop,
the woman had barely spoken to Abby, and underneath
her silence was a layer of hostility that she did not
understand.

"Well, I'm Big Mama Linda, purveyor of this
establishment." The big woman sat in the chair across
from Abby, her arms crossed over her ample chest. The
expression in her eyes was not a glare, but very close.
"Your daddy Gregory Kayne?"

"Yep."

"Your mama that Isobel woman?"

"No way. She's just his wife. My mother died
when I was little. Isobel and I don't exactly see eye to
eye."

Mama Linda nodded, seeming to be deep in
thought for a moment. "How did you end up getting
my message, I wonder? Got any theories about that?"

Not only did Abigail not have any theories, she
had no idea what the woman was talking about. What
message? Her phone hadn't even rung.

Mama Linda rolled her eyes. "How did you
know to come here?"

"I don't know. I just stopped. I needed something here."

Silence, then a thunderous roar of laughter from the big woman. Her entire body heaved and rippled, a meadow of fluttering purple flowers. "You sure did need something."

"What's so funny?" Abigail asked, defiantly. She did not like to be laughed at.

Abruptly, Mama Linda stopped her chortling and regarded Abigail with an expression that she could not read. Without another word, she crossed the room to where Ivanya sat and plopped herself onto a small sofa; the springs groaned in protest.

"I have something to show you ladies, but I need your word that you will keep it secret as you can." She looked at Ivanya expectantly, turned her head to the empty chair beside her and groaned. "Girl, why are you still standing over there? I told you to follow me."

Abigail wrinkled her forehead as she tried to remember that particular command. She couldn't, because it had never been uttered. "No, you didn't."

"I most certainly did, Miss Kayne." A smile played around the corners of her lips.

"I'm not a mind reader, you know," Abigail muttered, as she stood up and moved to the vacant seat next to Mama Linda.

"Maybe not yet, but that's a talk for another time." Leaning forward, Mama Linda took one of Ivanya's pale hands in both of her own. "How are you feeling, child?"

"In pain, but Dr. Smith gave me some pretty good drugs, which I plan on taking as soon as I'm done here."

"I wasn't talking 'bout the physical. How are you *feeling*?"

Ivanya floundered in her head for an answer, but all she found was a crippling mental agony that Abigail could read on her face.

"How do you think she is feeling?" Abigail shouted, drops of spittle flying into the air. "She's in pain from being nearly ripped to shreds, her daughter stolen from her belly and probably dead, and almost everything that made her a woman is gone! All she wants is to die, but I won't let her and she's pissed. How the hell would you feel?"

Mama Linda chewed on this for a second. "I would be wonderin' if maybe something good could come out of all this bad."

"No. It couldn't," Ivanya said, her voice weak with exhaustion. She looked like she wanted to say more, but had decided against it. "What am I doing here? I just want to go home."

Mama Linda left the room, the muumuu trailing behind her, flowing on the breeze created by her movements. She returned a few minutes later carrying a bundled blanket close to her chest. Abby watched as Ivanya's entire body tensed as if to spring out of the chair and run.

"Ivanya Devereaux? Meet the cutest little boy on the entire planet Earth: your son."

Abigail's head reeled as her brain put the words together and finally discerned the meaning. Ivanya's son? Impossible. Ivanya's baby was a girl, and taken by some maniacal crazy person that Ivanya was convinced was a monster. Her friend wore her scars and broken bones as a badge of honor.

Without waiting for her assent, Mama Linda dropped the baby into Ivanya's arms and stepped quickly aside, so she could not give him back. Sneaky old woman.

*****

Ivanya told herself that the child in her arms could not possibly be hers. Her child had been kidnapped before her very eyes, and had been a girl. Vetra was gone, probably never to be seen again. But there were some things that were beyond deniability, and this was one of those things. The face turned toward her with closed eyelids was almost an exact replica of her own. The pale skin with the peachy glow, lips drawn down into the most adorable pout she had ever seen, and the high cheekbones that were Grams' legacy. His eyelids were decorated with faint purple veins and a thick fan of white-blonde lashes. The eyebrows were the same color and thus nearly invisible against his skin. A mop of thick, blonde curls adorned his perfectly shaped head. He was easily the most beautiful baby she had ever seen; more beautiful, even, than she had dreamed Vetra would be.

"How is this possible?" Ivanya wondered aloud. She concentrated on the baby's long fingers and pudgy hands to avoid looking at Abigail and Mama Linda. She didn't want them to see the tears in her eyes.

"Ha! That's a big story. A minute ago you were itching to go home; are you sure you have time to hear it?" Mama Linda's voice was challenging and a little sarcastic. Ivanya thought about firing back an angry retort, but discovered, to her dismay, that she was mildly afraid of Mama Linda. Maybe it was her size, the big woman could easily crush Ivanya with one well-placed butt cheek. So she didn't say anything; she was pretty sure it was a rhetorical question and nothing short of death would stop Mama Linda from telling the story anyway. Sure enough, after seconds of silence, she settled back into her chair, crossed her feet, and breathed a long suffering sigh.

"I found you in the snow. Did Smitty tell you that?"

237

Ivanya shook her head.

"Good. I told him to keep his lips zipped, it's nice to know he listened. You were laying there, bleeding something awful, so badly that I was afraid to touch you. So I called Smitty. He's a good friend of mine, and also of your grandma's, and a damn good doctor, to boot.

"I had to bulldoze myself into the operating room, against everyone's wishes, of course," she said with a wry smile. "I had to be there. I had to know if I was right, and if I was, Smitty needed to be prepared for the insanity to follow. For your sake, my girl, I wish I was wrong. I wish you could grow up and be a normal young lady with a normal life, but that's just not in the cards for you."

"Because of the Ca'taal," Ivanya whispered, unsure why she had spoken the word. Mama Linda's head snapped back and her eyes widened.

"So you know this story." She nodded to herself. "Of course you would. Irena would have made sure of that. Did she tell you herself?"

"No. I found her altar room in the basement. And the book."

"Well, good. You're a step ahead of the curve."

Ivanya had begun to look at the baby again, marveling over his beautiful face and sweet, soft snore.

Her heart did not reject him as she had feared before Mama Linda had placed him in her arms. Rather, warmth and joy had exploded within her like fireworks, leeching some of the red pain from her world and replacing it with swirls of soft pastels. Baby pink and sky blue and the yellow of buttercups and she thought: *this is the color of happiness; the exact shade of motherhood.*

She still felt the agony of losing Vetra, nothing could take that pain away, but it was tempered with love for the boy in her arms. As plain as day, she saw that he was the key to her survival; he made her want to live. The revenge on the creature that had taken Vetra would have to be carefully planned, not the kamikaze mission she had been bent on. Within seconds her whole world had changed, and for the better.

"Girl, I know he's gorgeous, but you need to pay attention. This stuff concerns the rest of your life." Mama Linda's gaze softened, and a smile played on her lips as she watched Ivanya nudge her index finger against the baby's fist. He opened his hand and accepted it, then promptly jammed it in his mouth. "What are you going to name him?"

Without any thought, the name popped out of her mouth, just as it had with Vetra. "Vincent."

Abby, who had been silent and still through the whole thing smiled broadly. "Vinnie! That's a great name." She approached the baby and lovingly stroked his cheek. "Hi, Vinnie."

"No, it is Vincent. Not Vinnie. My son," she felt a thrill of joy at the word, "is not a porn star; do not call him that."

"Whatever, Vani," she chirped, happily. "Can I hold him?"

Ivanya hesitated, looking from Vincent to Abigail and back again. She didn't want to offend her friend, but a large part of her did not want to give him to anyone. Mama Linda interjected on Abigail's behalf.

"Maybe she should hold him so you can concentrate on what I'm tellin' you."

"But—"

"No buts, girl. I got the biggest butt in here and what I say goes."

Obediently, Ivanya lifted Vincent up, carefully holding his head. Abigail folded her arms and Ivanya set the precious bundle in the cradle they formed. Looking satisfied, Abigail trotted back to her chair and held him close. "You can proceed now," she said, under the mistaken impression, as always, that the world revolved around her.

"Thank you ever so much, Miss Kayne," Mama Linda said, dryly. "I'm glad I have your permission to speak freely in my own home."

Hearing, but likely not caring about, the sarcasm in the older woman's voice, she said a perky you're welcome and went about the business of inspecting Vincent's fingers and toes as he slept.

"I'm sorry," Ivanya said, sheepishly. "But I just can't stop looking at him. He's so perfect."

Mama Linda nodded her understanding. "He is the most beautiful child I have ever seen and it's good that you can't take your eyes off him, because you're going to have to watch him like a hawk from now on. Did you see who attacked you?"

"Not who. What."

"Here we go again," Abigail muttered.

Mama Linda showed no disbelief at Ivanya's description of the attacker, just a growing unease. She listened raptly, filing away details to be used at a later time. Abigail, however, started to get angry.

"Just knock it off, Vani. No monster attacked you. It was a human bad guy. The other kind does not exist."

"I believe her, and you need to start believing in the unbelievable, too. Considerin' what you are and all." Mama Linda had both hands on the armrests of the chair, looking as if she were going to get up and throttle Abigail.

"What I am? What are you talking about?"

241

"You're kinda witchy, kid. I could practically smell it on you when you walked in the door. And you got my message." Her voice rose in anger as she spoke, her cheeks becoming an alarming shade of red. "I don't know how you skated by all this time not knowing what you are, or having anything unexplainable happen to you, but it seems to be coming to you now, and you better believe it will crush you flat if you let it."

As if the heated exchange between Mama Linda and Abigail had never happened, the woman turned her brown eyes back to Ivanya. "No one can know about your little Vincent for now. The thing," she looked pointedly at Abigail, "that attacked you and took your baby, might have killed her. Sorry, I know it hurts, but true is true and you're gonna have to face up to it sooner or later. I hope I'm wrong, but in case I'm not, you need to prepare yourself. If it finds out about the boy, it might come back and take him, too. I know you don't want to risk that."

Of course she didn't. She would rather be flayed alive than see a single hair on his head even touched by that thing. Already, Vetra was gone. Mama Linda was right about that she had to prepare for the possibility that she was dead. But Vincent, he was real and precious and here. She would protect him with every fiber of her being. Losing another child was out of the question.

Mama Linda stood suddenly and pulled Ivanya carefully off the sofa, embracing her with hefty arms. "Take him home, my girl. I have things to think about and research to do. If you need anything, give me a call." Then she brought her lips to Ivanya's cheek, planting a dry kiss on her skin.

Ivanya and Abigail took her son home.

Chapter 24

The first thing Ivanya noticed as they pulled in the driveway was the porch light blazing in the darkness. The house looked lonely, with thick drapes covering the windows and a pile of newspapers in plastic sleeves stacked on the porch swing.

"You didn't take the papers in?"

Abigail shifted the car into park, turned it off, and removed the keys. "I wasn't really here much. I came to get stuff for you and to shower, but I was pretty much at the hospital the whole time."

Ivanya looked at her dubiously. "You weren't in my room the whole time."

"No, I hung out in the cafeteria some and caught some z's in the doctor's lounge after you woke up. I slept in a chair by your bed every night while you were unconscious, though."

Abigail helped her out of the car, jarring her leg in the process, which made it throb inside the cast. Ivanya jammed the crutches under her arms and carefully climbed the porch, making slow and painful progress. She tried the knob, expecting the door to be locked, and was more than a little miffed when she discovered that it wasn't. But she bit her tongue as she pushed the door open and stepped inside.

The air was flat, as if no one had breathed in here for a while. The scent of vanilla was on the air, courtesy of a plug-in by the couch, but it did little to detract from the almost artificial atmosphere. Everything was frozen exactly as it had been when she left. The couch cushions were still slightly askew, and the blanket still lay on the floor. Her teacup sat on the coffee table, no doubt with the moldering dregs of the last sip in the bottom. Ivanya leaned heavily on the crutch as she shrugged first her left, then her right arm out of her coat and tossed it at the rocking chair. She missed, and it landed in a heap on the floor. She maneuvered the crutches out in front of her and gingerly lowered herself onto the sofa. She could really use one of those pain killers about now.

Abigail blundered in behind her, juggling the infant carrier and two small duffels. She dropped the bags near the shoe rack and kicked the door closed behind her. She removed Vincent from the carrier and brought him over to the couch, where she sat, sighing happily.

"He is so beautiful," Abigail breathed, running a hand over his curly locks. The baby squinched his closed lids tighter and wrinkled his nose. In seconds, he was calm and once more breathing softly with the sweet peace of sleep.

"Is he just going to sleep forever?" she asked, wistful longing in her voice. "I want to play with him. He needs to wake up."

"He's a baby, Abs. They eat, sleep, and poop. It's like their only job."

Abigail narrowed her eyes and scowled at Ivanya. "Don't you think it's a little weird that he hasn't woken up yet?"

Ivanya shrugged, her stitches tugging painfully at the movement. She winced; she really needed those pain killers. "I don't know what's normal, dude. I've never had a baby before. I don't know anyone with a baby. I never even babysat for anyone younger than three. Could be normal, might be weird, who knows?"

"I'm gonna poke him."

"Really? That's your great idea? To poke him?" Ivanya mocked, though she was seconds away from doing it herself. She wanted to see what he looked like awake. Maybe he would get gas and smile. "You're so mean, like an evil fairy godmother."

"Just call me Maleficent," she said wickedly. She pointed out her expertly manicured index finger, holding it about an inch from his belly. Her lips pulled into a smirk and a devilish glint flashed in her eyes. The finger poked gently into the soft, blue sleeper and he jerked, his eyes popping open. His brow creased and his lips jutted out into a pout.

Ivanya and Abigail gasped in unison, too surprised to say anything. His eyes were the soft, vibrant blue of a spring morning. It wasn't just the irises that were blue, but the area around them as well. Nothing marred this field of sky; there was not even the slightest hint of a pupil. There was no multifaceted jewel effect, the orbs were opaque like a turquoise stone instead of sapphire.

"Whoa," Abby breathed, leaning closer for a better look. "Do you think he's...?"

"Blind. Yes. He's blind."

Abigail waved a hand in front of his face and sure enough, his eyes did not track the movement.

Ivanya looked at Vincent as if he were a strange new species of animal instead of her son. *This is it,* she thought. *This is more than I can handle.* It all crashed home for her then, a battering ram to the chest. Not hard enough to kill, of course, but enough to crack a few ribs and hurt like hell. This was not what she asked for. Ha! As if she had asked for any of it. She never wanted to have a baby and never expected to love it. And she didn't want to love this one. She recognized her joy at Vincent's arrival for what it was, a chance to bask in stolen motherhood for just a little while. It was Vetra she needed, not this other baby, this strange child she had never asked for.

Without a word to Abigail, Ivanya used the armrest to stand herself up, leaned heavily on her crutches and lurched down the hall, trailing the useless leg behind her. She flopped herself down on the bed, knocking the surgical boot against the bedframe. Her eyes watered, but she took solace in the agony. Physical pain was much easier to endure than the mental anguish she now found herself facing.

She crawled awkwardly to the head of the bed, and thought of the pain-killers in her coat pocket. In the living room. With the baby. She couldn't handle going back out there, and to be honest, she wasn't sure she could make the walk. Instead, she searched the bedside table for the bottle of ibuprofen she kept in there for cramps. She shook four into the palm of her hand and dry swallowed them. Leaning back into the pillows, she inhaled deeply in an effort to calm herself. The scent of gardenia and Icy Hot tickled her nose. That was Grams' smell. Ivanya inhaled again, deeper this time, submerging herself in the memory of her grandmother.

"Grams?" she whispered, tentatively, feeling hopeful and like an idiot at the same time. As ridiculous as she knew she looked, she kept talking. "I'm in trouble. I wish you were here. Everything is so messed up. I was so happy—for about three seconds. I didn't want the baby, but then I did and then she was gone…and now I have this new kid. One I didn't plan on." She paused for a second, half expecting to hear a reply. "I don't know why, and I would never admit it to Abby, but he scares me.

"The thing is, I don't know why. I should be the happiest person in the world. All of the crap I went through in the last few months wasn't for nothing. I have a child." She sniffled, wiping a string of snot from her nose. How were there no tissues in here? "But I looked into his eyes and, Grams, they are so…creepy. They're beautiful, but they are flat, like stone. Yet deep at the same time, like he knows everything there is to know.

"I'm supposed to protect him; that's what Big Mama Linda said, but how am I supposed to do that? I can't even take care of myself. How can I save him from whatever evil thing is coming?"

Ivanya continued to speak, but the words soon turned to mumbles, then unintelligible groans. Finally, after only a few moments, Ivanya lay snoring with her mouth open, just a lump of girl on top of the blankets.

*****

Corl wadded up a piece of paper and tossed it at the garbage can in the corner of the room. It smacked into the wall and fell to the floor to the side of the trash can.

249

"Well, there goes my career in the NBA," Corl said. He looked at Kingston for a reaction, but there was none. He tried again. Missed again. Dammit. "What are you doing over there?"

Kingston lifted his notebook up, but did not meet Corl's eyes.

"The notes again?"

Just a nod as Kingston went back to scanning over his jottings.

"What are you hanging up on? Same thing I am?" Corl was, of course, talking about the description from Ivanya Devereaux of her assailant.

Kingston sent a quick text to Corl.

I believe her. She was telling the truth.

"You know that's crazy, right?"

She believed it.

"She was delirious." Corl thought about it for a moment. And he was starting to think that maybe she wasn't. At least, not when they spoke. Ivanya Devereaux's eyes had been clear and hard, like marbles. She spoke with the conviction of a pious nun and there had been that ring of truth to her words, hadn't there?

She seemed fine to me. Pretty angry, but lucid.

Corl thought of Peggy Lofton, then, about her tales of a black thing that threatened to take her baby. He had no doubt that Peggy had believed what she said and she had a lot of detail to back it up, but was it a truth that others could see, or something manufactured by her illness? No one could be sure. A lightbulb went on in his head. Or maybe they could. Maybe there was evidence.

"Peggy Lofton," Corl said, grudgingly. Once he opened this can of worms there was no closing it. "Peggy said that some smoky thing threatened little Adam and that was why she had to 'save' him. I wonder if she were asked to describe it again, if it might sound a little familiar to us."

It might be worth it to talk to Peyton Crane again, as well. Maybe she wasn't telling us everything. She was *delirious.*

Corl made the call and Peyton agreed to come in around two o'clock that afternoon. Then they would see.

Chapter 25

He called it Maggot, because it was a writhing, white, fat parasite. The Maggot had been his responsibility for nearly a month, and in that time he had suffered repeated indignities. He was required to hold the thing in his arms to feed it the blood it needed to grow to maturity. It gurgled, mewled and sometimes laughed at him, a high pitched sound that made his ears want to bleed. It shat on him on more than one occasion, and each day a bodily fluid of one type or another would come spewing out of it, drenching him to the point that he needed to bathe.

However, there were things about the Maggot that were interesting. Its eyes, for instance, were inky pools of black set into the chubby face; no pupils were discernible and no whites marred the surface of the marble-like orbs. They were perfect, bottomless ebony. Two pointy canine teeth protruded from its slimy, pink gums. The Maggot also had a tangle of wild, black curls on its head. Contrasted with its pale skin, these features made it seem otherworldly, as if it were not human at all, but a denizen of this underworld. Perhaps even more than he was.

According to Lykah, who came to check on the Maggot every day to gauge its progress, it was coming along nicely. Already it could hold up its own head and played ridiculous games with its fingers and toes. It shrieked things at the top of its lungs that sounded suspiciously like words. They could not quite understand it yet, but it was only a matter of time before it would be speaking coherently. And there was power. The Maggot was exhibiting abilities that were beyond what anyone should be capable of, especially one diluted with human genes.

Tarik still hated the thing; still resented his entanglement with the little parasite, but there was nothing to be done about it now. Something was not right with the whole scenario. There were emotions flying around the underground lair (he loved that human term; it had a certain zest to it) that boggled his mind. He had the distinct feeling that he was being used. Tarik was not accustomed to being exploited—he was the manipulator in any business relationship. He had always come out on top. Until now.

Maggot stretched out a tiny hand and captured his index finger in its fist. Before he could stop it, the Maggot plugged the finger into its mouth and bit down hard with her dagger sharp teeth. Nausea roiled in his stomach as the slimy mouth substance breached the punctures from its teeth and invaded his body. He felt it coursing through his veins, polluting him with Maggot's poison.

Grabbing it under the armpits, Tarik threw the parasite to the floor. To his amazement, it bounced off the hard packed dirt and back onto the cot, as if it had never moved. He'd never considered it before, but were humans composed of rubber? However, he did not get a chance to ponder this before a searing pain stabbed his brain. He screamed, something not many creatures had been able to make him do.

Derisive laughter echoed through the cavernous room.

"Tsk, tsk, Tarik," Lykah intoned. "What did I tell you? Your job is to protect her, even from yourself. You cannot hurt her, no matter how you may want to."

"The parasite bit me! I was defending myself." Even to his own ears the excuse sounded feeble.

Lykah's face shifted with a beauty born of power and satisfaction. "It couldn't have come at a better time."

"What is that supposed to mean?" he snarled. He was sick of her riddles and games. Just once, he would like an actual answer.

"You'll see soon enough. In the next few moments, as a matter of fact." She laughed mirthlessly as she turned away. "The pain will be exquisite. Enjoy."

He liked it better when she was plying him with charm. Instead, she acted as if she owned him.

And he hated her for it.

*****

That bitch Lykah was right. This was the most excruciating pain he had ever known. During the ritual, the agony had made him feel like he was dying. What a fool he'd been. This was a million times worse. He didn't feel like he was being burned alive, he actually was.

His entire body erupted in flames. Black flesh bubbled and blistered before peeling from his bones in long strips and falling to the floor. Thick, black smoke clouded his eyes. They sizzled in their sockets, growing hotter and hotter until they finally deflated and oozed down his cheeks like snails.

Tarik was not afraid of many things; in fact, he could count all of his fears using only one finger. Being ordinary and powerless had been his greatest fear, but now, as he broiled, he discovered a new one. Blindness. He enjoyed the darkness because on some level he knew that he would see again. He knew no such thing now. There was no choice here. He was weak.

The screams quieted after a while, because his tongue had dried to a crispy wafer and fallen down his throat. He choked on it for a few seconds and a new fear held him in its clutches. He was dying. Never before had he been faced with the possibility of his own mortality. He had not even been certain that he *could* die. Now he knew. The only comfort left to him was that he would finally be rid of the Maggot, and there would not be enough left of him for the parasite to feed on.

He writhed in agony, his talons snapping off as he dug their charred remnants into the floor. Hours passed slowly; he no longer feared death, he yearned for it. In the background, above the crackle of flames and his own tortured groans, he could hear the Maggot laughing and clapping its hands. It was enjoying his pain.

Light pierced the darkness. Tiny pinpoints at first, and then larger splotches. A strange feeling tingled his face as his eyeballs re-inflated, swelling until they nestled comfortably in the sockets. He watched in fascination while new layers of muscle grew up his arms, adhering themselves to the bones with thick ropes of tendon. The muscle was even denser than before. Thicker. His body was still steaming when he managed to stand and maneuver to the looking glass on the wall. Gone were the blood red runes; he was now decorated with an intricate design of light blue markings. They glowed as they had during the ritual, but as the shimmer faded, they became the royal blue of a twilight sky. And his eyes, these new eyes, matched.

Somehow, he had been broken down, every piece of him destroyed in order to give birth to a new, stronger demon. He glared at the Maggot, who was smiling open mouthed now, and though she still annoyed him, the hatred that had burned within him for so long dissipated.

This new demon, this superior Tarik, had come into being for her.

*****

She walks through the fire in bare feet. Flames lick her toes, but there is no pain. It is strangely comforting. The warmth. The jagged rocks beneath her feet.

There is blue above, but she continues to look down. She doesn't like the sky, it is too bright. The reds and oranges of fire, the shadowy tendrils of smoke rising from wreckage. These things give her comfort. It smells good. Like home. She flicks her tongue out to taste the air.

A sizzling sound. The sweet smell of burning flesh. Her stomach growls. Hunger cramps her stomach.

Lightning stabs down from the sky, striking a heavily leafed tree. The leaves burst into flame and float to the ground like moths. A savage sound of glee escapes from her throat. She doesn't know why. Seeing the living thing burning, turning to ash, brings her joy.

She continues walking. People run, screaming. Fear rising from their bodies in streams. It makes her body hum. There is power in her limbs now. As if the fear was food for her. She revels in it.

Blood is on the air. This makes her hungrier still. She wants the screams, the fear to get bigger. She wished she knew how to make it so.

A voice floats on the air. It is high and soft, echoing off everything. Flowers spring up from the chaos. She does not like this. She covers her ears with sooty hands, begging it to stop. Rage cripples her as she stomps on one of the flowers. She laughs as it turns to pulp beneath her foot.

At first, she doesn't hear what the voice is saying. She doesn't care.

Then it comes to her...a soft whisper.

Vetra...Vetra...

She shakes her head. She screams for it to stop.

The voice grows louder.

Blackness surrounds her. She welcomes it. It is soft, familiar. Like a blanket. Darkness is home.

When she awoke, he was there. His eyes bored into her. She felt no fear, only comfort. He protects her. Tarik is her Guardian. She reached up and traced the markings on his face with chubby fingers. He was beautiful.

Her eyes moved to the fire burning quietly in the corner. A smile lit up her face. She could stare at its beauty for hours and frequently did.

"What did you see, Maggot?"

She said nothing. The words did not yet exist to explain it to him. Later, she would. When she knew how. That moment would come quickly. She changed every day. Her limbs were growing long and filling with power. Her brain developed quickly. Not enough to understand everything she saw; not even to understand what she was. But soon, it would come.

With a sigh, she closed her eyes against the fire and drifted off to sleep, the ghost of a smile on her face. One day, the world would burn.

*****

Lykah met Kabe in the corridor outside her chambers and quickly ushered him inside. She approached the table in the center of the room and picked up a small glass vial that contained a shiny, gold liquid. She hurled it against the thick door of her chamber, where it broke with a satisfying smash. As the liquid seeped into the wood, the door took on a golden hue for a moment, before fading back to its original shade. Now she would not need to worry about being overheard. Silence was golden, after all.

"Have we found the reason she has not manifested yet?"

"I ran the tests as instructed, and there is a problem." He paused, unsure of how to continue. Lykah was not the type who tolerated bad news well.

"And the results?" she asked, the hint of acid in her voice.

"It seems the vessel is short a soul. There are only six in her body. Before you ask, the other infants were scanned as well, and their souls are gone. Presumably, housed inside the vessel." Kabe clenched his fists and leaned backward, eyes shutting tightly as if in anticipation of being struck. She almost smiled—he knew her well.

Lykah knitted her brow ridge in confusion. She did not like the feeling. "But that would suggest...impossible! Are you certain?"

He flinched back, fully expecting to be eviscerated for his answer, but managed to force it out anyway. "Yes, I'm sure. The vessel was born without one."

Rage exploded out of her in the form of a shriek, the likes of which Kabe had never heard. It reverberated off the walls and ceiling, filled with anger and the longing that comes from a plan well laid. She paced the chamber, upending the table near her bed, sending a hail of vials and papers to the floor. She stomped on them as she strode through the room, glass crunching beneath her feet. A few shards sank into the heel of her left foot, and another caught just behind the pad of her big toe. She kept walking, the glass digging deeper, leaving footprints of blood on the floor, but she didn't care. The scroll was crumpled in her hands and she had almost ripped it in half before she realized what she had. Almost rending the prophecy to shreds was what finally snapped her out of her angry fugue. She thrust the scroll at Kabe.

"We both know that she is the child in the prophecy. Find the reason for this. Find the seventh soul."

Kabe scuttled quickly to the door, the scroll tucked under his arm.

"And Kabe," she called over her shoulder. "Remember, we are the only ones who know the true purpose of the ritual. Keep this to yourself."

He nodded and left the room, abandoning Lykah to the machinations of her own mind. The prophecy swirled around in there, bits and phrases echoing inside her head. 'When six meet the one' could really only mean one thing, but the rest could be open to interpretation. What wasn't she seeing?

Chapter 26

Kingston's first thought upon seeing Peyton Crane again was that she looked good. She was standing straight and tall, instead of hunched over and trembling as she was when they first met. Blonde ripples of hair spilled over her shoulders in a soft cascade, complementing the blue plaid shirt she wore. Her cheeks had filled out, and through rest or the magic of concealer, the purple bruises beneath her blue eyes were gone. In short, she looked like a normal, healthy, twenty-something woman with her whole life ahead of her. That was, until he met her gaze. Her eyes were stark and haunted, broadcasting a pain that would make others look away. For the first time, Kingston hated his job. He was going to have to delve into that pain to get answers. It was going to hurt. And her husband, who sat next to her, his fingers intertwined with hers, would have to see it.

"We just wanted to touch base with you, see how you're doing," Corl said, Kingston nodding in agreement beside him. Ryder brought in four cups of coffee and placed them on the table, before grabbing his own and leaving the room. Peyton grabbed hers eagerly and took a sip, grimacing in disgust.

"God, this stuff is still just as bad as I remember."

Corl smiled, just a little. "They make that brew special for law enforcement. You hear cops talking about their gut? It's just bad coffee. But it goes good with donuts." The joke was a bad one, but both Peyton and her husband, Ben, visibly relaxed.

"So, how are you doing?"

"Cop speak for do you remember anything else?"

He smiled again. "Something like that."

Her breathing was slow and steady, but Kingston could see her eyes flicking toward the exits and knew she was planning for the eventuality that she would have to escape quickly. Abduction survivors often suffered from hypervigilance after their ordeal. She dropped the remains of her smile and gazed intently between them both.

"Have they found any of the other girls, yet?"

"No, ma'am."

"Same with the babies?"

"Unfortunately."

She sat there contemplating his answer while she sipped on the bitter coffee, without making a face. "Ok. What do you need?"

"We would like to do something called a cognitive interview with you. It is designed to bring forth information that you may not consciously remember. The questions were written by Dr.

263

Kingston, here. If you hear my phone vibrate, that is just my phone asking a follow-up question, which I will then ask you. Do you have any questions?"

"No, I get it. Where do we start?"

Corl cracked his knuckles and took the typed sheet of paper in his hands. "I would like to go back to the night you were taken. Your husband was just leaving for work. You kissed him goodbye. Then what happened? You can close your eyes if that will help you concentrate."

Kingston was glad to see her take the suggestion. Not being able to see her husband's facial expressions would bring forth more genuine answers. If she thought she was causing him pain, she could decide to edit herself to make it more bearable for him.

"I shut the door behind Ben after watching him go down the porch. I was looking at his butt. Still gets me." A short giggle broke the tension in the room. "Then I locked the door."

"You're sure you locked it?"

"Yeah. I remember because we had been watching a scary movie on TV and I was nervous about being alone at night."

"What did you do next?"

Her answer came quickly, with zero forethought, exactly what Kingston had been hoping for.

"I went to the kitchen to make a sandwich. I was hungry."

"What kind of sandwich?"

Good. Corl was probing the details to keep the scene real in Peyton's mind. Kingston was a little surprised that he was so good at this. Normally, Corl had all the subtlety of a sledgehammer. He was conducting this interview the same way Kingston would if he had been able to speak.

"PB and J," she replied. "I crave, sorry, *craved* that a lot when I was pregnant. Especially at night. I always slept better afterwards."

Peyton walked them through her evening. She had taken the butter knife to the kitchen and quickly washed it as she watched the snow fall outside the window in big, fat flakes. She stood, transfixed by their beauty, then shook her head, dried the knife and put it in the drawer. From there, she went to the couch, sat down, and pulled a blanket onto her lap.

"Then I heard a car door slam. I thought it was Brett Murphy leaving, because he's out at all times of the night, but I didn't hear an engine start." She took another sip of the coffee and Kingston noticed her hands begin to shake. "A few minutes later, I heard the knock at the door."

Kingston perked up. This was what he needed to hear.

"I got up to open it, and looked through the—"

Kingston buzzed Corl. *Go back. Walk her to the door. We need the senses.*

"Hold on, Mrs. Crane. You're walking to the door. Are there any noises that you hear? Anything out of place?"

Peyton shut her eyes tighter, her brows drawing together. She squeezed her husband's hand to the point that he drew in a sharp intake of breath. To his credit, he just stretched his fingers and clasped her hand again, instead of pulling away. It was refreshing to see couples cling to each other in moments of profound sadness, when usually they would drift apart.

"I hear feet on the porch and a kind of...scrabbling sound that I can't place." Peyton slid smoothly into the present tense. That was good, it meant she was there. They would be getting the raw experience. "There are people talking, but when I look through the peephole, I only see her." Her breaths came a little quicker now, more urgent than before. "She's pretty and I know her from somewhere, but I can't place it. But I've seen her before. I know I have."

266

Kingston didn't know why, but he hadn't expected the perpetrator to be a woman. Typically, men kidnap women, women kidnap babies. Although it made a little sense, because weren't the babies the targets all along?

"Freeze, Mrs. Crane. What did she look like?" Corl's voice deepened with anticipation at the first actual lead they've had in a while.

"She has brown hair, long and glossy, like it had just been blown out at the salon." Peyton's tongue poked out of the corner of her mouth as she tried to picture the woman. "Her eyes are brown, too. Big, like a cow. She has pale skin and thick red lips. Holy shit, I just described Snow White."

Kingston did not allow himself even the smallest of smiles. He needed to appear professional, to exude an air of authority. Whether Corl was his mouthpiece or not, this was his interview. He recognized her humor for what it was, a defense mechanism meant to deflect her fear and pain.

"So, you saw the woman and opened the door."

"Yeah. She was high class and looked important. It was weird that she was there at night, but I honestly didn't think about that until later." Sweat popped out on her forehead and she squeezed her eyes shut once more. "I didn't see it until it was too late."

"Didn't see what?"

"The needle. I felt it though. Someone jammed it into my neck."

Damn it. They drugged her. Kingston felt defeated. Peyton might not remember anything else. Anything they can use anyway.

"That's when it got weird. The world got all swirly, like I was in one of those cylinder things in a haunted house. You know what I mean? Just as you exit, it starts turning and lights are flashing and if you're not careful you end up on your butt. That's when he came in."

Corl kept his mouth shut to let her speak. Good.

"He was like nothing I'd ever seen before, and I hope I never do again. He was black with red tattoos on his body, all over his head and chest. He reached for me with these long fingernails and I ran. Well, tried to run, but I wasn't seeing very well. I ran into the counter and banged my hip pretty hard." She tipped her head back and drained her coffee, crinkling the paper cup in her right hand. "He was on me like that. Spit flew from his jaws and he hissed at me. It was then that I knew."

"Knew what?"

"Whatever this thing was, it wasn't human. And that I was in big trouble."

Yes, Kingston thought. *Confirmation of Ivanya's story. Crazy as it sounds, it's real.*

Ben Crane had sat silently through his wife's entire story. "I tried to tell her that it was just the fear that caused her to see this man as a monster. She won't listen. I'm trying to get her to counseling, but she won't go."

Kingston typed quickly to Corl.

"Dr. Kingston thinks it is a good idea to get some counseling for your loss and the post-traumatic stress that you are displaying symptoms of. As for your story, Mrs. Crane, we believe every word. That stays in this room. It will be easier to find this man if he doesn't know we are looking for him. Thank you so much for coming in and talking to us."

Peyton stood up and Ben helped her with her coat. They moved toward the door, his arm draped protectively around her shoulders.

"Detective Corl, can I ask a question?"

He raised an eyebrow and nodded.

"What's it like having a partner that can't speak?"

He laughed, right from his belly. It was a jolly sound, like Kingston imagined Santa Claus would make.

"Peaceful."

Chapter 27

Abigail cradled Vincent against her shoulder, gently patting his butt and praying he would stop crying soon. He was getting heavy and her arms were tired, but every time she put him down he just started screaming again. And Ivanya was no help. She had barely come out of her room in over a week. Abigail felt bad for her friend, knowing she was in pain and grieving, but she was a little pissed at her, too. Like it or not, she had a baby to bond with and take care of. Abigail loved him. She had been taking good care of him, but was a poor substitute for a mother and she knew it.

Vincent had quieted down and a soft snore issued from the back of his throat. She continued pacing and patting, trying to lull him deeper into slumber so she could finally put him down. She needed to clean up this living room and do some laundry, this kid pooped a lot. Slowly, she moved to the bassinet, carefully removed him from her shoulder, and laid him gently down. She stepped back, waiting with bated breath for the inevitable wail that was coming. He continued snoring. Yes! Abigail threw her hands in the air and did a little happy dance. A quiet one.

There was a dirty diaper on the floor that she scooped up and took into the kitchen to throw away. Dishes needed to be done, the floors were in desperate need of a good mopping, and the trash needed to go to

271

the curb. There was a barrel out back, but Mrs. D. had only used that to burn cuttings and leaves from the yard. Abigail wondered if it would be cheating to call the maid at her parents' house and hire her to come over for the day. The house would be clean and Abigail would get a much needed break.

She whipped the phone out of her pocket and called her brother. If she called the house, there was a chance that she would get Isobel and she did not want to deal with her step-mother's drama today.

"Hello?"

"Hello, my dear brother. How are you today? Long time, no hear. How's life and all that?"

Abigail could hear Spencer's befuddlement through the phone.

"Why are you calling me? Aren't you mad at me still?"

"For what?" she asked, but she knew.

"For dating your friend."

She had been more than mad about that. Ivanya liked Spencer—a lot. She didn't think anybody noticed, but it was an open secret that everyone was in on. It was gross, but Abigail didn't like it for an entirely different reason. Spencer was a player. He'd practically dated everyone in town, leaving more than a few of them broken-hearted. Abigail did not want that for her friend. She knew Spencer had no plans to settle down and that that was all Ivanya wanted. She had some severe abandonment issues. That kind of thing happens when your entire family dies before you do.

"Do you have any intentions of taking her out again?"

"I would like to. After she heals and stuff." Huh, he sounded like he really meant it.

"Listen. I'm not still mad at you, but remember this: if you hurt her I will make you wish you had never become a part of this family. I will be the worst thing that ever happened to you."

"You kind of already are," he quipped, guffawing loudly at his terrible joke.

Abigail shook her head in exasperation. "I called for another reason, Spencer. It's not always about you."

He laughed again, louder this time. "Have you met you?"

"Will you just shut up and listen? Is Mrs. Garvin there today?"

"No, it's Tara and Michelle."

Abigail cursed under her breath. She'd really wanted Mrs. Garvin, she was the best. Oh, well, one of the others would have to do. "Can you send Michelle over to Ivanya's house? I want to have a deep cleaning done as a surprise for her. You know, one less thing to worry about."

"No can do. Mom has them cleaning out the third floor. Apparently there are guests staying here for the gala this weekend. You're going to have to spring for someone from a service." He snorted. "Or wash a dish yourself."

Abigail was about to deliver a scathing retort, but Vincent chose that moment to begin wailing again. It was a mournful sound, akin to the howl of a wolf.

"Hold on, Vincent," she called in a singsong voice.

"Who's Vincent? What is that godawful noise?"

Oh shit! Abigail knew that at some point the secret would be out and people would know about the baby, but she did not want to be the one responsible for telling them. What was she going to say? What had she been thinking? Bringing a maid in would blow the secret for sure. She could have kicked herself. This proved that she was in desperate need of some rest, her brain obviously wasn't working.

"Dog."

"You have a dog."

274

"Yep. Just got him. Named him Vincent. Whines a lot."

His voice was laden with suspicion. "You are going to take care of a dog? Are you qualified to do that?"

"Sure. Feed him, water him, walk him. Simple."

"What kind of dog is this Vincent?"

"Schnauzer." Abigail searched for a valid reason to end the call. Vincent was getting louder. "I got to take him to the groomer. Bye."

She ended the call and whistled softly. She had no idea if he bought that mess of an excuse. Probably not. She was going to have to do some damage control later.

"Abs! The baby is crying! Will you get him already?" Ivanya screamed from down the hall. Abigail rushed to the bassinet and picked up the squalling child. She cooed at him and jiggled him up and down gently, trying to soothe him, but nothing worked.

"Maybe he's hungry!"

"Well, why don't you come out and hold him while I make him a bottle, then," Abigail shouted back.

"I can't. My leg hurts."

That was it. Abigail couldn't take it anymore. This baby was Vani's, not hers, and she needed to at least take part in his care. Abigail was close to completely losing her mind and crumpling into a drooling heap on the floor. She needed to get out of here. It was time for some tough love. She placed Vincent in his infant seat and carried him down the hall to Ivanya's room.

Ivanya was propped against the pillows and had another one elevating her broken leg. A pink chenille blanket was draped around her shoulders. Her hair was tossed up on top of her head in a messy bun, ends sticking out haphazardly. She looked like an old woman. If she'd had some reading glasses on a chain around her neck, she would've looked just like Mrs. D.

"He needs to sit in here with you, while I make him a bottle," Abigail said, as she sat the carrier on the floor next to the bedside table. Vincent's cries slowed to a soft sniffle, then stopped altogether. Sometimes Abigail wondered if he was actually blind, because when he heard a person or sensed them near him, he would turn his face to them and open his eyes. He did this now, staring sightlessly at his mother. She left the room before Ivanya could protest and ran to the kitchen. When she returned a minute later, Vincent's face was still turned toward Ivanya and he was cooing at her. Ivanya pointedly ignored him, content instead to flip through channels on TV.

"Ok, Vani," she said, plunking the newly made bottle of formula on the night stand. "I have to go out for a while. You need to take care of Vincent. I'll be back later."

Ivanya's eyes were wide with horror. "No, I can't watch him. I can't even get out of bed."

"Yes, you can. I've seen you do it. You're going to have to suck it up. I have to go."

"Where are you going?"

"To buy a goddamn Schnauzer," Abigail grumbled, as she left the room, letting the door slam shut behind her.

*****

The odds that two people who've never met are suffering from the same delusion are infinitesimal.

"I know that," Corl growled. "But the other option is insane. A monster, an honest to God monster with fangs and claws took her baby? How do we find something like that? How do we *arrest* something like that?"

This whole thing bothered Corl right down to the core of who he was as a person. He lived an ordered life and relied on logic to get him through the tough spots. When he worked a case, he followed the evidence, tracked down the perp, and sent them to jail. Sometimes it went well, sometimes it didn't, but it always made some sort of sense. This didn't make sense. There was no order to monsters, no prescribed set of rules to tell him how to proceed. Nothing to tell him how to feel.

You find it the same way you find the other perpetrators. You work the evidence and follow the leads. What do we know?

There was one thing, one little thread they could pull. The woman who had come to Peyton Crane's door had been someone she vaguely recognized, someone she'd seen before. It was possible she was local. That's where they start.

"We got that sketch they did for Mrs. Crane?"

Kingston handed it to him. Corl placed it on his desk blotter and stared at it, allowing the details to sink into his brain. She was pretty, around his age with dark hair that spilled over her shoulders. Wide brown eyes were set under perfectly sculpted brows and above razor sharp cheekbones and a patrician nose. She *did* look familiar—he'd seen her before as well. He snapped a picture of the image on his phone and handed the sketch back to Kingston.

"Who is that? We know who that is, but I can't place her."

It was bugging Corl. He knew he would remember where he'd seen her eventually, but it was right on the tip of his brain and that pissed him off. He knew he would wake up out of a dead sleep in the middle of the night, the name falling from his lips with ease. But for now, he was stumped. He did not like the feeling.

She does look familiar. Is she famous or something?

"I don't know. Maybe."

The idea came from nowhere, as all great ones do, and Corl snatched up the newspaper that lay rolled up on top of his file cabinet. It was the nose. No one's nose was that perfect. Nose job, maybe. Whether it was fair or right or not, it made him think one thing: money. He flipped the *Sentinel* open to the society pages and sucked in a deep breath. There, next to an article about a charity event, was the woman from the sketch. He passed the paper over to Kingston, who whistled softly.

What do we do about that?

Corl didn't answer. He had no idea what they would do about that. He could already see the shadow looming over what was left of his career.

*****

Lykah sat with her eyes closed, repeating the lines of the prophecy in her head. She was so involved in what she was doing that she gasped in dismay when Kabe touched her shoulder. She whirled on him, ready to rip his head off. Whether literally or figuratively was unclear; she hadn't decided yet.

"The Grey One is here," he whispered, turning his back and hurrying out of the room. Perhaps he sensed her ire. Or perhaps the Grey One frightened him. Then again, everything frightened Kabe.

He entered, moving slowly across the floor as if he were in a procession. She loathed his inflated sense of self-importance. There was no one here to watch him, he needed to get to the point.

"What can I help you with?" Lykah asked, sardonically. She had no intention of helping him. If anything, he should be groveling at her feet and begging for his life while apologizing profusely for altering the timeline. This whole debacle could be traced back to the Grey One's impulsive behavior, and anything that wasn't his fault would be placed on his plate anyway. Such was the way of leadership, scapegoats were indispensable assets.

"How is the vessel?" he asked, his pale grey face arranging itself into an expression of concern. "Has the Spirit manifested yet?"

Lykah scowled. "No. There is a problem. The vessel seems to have been born with no soul. We are working on a solution."

He smiled, a truly disturbing gesture. He had no lips at the moment, so it was just open space and sharp teeth. While Lykah preferred beauty and youth in her manifestations, the Grey One preferred the grotesque and unnerving. This may have been for intimidation, but it also could be due to the fact that the Grey One was a truly unbalanced individual.

"I may have one for you. That is why I have come. I stumbled on some information that could prove useful." He paused with a brow ridge raised, teasing her. She didn't like it.

"Please put on your human face, you're very distracting right now."

"Only if you wear yours, Mother."

She obliged, her doughy face gaining definition and hair. She looked in the mirror as she always did when she donned this form: the face of Isobel Kayne.

"I was speaking to my dear sister, and it seems there is another child. I heard it crying in the background." Spencer laughed, derisively. "She tried to tell me it was a dog, apparently thinking I truly am human and therefore stupid."

The lines of the prophecy once again played in her head. *Born with light, the darkness grows.* Clarity broke over her like sunlight on a dreary day. She finally understood. The vessel was the darkness, this other child was the light. They needed that baby, now. Isobel stalked down the corridor, yanking a torch off the wall. She made it to Tarik's chamber in record time. He was holding the child and attempting to soothe it, as it wailed forlornly.

"Tarik. I have a job for you." She decided to bait him a little. "This task will allow you to unleash whatever Hell you wish upon the girl."

Tarik deposited the child that he had dubbed Maggot on the cot and approached Lykah. He didn't stop until he was almost nose to nose with her, now that she had a nose. "I can do whatever I want? No restrictions?" He licked his lips in anticipation, the new blue markings on his body pulsing like a beating heart.

"You may proceed however you wish. Kill the girl, murder her friend, level the house to rubble if that is what you desire. I only ask that you bring me the child that lives there."

His eyes widened, burning blue orbs in his night black face. "No. I will not touch another human youngling. One Guardianship is enough." He thought for a moment, his runes blazing brighter with each second. Lykah squinted against their glow. "However, I have been growing bored. I will take care of the

282

gypsy girl and her friend, but someone else must be there to acquire the child."

Lykah smiled her Isobel smile as she rubbed her hands together. "Excellent. The Grey One and a small group of warriors will accompany you."

Tarik watched Lykah leave, presumably to plan the siege. He couldn't wait. He would finally get to release some pent-up aggression and punish the girl for not dying when she should have. *Why was that?* he wondered. He knew she had felt less than the expected amount of pain because of the paralytic that coated his claws, but the blood loss should have killed her. It must have been this other parasite, keeping its host alive long enough for it to survive the ordeal. Whatever the case, it was best he had nothing to do with the thing. One Maggot in his life was plenty.

Chapter 28

Faster than anyone would have imagined, even herself, Mama Linda bustled around the room, gathering supplies in her arms. Candles, one of each color, except the black of which she grabbed two. Incense, cowry shells, lavender. She needed much more, but the rest of the items, the really potent ingredients, were in the hidden room where no one but her could find them.

She retreated to her chamber, the one place where she could be herself. Watson was a pretty progressive place. It wasn't the seventeen hundreds anymore, but still, her craft was looked down on by some people. People feared what they could not understand, and not many wanted to understand Voodoo. It was often described as a black art, expressly used for evil workings, but that wasn't true. She loved God and hated Satan as much as the most devout Catholic. She used her knowledge to communicate with nature and the spirit realm, but not for reasons of darkness. Rather, she used it to see more clearly, to learn, and to help.

And help she could. After spreading out her supplies on the round table, she lit a large, black candle and two smaller white ones, as well as a cone of frankincense for concentration and protection. From the small pocket she had long ago sewn into the seam of her muumuu, she extracted a vial of blood she had taken from Ivanya's wounds before the ambulance arrived. Anointing one white candle with the blood, she whispered the girl's name and prayed to the ancestors for guidance.

Once again, she delved into the secret pocket, pulling out a small wad of Kleenex. It was disgusting, the piece of mottled flesh that had been found under Ivanya's thumbnail, and when the tissue was opened the odor was enough to make Mama Linda retch. She cut the piece of flesh in half, placed one section on the clean, white candle and the remaining bit was cast carefully into the flame of the black candle.

Immediately, she was deluged by a barrage of images. Ivanya screaming in terror and agony as she fought for her life, blood gushing from long, jagged tears in her flesh. The pale skin becoming even more so as her life spilled onto the snow. The screaming baby as it was ripped from her womb. Her trembling hands reaching out for the child. And then...the creature.

Mama Linda had seen many demons in her time, some in the many journals of her ancestors, plus a few in person. There are as many breeds of demon as there were species of animal and insect on the earth. Some were relatively harmless, but most were ruthless murderers. This creature, however, was of a type she'd never seen, and a great cause for alarm. She could not decipher the red runes on his body, but looking at them brought to mind feelings of hatred and hunger, torture and terror.

The most worrisome thing of all, though, was the reaction of the child. At first, she had been screaming with abandon, wailing and pumping tiny fists in the air. However, just before the creature faded out, she became docile, even cooing at the monster that held her.

The scenery shifted and Mama Linda found herself in an underground cavern. Torches burned brightly on the walls and small groups of demons milled around, talking amongst themselves. She walked among them, unnoticed in her spectral state. She entered a small alcove on the north side, equipped with a cot, a fireplace with banked embers inside, and a stone cradle in the center of the room. She approached the cradle, gasping at the sight before her.

The child—what had the girl called her? Vetra?—was too large to be only six weeks old. She was a portly little thing, with a pair of chubby cheeks and rolls even on her fingers. She was beautiful, with ebony hair that fell in ringlets to her shoulders and thick black lashes that fanned against her cheeks as she slept. Beneath the cradle was a vat containing what appeared to be the last dregs of a large quantity of blood. Mama Linda stepped forward and touched the scarlet liquid with her index finger. Images stormed her again—a vision within a vision. Faces, screaming and crying in

286

pain and anguish and she had time to think *oh, my god, it's human*, before everything changed again. The chubby little girl suckled greedily on a bottle filled with the red liquid. Her lips smiled around the nipple as she devoured it. Her eyes fluttered open, black and sparkling, like polished volcanic rock. A feeling of pure dread washed over her as those eyes seemed to focus on her face. Vetra dropped the bottle as she pointed a pudgy finger in Mama Linda's direction. A bloody gurgle erupted from the baby's throat. It was a low rumble at first, but morphed into a long, urgent cry.

Footsteps sounded outside the alcove, growing louder as they drew closer. Four demons burst through the door, accompanied by the creature of her nightmares. He looked different now, with blue runes instead of the red, but she recognized the same feelings of malice and morbid glee that she had felt in the alley that day. The other demons looked around the room, blind to her presence, but not the creature. His eyes burned blue fire right through the mystical protection she had cloaked herself in, and he took a deep, greedy breath. He reached out for her, arcs of electricity snapping across his claws.

Then, it all disappeared. The hard chair beneath her bottom told her that she was home. Dazed, Mama Linda looked around, her eyes wide and unable to blink. The white candle still blazed brightly, the flame dancing in the darkness. The black one had gone out. Apparently, after consuming the flesh she had put in the flame, the connection had severed. A good thing, too, because she had a feeling the demon could do more with it than see her.

Hastily, she blew out the remaining candles and flipped a switch on the wall. She didn't really need the light, she knew where everything in this room was, but it provided a much needed sense of reality to her situation. From an old trunk, she removed a large satchel and a smaller duffel bag. First thing into the bags was the ancient tome of her people. She covered it quickly with two cloths that she used for table coverings, all of the candles in the secret room, and various bottles of crushed incense. She rushed back through the tunnel that connected her inner sanctum to the store, towing the bags behind her. Once inside, she moved from shelf to shelf, like a huge hummingbird, tossing bottles and sachets and boxes of powders into the duffel. She did this for almost an hour until, satisfied, she heaved the bags onto her back and began the walk to the Devereaux house.

*****

Tarik stood against the wall of the ceremonial chamber while the Trynok warriors pored over blueprints for the Devereaux house. They bickered back and forth about ingress and egress points. They tossed out ideas, most of them bad, for infiltration. Nobody asked Tarik for his opinion and he didn't offer it. He pictured the house in his head, no blueprint needed. The last eight months of surveillance had gifted him with a wealth of knowledge the others didn't have. The blueprints might detail doorways, stairs and various rooms, but they didn't show furniture placement or possible hazards. They would definitely be no help in determining the behavior of the targets.

"What about the wards?" Tarik said quietly, drawing the attention of the Grey One.

"What wards?"

Tarik shook his head with disbelief. "The wards of spiritual protection around the entire outside, and probably the inside as well. The old woman knew what she was doing when she landscaped the lawn. There are holly trees and lavender around the perimeter. Wind chimes of cowry shells hanging from the eaves. And her potions were powerful. There is nothing to suggest that the girl has her grandmother's abilities, but we would be foolish to proceed as if she doesn't."

The Grey One knitted his brow in concentration. "How powerful are these wards?"

"Strong enough to hurt me," Tarik muttered, mildly embarrassed to be saying such a thing.

The Grey One's features arranged themselves into an expression of shock. Tarik's power was legendary and anything that could hurt him was a threat to be taken seriously. "Any suggestions?"

"We need to take out the wards. Get your best potion makers to take care of the plants. Maybe an archer or two to get rid to the chimes. I can get rid of the amulets and anything else now that I don't have to be concerned with stealth."

"You plan to what? Barge in there? Advertise our presence?"

Tarik licked his lips. "I want her to see me. I want her to know I'm coming for her." The imagined scent of her fear held the promise of the gourmet meal to come. He savored it, salivating at the thought, knowing it would be all that it promised.

More orders were given, plans were made, but Tarik was no longer paying attention. He thought only of the target. Green eyes open in shock and fear. Skin parting beneath his talons like warm butter. And the scent. Oh, the sweet scent of fear and latent magic, simply mouthwatering. He could see it, the crimson ocean of blood on the hardwood floor. They could try to clean it, but it would never come out of the cracks between the slats. Her fear would be forever entangled in the very heart of the house.

A gurgly laugh interrupted his thoughts and he looked around, fully expecting to see the Maggot, but she was not there. She was still in the chamber where he had left her. A vision of toes invaded his brain, wiggling and waving on a chubby foot, accompanied by another chuckle. He shook his head to dislodge the picture, but it was still there in the back of his mind. He could see everything happening in the war room, but now he could see what was happening in the Maggot's chamber as well. What had she done to him? Now he could see through her eyes. It was wildly disconcerting and he didn't care for it. He would talk to Lykah and figure out how to make it stop. He concentrated intently on what the Grey One was saying, while formulating his own plans for bloodshed.

Chapter 29

Ivanya stared at the child in the carrier, growing more uneasy with every second. Something was wrong with him and that was a fact. Sometimes she noticed the weirdness through a medication induced haze, making it easy to doubt, even deny, what she had seen.

It was the lucid times that bothered her. Whenever she gazed at him-rarely touching him—she couldn't bear to do that—trepidation swelled inside her. His skin was golden, a term Mama Linda had used to describe a mild case of jaundice. No hospitalization was required and he didn't need any medication. The treatment was to simply place him in sunlight as if he were a plant. Strange, but true. No, the condition was not serious, but it did make him look much older than his six weeks.

He also grew quickly. Alarmingly so. When born, he had weighed five pounds, ten ounces. When Abigail weighed him yesterday, he had been nearly seventeen. According to Abs, who had acquired an encyclopedic knowledge of all things infant related, Vincent was at his target weight for six months. Months, not weeks.

But it was the eyes that filled her with a grim foreboding. The absence of a pupil was disconcerting to say the least, but it was the fact that nothing reflected on the surface of his eyes that upset her the most. They were fathomless. Ivanya could only look at them for short amounts of time before succumbing to the fear that if she stared too long she would drown in them, lost forever.   He moved as though he could see. Whenever Ivanya or Abigail spoke, his eyes, with not even a flutter of the eyelids, would find their way directly to the face of the speaker. Without seeing, he could pinpoint the exact location of everyone in the room. It was surreal. Ivanya had begun to believe that perhaps she was the one that was blind. Perhaps this child lived on an entirely different plane of existence, seeing things that were infinitely beautiful and frightening.

He was alien to her. A stranger. One she did not care to get to know.

And Abigail had abandoned her for some mysterious errand. Her leg began the slow ache that would soon blossom into fresh blooms of agony. She grabbed the prescription bottle and tapped two pills into the palm of her hand. She took a greedy sip of stale water to wash the already dissolving mess down her throat. She relished the bitter taste. It let her know that soon, very soon, sweet oblivion would claim her. She explicitly ignored the now softly cooing baby on the floor, closed her eyes and fell into a fitful sleep.

*****

Ivanya awoke in darkness, barely able to discern the glowing green digits on the alarm clock that read four p.m. It got dark during northern Michigan winters, but generally not for a couple more hours.

The baby cried lustily from his car seat, arms and legs stretched out rigidly in distress. She shushed him as she maneuvered her booted leg out of the bed, noticing that for the first time there was no pain. She tested it, gingerly pushing it into the floor and half standing to see if it would bear weight. After the test proved successful, she moved to the window and threw the drapes open. Farther down the block, right at the property line that marked the Gulleckson domain, the sun shone brightly. Snowbanks glittered like piles of treasure around newly shoveled walkways. The darkness was confined to Ivanya's house, cloaking it in a shroud of premature night.

Vincent began to cry louder as she noticed a vibration in the house. The walls hummed, a ringing invaded her ears. It was in her head, a sound deep in her brain, like a tuning fork accompanied by the buzzing of a thousand flies. They ricocheted off her skull, crawling through the grey folds of her mind.

"Shh," she cooed, then began to hum a nameless tune she had learned from Grams. She unbuckled him from the seat and nestled him into her shoulder. She walked across the room, gently jiggling in an effort to soothe him. After depositing a calmer Vincent into the crib, she undid the Velcro straps on the boot and removed it, marveling at the absence of pain.

From the corner of her eye, Ivanya caught a movement out the window. It was just a slight thing, there and gone in a flash, but it made the hairs on her arms stand up in alarm. It could have been a cat or a raccoon, but in her heart of hearts she knew it wasn't. It was a Bad Thing—and it was coming for her.

With her body on autopilot, she snatched up the tote bag she had brought up from the basement and removed Grams' book. She placed it carefully in the end table drawer. She withdrew amulets, powders, and vials of liquid from the bag, placing them in a neat row on the nightstand. Not understanding her actions, but trusting them just the same, she walked over to the squirming baby and placed a medallion engraved with an eye on his chest. He instantly stopped moving and a wide smile lit his face. His eyes turned in her direction, wide and opaque, and in that moment she was certain that he could see her. She knew it wasn't physical; it was more like his soul was speaking to hers. A tremendous love burst from her, her head filled with a light that was nearly blinding. Ivanya understood that she had been afraid to love him, lest he be lost like Vetra. Now she claimed him. He was hers and hers he would remain.

The tinkling of the wind chimes outside put her back on high alert. The smell of rot and refuse, like moldy leaves and garbage, permeated the house, gagging her. She caught the movement out the window again, a large shape looming beyond the glass. Terrible recognition struck her, ripping the breath from her lungs. The feeling of dread that seeped into her bones was identical to what she had experienced that day in the alley. He had come back for her. No, he had come for her son. An icy fist of fear gripped her heart, freezing her in place.

Glass and chunks of wood rained over her as the wall exploded from the outside. A chunk of the window laid open her cheek and blood dripped down her skin. The sting broke her paralysis and she retreated, standing next to the nightstand and in front of Vincent.

The nightmare waited outside, the creature from her dreams. The thing that created the screams she bellowed in her sleep each night. It looked different, with glowing blue runes instead of red, but she knew it was the same one, the same thing that had taken Vetra. This was the one that had ruined her life. The one that murdered her soul.

It stared at her, its head cocked to one side. The teeth were bared, dripping saliva onto its chin. It moved slowly, sinuously, reaching its arm through the window, straining against some unseen barrier. The flesh on the tips of its fingers erupted into flame. It screamed, an inhuman roar, many layers all saying the same thing.

I've come for you.

An almost invisible ripple appeared in the air, one black talon in the center. As its hand pushed through the field, she noticed men behind him with faces of clay staring. She followed their hot and hungry gazes to Vincent.

"So woman, we meet again," the creature said. Its eyes burned neon in their sockets. It inhaled a deep breath through its nostrils and held it in for an uncomfortable moment. He exhaled in a satisfied hiss.

"I guess we do," Ivanya said, voice firm with a bravado she didn't feel.

The posse of clay-faced men stood behind the creature, practically shaking with excitement. On the mark of her nemesis they moved forward with measured precision, led by one with ash colored skin. They marched with purpose, directly toward her and Vincent.

"Give us the child," the ashen man said, venomously.

"Never," Ivanya spat.

"Then we shall take him."

"You're welcome to try," she said, fear hidden beneath a thick layer of sarcasm. She silently vowed that they would not touch her son, but she wasn't sure that she could keep that oath.

Vincent began to scream again, a high pitched wail that hurt her ears. The faces of the clay men shifted and their ears were gone. They continued to advance on Vincent.

Ivanya took a vial of red liquid in hand and threw it at them. It struck one near the back in the chest, leaving behind a large crater that she could see the wall through. She followed it with another, this one the green of an isotope, and smashed it against the skull of one who had gotten too close. His flesh began to run like candle wax. Cheeks drooped to the jawline before ripping off and splatting on the floor, where they continued to melt into twin puddles of slime. He fell to the floor, sickening gagging sounds issuing from what was left of his throat. It seemed that time had stopped as she watched him die. No one moved.

The one with grey skin looked at her quizzically, a new perception of her in his eyes. He stepped back, drawing the last three of his compatriots with him. He stood near the hole in the wall behind the creature that had ruined her life and was now here to end it.

She stared at him, her eyes boring holes into his as she assessed him as an adversary. He was strong, she was not. His entire body looked like a finely honed weapon of destruction, she was human.

"What is your name?" she asked it.

He raised a brow ridge in suspicion. "Why?"

"Because I want to know who I'm killing."

He laughed then, a sound like grating sandpaper filled with genuine mirth. "Very well, woman. I am Tarik, destroyer of whatever inspires me. Today, that is you, gypsy."

He swiped his talons at her, but she jumped back and they sailed harmlessly through the space her body had just occupied. She plucked another potion from the table and hurled it at his head. It exploded against his skull, glass falling to the floor, liquid dripping into his eyes. He did not blink it away. He did not move at all. He stood frozen before her, fingers curled, face paralyzed in a mask of rage. She used the precious seconds this afforded her to grab Vincent from the crib and drape the eye emblazoned medallion around both their necks. She did this instinctively, with no conscious thought muddying the waters.

Tarik moved. Just minutely at first, fractions of inches before the freeze wore off and he was lightning quick again. He approached them, drool dripping off his pointed teeth, as he snarled angrily. He reached out a hand and pushed it toward her, pulling it back in dismay.

"This didn't work when your grandmother tried it and it won't work for you," Tarik sneered.

Ivanya's breath caught in her throat. "Grams," she whispered, tears welling in her eyes. He'd killed her. But she didn't have time to worry about that now, because his hand was fighting through the protective shield provided by the medallion. His skin bubbled and blistered, oily black ichor splattering to the floor, but the hand kept coming. Ivanya crushed Vincent to her chest and knelt to the floor, curling her body around him like a shield. She waited for the slash of talons that she knew was coming and for the first time in a long time, she prayed.

Chapter 30

She knelt, her body huddled over her son to protect him from the claws that kept coming. Energy crackled all around her, some from the lightning arcing off the demons talons and more from the protective field around her. But most of it seemed to be coming from within Ivanya herself. She could almost hear it, a low buzz thrumming through her muscles. It built within her, growing more pronounced with every second.

It was just as Tarik's hand closed around the medallion and ripped the chain from around her neck that it happened. The thick, black talons nicked Vincent's sleeper, slicing through the yellow fabric like hot butter. A thin runner of blood appeared on his golden skin. Something inside her snapped and a scream tore from her throat. There was no fear in it, just a white hot, undiluted rage. The sound of a lioness protecting her cub. In that moment, she fully understood how a mother could lift a car off her child.

Ivanya shifted Vincent to her hip, freeing up her left hand to fight. She glared at Tarik with flinty eyes, her free hand balled into a fist. She concentrated that rage into the one hand, visualizing herself ripping and tearing at him. She never broke eye contact as she whipped her entire arm to the side. The demon screamed as large slashes appeared in its flesh. Over his head and down his face, piercing one hateful blue eye. Black blood spurted from the wounds and what was left of the eye dripped down his cheek and landed on the floor.

She had no idea where this power had come from, but she embraced it, slashing at him again and again.

The door banged open and Ivanya thought she might have made that happen, too, until Abigail and Mama Linda stormed in, stopping just a few feet behind Ivanya. Mama Linda launched glass vials from her pockets at Tarik like missiles. He retreated a few feet, clapping his hands over a wound that had opened in his chest. He fell to the floor, his glowing runes fading quickly.

"Take the baby!" Ivanya shouted at Abigail. When there was no answering word or shift of the baby, Ivanya turned to look at her friend. Abigail stood stock still, fingers gripping the flesh of her cheeks, parentheses to a mouth wide open in shock and horror. She was not looking at Tarik screaming in pain, but at the clay man in the corner. The threat that Ivanya had forgotten.

"Abs!" Ivanya yelled, shoving Abigail in the shoulder. "Take Vincent."

Ivanya thrust the baby at Abigail, who latched onto him like a drowning woman with a life preserver. Abigail snuggled an oddly calm Vincent into her shoulder and moved over by the closet, hopefully out of the line of fire.

Seeing this, the ashen demon moved away from the wall and bolted after Abigail. Mama Linda stepped in between them, hitting him in the shoulder with another potion.

"You stay away from that child," Mama Linda cried, her voice strong and commanding. "You have no claim to him."

"I have the highest of claims on him, woman," he sneered.

Ivanya watched as the face began to move, hills and valleys forming from the clay, the skin becoming peach toned instead of gray. Sandy brown hair sprouted from his scalp and matching eyebrows settled atop eyes the color of molten chocolate.

"No…" she breathed, the sound barely escaping her lips, as there was suddenly no air. No air in her lungs, no air in the room, no air on the earth. "Spencer?"

He took another step toward Abigail, palms open in surrender. "Give him to me, Abigail. I sired him, he is mine."

Abigail's arms closed tighter around the baby, as if she were trying to push him into herself to keep

302

him safe. "You *sired* him? You...you're his father?"

Ivanya found her voice, screaming as she launched herself at Spencer. She pummeled him to the ground, smashing his face with her hands. She tore into him, his clay skin coming apart beneath her nails. A couple of nail tips pulled off, embedding themselves into the flesh under his eyes. She poured all of her rage into the attack, thinking of the assault that had begun it all. It was the portal to her pain, without which none of the other things would have happened. She placed her hands against the sides of his face, letting her anger flow through her palms and fingers. It manifested in a surge of heat, which combusted into a flare of violet flame. His flesh began to melt against the fire, smelling much like a turkey forgotten in the oven. She held on while he thrashed, held on when the screaming began, and she was still touching him when it ended. She stared at the mess that had once been Spencer Kayne lying on the floor. He had started this.

Mama Linda approached the burning mass, breathing in shaky breaths and pressing a hand to her chest. She suddenly looked her age, old and haggard, weariness etched in all of her features. She pulled a stone from her pocket, a piece of rose quartz that smelled like peppermint and rosemary and placed it on the still smoldering remains of Spencer's forehead. "He won't be rising again." She reached out and placed a hand on Ivanya's shoulder, using her to steady herself.

Ivanya could feel the adrenaline seeping from her muscles and a full body fatigue stole over her. She glanced back to where Tarik had been laying on the floor, but wasn't surprised to see that he was gone. There was only an oily black pool of blood and the mutilated remains of one blue eye left behind. In the darkness, beyond the shattered wall, snarls of rage punctured the night, receding into the distance and fading into nothingness.

She sank to the floor, leaned against the wall for support, and drew her knees up to her chest. She breathed heavily and waited for the vertigo to pass.

"How's Vincent? Is he hurt?" Ivanya held her arms out. "Give him to me."

Abigail brought him over, placing him carefully in Ivanya's arms before plopping down next to her on the floor. Ivanya checked his fingers and felt the feet of the sleeper to ensure his toes were intact. The hole in his sleeper had widened. She investigated the tear in the fabric, looking for the scratch, the demon-made imperfection in his skin. It was gone, his skin was perfect.

"I told you he was special, girl," Mama Linda said, as she bent over and scooped Tarik's eye up with a tissue. "And apparently, so are you. I guess your grandmama's power didn't skip a generation after all. Come on, girls, I'll make you some tea while we wait for the police. Goodness knows one of these people around here called them when they heard all the ruckus."

Ivanya cradled Vincent in her arms, leaning heavily against Abigail for support as they ambled down the hall toward the kitchen. The rest of the house seemed fine, it was just her room that was destroyed. Mama Linda was a hurricane in the kitchen, slamming cupboards and drawers, plunking the kettle on the stove and turning the burner on. Ivanya supported Vincent on the table, watching in amazement as he pushed his little legs under him and stood up, grasping her hands tightly for balance.

"That happened," Abigail said, her voice mystified. "That really just happened."

"Yes," Ivanya replied. "I told you about this. Do you believe me now?"

She could see the conflicting emotions on Abigail's face as her brain tried to reconcile what she had seen with what she thought she knew. It didn't seem to be working. Her face contorted in confusion and horror. "I knew he wasn't good enough for you."

"What?"

"Spencer. I always thought he was an asshole. Looks like I was right."

Ivanya widened her eyes incredulously. "That's what you're doing with this new and frightening information that demons exist? Using it to justify your abhorrence for my taste in men?"

Abigail nodded, her eyes sparkling with glee. "Yep."

Mama Linda plunked steaming mugs of tea in front of them and settled in at the table, chucking Vincent beneath the chin. She gazed at him, a small smile playing around the edges of her mouth.

"What are we going to do with the body?" Ivanya asked, as she placed Vincent in her lap and took a sip of tea. The hot liquid hit her stomach, warming her from the inside. "We can't just leave it in my room."

"It'll be gone soon, child. It will melt away as if it had never been. That's the one good thing about demons." Mama Linda sipped her tea. "The same can't be said for your wall, I'm afraid, but even that can wait. I have something important to say to you."

But Ivanya didn't get to find out the important thing, because once again there was the distinctive sound of a cop's fist on the front door.

*****

Corl and Kingston were already on their way to the Devereaux house when the distress call came over the radio. Less than five minutes later they were pulling up the drive and climbing the porch. He pounded on the heavy door, the sound echoing through the house. It seemed like forever waiting in the frigid cold, before the door creaked open and Abigail Kayne ushered them inside, favoring Kingston with a seductive look. His face burned and he looked at the hardwood floor as Corl pushed past them with a smirk, heading to the kitchen.

Ivanya was there, lounging on a kitchen chair and holding a baby that was gurgling happily. That woman from the occult shop was there, too, sipping tea and smiling.

"Miss Devereax, and…"

The large woman placed her palms on the table, using the surface for leverage to rise. "I'm Mama Linda, Detective. Would you like a cup of coffee before we get on down to business?"

"Coffee would be great, ma'am," he replied, as he sat at the table opposite of Ivanya. "Whose baby?"

The girl glared at him, obviously still holding a grudge. "Mine. Turns out I had twins."

"Congratulations. He's a cutie." Corl fiddled with his phone while he waited for the coffee, feeling awkward and out of place. He needed to buck up. He was the authority figure here. From the living room came a high peal of delighted laughter. The Kayne girl sauntered into the kitchen, pulling Kingston behind her by his tie. The man looked suitably mortified, but sort of happy at the same time. Kids.

"Paul. We're supposed to be working."

Kingston took the seat next to Corl, embarrassment written all over his face. Served him right. They were supposed to be professionals.

It wasn't long before two steaming mugs of coffee were placed on the table before him and Kingston. He took a sip of the brew, half expecting the battery acid they served at the station. This was warm and woodsy, with an almost fruity component. It was the best cup of coffee he'd ever had. He tipped the mug back and drained the liquid down his throat, then got up to serve himself another cup. When he sat back down, he was refreshed and ready to work.

"I have something to say to you, Miss Devereaux." This was hard, apologizing was not his strong suit, as in he never did it. Never. That was why he was divorced. "I know you thought that I didn't believe you when you gave us the description of your attacker, and for good reason. I didn't. But recent information has come to light that corroborates your story. Peyton Crane, the first of the missing women, described a thing much like the one you did. I wanted to say I'm sorry."

Ivanya eyes widened in shock, then narrowed in suspicion. "Just like that. You believe me."

"Not *just like that*. I had to put aside my own stuff and really think about it. And I came to the conclusion that something more is going on here. I came here tonight to have you explain it to me. And to offer some information about a suspect."

Now she seemed interested. She sat straighter in her chair and transferred the now snoring child to her shoulder, patting his butt absently. "You really want to hear this? You can't really go back to seeing the world the same way once you have irrevocable proof that things go bump in the night. I have some proof in the back, if you would care to see it before it melts."

The large woman, Mama Linda, glared at Ivanya, a shoosh dying on her lips. She shook her head in disappointment, then rose from the chair again, having more difficulty than last time. She led them down the hallway, past a bathroom and another door that was shut. Corl wondered what was in there. He froze just inside the door to the bedroom, eyeing the smoky thing lying on the floor. It lay in a puddle of what looked like melted wax, the grey of concrete. There were still some humanoid features that could be discerned, but for the most part it was just a pile of inconsequential goo. Corl surveyed the rest of the room, noting the bed pushed against the wall with one corner of the frame crushed into the wood floor. That would need to be sanded and re-stained. The outside wall had been blown apart, a spray of debris strewn all over the floor. Part of a pane of glass hung precariously from what was left of the window frame.

There was a fundamental difference between believing something, and seeing absolute physical evidence that it was true. That the thing, the horrifyingly impossible thing, was undeniably real. The two sides of Corl's mind battled, the logical versus the irrational. Eventually, after long moments of warfare, logic lay beaten and bloody on the floor of his brain. It was real. All of it.

"Anybody I know?" Corl asked, trying for nonchalance, but not quite making it.

"Yeah," Abigail replied. "My rotten step-brother. Spencer Kayne."

Corl couldn't believe that he'd been so distracted that he'd forgotten why he had come in the first place. It took an almost Herculean effort, but he tore his eyes away from the barely recognizable mess on the floor and looked at Abigail.

"Peyton Crane, who barely lived through her butchery, provided us with a sketch artist's rendering of one of her abductors." Corl paused, wondering how to say it. He decided that just getting to the point was the best way. "It was a perfect match to your step-mother."

Incredibly, the girl began to laugh. Before long, she was bent over at the waist, arms wrapped tightly around her middle as tears squirted out the corners of her eyes. Her breaths came in sharp wheezes, punctuated by bouts of infectious giggles. Corl looked to Ivanya desperately, hoping he hadn't driven the Kayne girl completely insane. Ivanya was no help, as she wore a wry smile and shook her head indulgently.

"Did I miss something?"

"I knew it!" Abigail screamed, maniacally. "I knew she was a crazy demon bitch from Hell. Didn't I say that, Vani?"

"She really did."

Corl, relieved that everyone seemed to be taking everything so well, approached the smashed wall, gazing at it speculatively. "Well, I guess we should throw a temporary fix on this before nightfall."

Chapter 31

"Aahhhhh," Tarik hissed his discomfort as Lykah stuffed a hot ball of herbs and sulfur into the hollow where his right eye had been. She placed a leather patch over the wound and went on to tend the gashes across his head and neck. She smeared a poultice across the lacerations, then sewed them closed with cat-gut sutures.

After she finished, she handed him a potion for the pain, which he guzzled greedily. It warmed him from the inside and caused his wounds to tingle. Lykah lowered herself to the chair next to him and met his remaining eye.

"You're absolutely certain that my son is dead?" Her voice held anger mixed with a barely restrained thread of hope.

"Yes, Priestess, I'm sure," Tarik replied, treading the conversation lightly. In his weakened state, he did not want to deal with her unpredictable ire. He could smell her rage and anguish on the air, but her expression remained controlled. Determination narrowed her eyes and set her lips in a thin line.

"That's...unfortunate. I had high hopes for the boy."

But Tarik knew that the words were only to preserve her pride. Lykah had cared for her son as much as her kind was able to. The devastation of her heart was nearly complete; what mercy was there had dried up, leaving behind only a powerful thirst for revenge.

"That girl," Lykah spat the words as if they were poison, "will know loss and torment. Then, when I've taken everything there is to take, I shall finish with her life. Leave me, Tarik. I must plan."

He did not need to be told twice. He trudged down the corridor toward the chamber he was forced to share with the Maggot. It was dark, but he didn't need a torch to find his way. Whispers from his den found their way down the hallway to his ears. Why were there people in there? All he wanted was to fall upon his cot and sleep, until the events of the past few hours faded away like the last vestiges of a nightmare. He rounded the corner and poked his head past the open chamber door, wishing he could turn around and flee. Three handmaidens lounged around the fire, talking of inconsequential things. The Maggot and her Six sat in a loose circle on the floor, waving hands as they babbled animatedly. It was as though the Maggot were holding court with her council—every time she spoke a garbled word or two, they nodded assent and gurgled back. Squeals of laughter ice-picked his brain.

Breathing a deep sigh, Tarik entered the room completely, drawing the attention of everyone. The handmaidens jumped from their seats as if poked by a cattle prod and busied themselves with preparing the belongings of the children for departure. The Maggot grabbed her chubby toes and began smacking the soles of her feet together.

"Geek, Geek," she chattered, happily, her black eyes glittering in the firelight. "Tar-geek!"

The other younglings followed suit. "Tar-geek!"

The ice pick drilled into his head again, more forcefully this time. The handmaidens approached, each scooping up two younglings and fitting them neatly onto their hips. They said nothing as they hurried out of the room, peeking out the sides of their eyes at Tarik's wounds. He didn't like it, but he understood. He was the most ruthless being they had ever known, second to none in battle. Anything that could injure him so grievously was a threat to be taken seriously. That is, until they found out the threat was a human. And a girl. Then they would laugh, as he would if the victim were anyone else.

Once the room was cleared of everyone but the Maggot, Tarik fell onto his cot. A strange vertigo surged over him, tossing his brains around his skull like a tidal wave. Everything in the room moved, rolling on waves before his eye. Even the Maggot moved, her eyes and features swirling on her face. She giggled again, reaching her doughy hands toward him.

"Tar-geek!" she squealed.

Sighing heavily, he sat up and leaned forward, slipping his hands under the Maggot's armpits and lifting her up. He sat her on his lap, watching as she cooed happily. Her tiny brow furrowed with worry as she looked at him, taking in the wounds on his head and neck. She reached for the eye patch, but he held her hands away from it. It was unclear even to him whether he did this to stop her from touching it, or to stop her from seeing it.

"Geek," the Maggot whispered, mournfully, tears pricking the corners of her deep, black eyes. She gave him a stern look then reached forward again, this time touching one of the gashes on his neck. Her hand was warm to the point of discomfort, but when she removed it, the pain went along. He gingerly touched his neck, feeling the ridges of the laceration grow hard and scaly. She touched it again, her hand growing warmer still, and the cat-gut burst and burned off, leaving only healed scabs instead of open wounds. She continued this with the other gashes, not healing them completely, but closing them up and making them much less painful.

"Thank you, Maggot."

She gurgled again, a happy sound that did not annoy Tarik as much as it had before, and leaned her head against his shoulder. Before long, soft snores filled the cavernous room, coming from both the child and her Guardian.

*****

After fitting two sheets of plywood over the demolished wall and nailing them in place, Corl called the station to put out an APB on Isobel Kayne. Ivanya could hear him speaking in hushed tones to the dispatch operator, using phrases like 'suspicion of kidnapping' and 'accessory to murder'. Ivanya was still reeling. The evil that wished her harm was so close and she never suspected them, not for a second. Isobel had always acted like Ivanya was dirt beneath her feet, but she had no idea that her hatred had run so deep. And Spencer. Spencer was the reason for all of this. The man she'd thought she loved had taken what he wanted and caused all this misery and heartache. She was glad he was gone, and even gladder that she had been the one to kill him.

Ivanya held Vincent in the crook of her arm while she fed him some formula. He placed his hands on the sides of the bottle and held it to his lips, breathing contentedly. A dribble of the milk ran from his lips and puddled on the collar of his sleeper. Peace stole over her while she watched her son eat. It was all right. Everything was okay. Vincent was safe.

316

Abigail flirted shamelessly with Kingston, who blushed and motioned for her to stop.

The gentleman doth protest too much, the voice said, and Ivanya had to agree. The only person Kingston could possibly be fooling was himself.

Corl and Kingston left with travel mugs of coffee and promises to call if any headway was made in the case. Abigail followed them to the door and locked it securely behind them. She leaned against the heavy wood with a sigh and a wistful smile.

"He is sooo cute."

"Calm down the hormones, Abs. That's how you get these," Ivanya laughed, lifting a now sleeping Vincent into the air. "I'm not ready to be an auntie."

Abigail snorted. "Dude. I'm adopting. None of that hard labor for me. I'll be this size forever."

It was Mama Linda's turn to snort. "Don't bet on it, child." She rooted through her bags, pulling out candles and dropper bottles of oils. She placed all of this on the coffee table in a neat row.

"It's starting to look like your store in here," Ivanya muttered. She snuggled Vincent to her chest and gently kissed his brow. A smile formed on his lips and he nestled in closer.

"You could only be so lucky," Mama Linda retorted. "Now, you're gonna want to put the baby down. Just lay him down in the playpen. I want him nowhere near what we are about to do."

Abigail took the baby from Ivanya, kissed his cheek and deposited him in the playpen, being sure to cover him up with a blue fleece blanket. She stared at him for a few seconds before whirling around and glaring at Mama Linda.

"And what are we about to do? I think we've had plenty of excitement for one night. Besides, I should go back to my dad's house. God knows how he's doing now that his dearest wife is about to be arrested."

"I have something to show you girls. And as much as it pains me to admit it, I'm a little tired after all the demonic activity in the other room." Mama Linda swallowed hard, as if the words she needed to say next were lodged in her throat. "I could use your help."

"My help."

Mama Linda shook her head and huffed in exasperation. "I told you that you had some talents. I need to use them. This will change life as you know it. Now get over here and sit down."

Ivanya slid from the chair to the floor and scooted over to the table on her butt. She picked up a chunky yellow votive and sniffed it. Nothing. Mama Linda handed her a dropper of liquid.

"Here. Anoint it with this. It's jasmine. Just drop the liquid on and then rub the candle between your hands until it is soaked in a little bit." She handed the white candle and a vial of what looked like water with little leaves floating in it to Abigail. "Do the same with this. When you're done, place it back on the table."

The oily candle slipped out from between her palms twice, the second time nearly nailing Abigail in the forehead. Abigail leaned back at the last second, concentrating on the one in her own hands, and the yellow votive fell harmlessly onto the couch cushion. Ivanya scrambled up to retrieve it and placed it back on the table where it no longer had the potential to be a missile. Abigail finished hers and set it down as well.

"Okay. Looks like we're ready. Light the candles, but make sure you're still touching them with at least one finger." The girls did as they were told, while Mama Linda took the piece of balled up tissue that contained the remnants of Tarik's eye from her pocket. She cut it in half and placed a piece on both flames.

Ivanya could feel her eyelids snap shut and the orbs themselves rotate backward in the sockets. Her ears rung painfully, as if a grenade had gone off near her head and she was plunged deep into something like a forgotten well. Violent shivers wracked her body as the nearly complete darkness enveloped her. A pinpoint of light hovered above her. She reached for it, fingers extended, but it stayed just out of reach. Ivanya concentrated on it, harder than she'd ever thought about anything before, and was rewarded with a light violet glow emanating from her fingers. The glow became more focused as she thought about it, growing and pushing back at the darkness. The circle of light grew bigger and closer, until, at long last, she was able to step through it.

Everything had taken on a violet hue and she began to understand that it came from her. Purple was her protection, her talisman against evil. Rock walls of a subterranean cavern formed around her. A fire burned brightly off to the right, spitting lavender tinted flames at the ceiling. The hulking black form of Tarik sat upon a cot to her left, his head leaning against the wall. And on his lap...

Without warning, she was in the living room again, her feet tingling with pins and needles as she sat on them. Mama Linda had moved across the room, looking down into the playpen with a grandmotherly gaze.

"What happened? How do I go back?" Ivanya half screamed at the woman. "I need to get back!"

320

"Just touch the candle again and close your eyes."

Ivanya touched the candle with her index finger. Just as she was about to yell at Mama Linda that it wasn't working, she was sucked back in. Her brain corkscrewed inside her skull, eyes bouncing around in the sockets. The world had turned a fast moving deep purple, as if she were hurtling head first down a wormhole through space. Then she was in the cavern again, looking at the demon and...her daughter. Her little Vetra.

Even though the child did not look much like what Ivanya had expected, she could see herself in the shape of the girl's eyes, the slight upturn of the nose, and the dimple that dented her right cheek as she stared up into the monster's eyes. She was alive. Alive and beautiful.

Something like grief tore at her as she watched her daughter reach out with a chubby hand and touch Tarik's cheek. He gazed at her indulgently as she touched the wound on his neck and began to cry. It was obvious she loved him, Ivanya could see the aura of soft pink surrounding Vetra. Jealousy ripped through Ivanya's gut. Her daughter should be touching *her* cheek. She should be sitting on her lap and gazing at her with the pure adulation she was showing that monster. Vetra belonged with her—not him.

Ivanya's eyes popped open to the familiarity of her own living room. The candle she had been touching had burned all the way down, leaving a pool of hot wax on the table. Abigail stared at her across the coffee table with wide, tear-filled eyes. Ivanya ignored her though, and sought out Mama Linda again.

"That's my Vetra. She's alive."

The old woman nodded, her eyes bright and crinkled at the corners. "Yep. That's what I was coming over to tell you when everything went to hell. Now, we just need to get her back."

Anne Langworthy is a resident of Cadillac, Michigan where she lives with her husband, Michael. She works in customer service and facilitates a group for at-risk teens. Anne has found her passion for writing after trying many other creative endeavors.

"Nothing serves my soul like bleeding out the stories inside me."—Anne Langworthy

Made in the USA
Monee, IL
11 March 2020

22800152R00184